REPRISAL

REPRISAL

AKIO REVELATIONS™ BOOK ONE

CHARLES TILLMAN
MICHAEL ANDERLE

DISRUPTIVE IMAGINATION®

LMBPN Publishing
PMB 196, 2540 South Maryland Pkwy
Las Vegas, NV 89109

First US edition, June, 2020
Version 1.01, June 2020
eBook ISBN: 978-1-64971-005-5
Print ISBN: 978-1-64971-006-2

DEDICATION

To my Wife Danette, thank you for being behind me while I did this.
A huge thank you to Michael Anderle who let me come and play in his world.
There are also two others who worked hard to help me bring this to you:
John Ashmore, Alpha reader extraordinaire
Tracey Byrnes, Alpha reader and first pass editor who kept me and my sentence structure on track. I couldn't have done it without you.
And most of all thanks to you the Kurtherian Gambit Fans for reading.

—Charles

To Family, Friends and
Those Who Love
to Read.

*May We All Enjoy Grace
to Live the Life We Are
Called.*

— Michael

THE REPRISAL TEAM

Thanks to our Beta Readers

Kelly O'Donnell, Micky Cocker, Daniel Weigert, James Caplan, Rachel Beckford, Larry Omans

Thanks to the JIT Readers

Dave Hicks
Veronica Stephan-Miller
Diane L. Smith
Jackey Hankard-Brodie
Peter Manis
Misty Roa
Dorothy Lloyd
Kerry Mortimer
Deb Mader
Angel LaVey
Paul Westman
Tim Bischoff

If we've missed anyone, please let us know!

Editor
Skyhunter Editing Team

CHAPTER ONE

Kume Island, Off the Coast of Okinawa, Japan

Just my luck, Taka Ogata thought sourly as he held the twenty-meter fishing boat steady in the current fifty meters from shore. *That idiot Issa forgot to tie the anchor, so I'm stuck minding the boat while he goes ashore. He should have gone over the side with the damn thing.*

The earthquakes that struck Japan after the day now called the World's Worst Day Ever, or WWDE, had destroyed the docks on Kume Island, and there had been no attempt yet to rebuild. The only way to get there was to take a small craft that could handle the shallow water near the beach.

Ogata watched through binoculars as the ship's dinghy approached the shore. A man waited with a group of what appeared to be teenagers. When the crewmen stepped onto the sand, the teens surged toward them in a wave. Ogata watched helplessly as they quickly swarmed his crewmates, whose panicked screams echoed across the water as they went down under the onslaught. He stared in horror as the group tore the men to shreds. When a young girl came into focus, Ogata's blood ran cold as he saw her glowing red eyes.

He shoved the throttle wide open and spun the wheel sharply, racing for safety as the powerful engines carried him away from the island and the demons who lived there.

She watched her opponent warily as he approached, her sword held ready and a look of determination on her face.

He moved with fluid grace, his feet seeming to glide across the floor as he nonchalantly stalked her. A slight smile played on his lips as he held his blade in a deceptively casual grip.

She struck with the speed of a snake when he came into range. He never slowed as his sword appeared, like magic, to push hers aside. She twisted and quickly leaned back as he reversed his motion in a counterblow, his sword-tip creating a breeze that ruffled her hair in passing.

She circled left, feinted with a strike at his leg, then immediately swept the blade up to slice his sword arm as she pressed the attack. Again, his weapon was there before she connected. He casually pushed her blade down, and she barely avoided his backstroke before it took her in the throat. She kept moving, her eyes never leaving his body as she watched for the slightest hint that would signal another attack.

They continued their deadly dance, both silent except for the clash of steel-on-steel that echoed through the room in a rhythm of strike and counterstrike. Neither gave an inch as they dueled. She defended more than she attacked, growing increasingly frustrated each time he effortlessly blocked her. After each failed attempt she changed her form, hoping to catch him off-guard with the quick changes.

When all her attacks proved unsuccessful, frustration turned to anger. The angrier she became, the faster she moved until their figures were colored blurs as they moved about quicker than the human eye could follow. They came together in a flurry of ringing blows and slid apart before the sound of the first strike died away.

The dance continued for several minutes, until her body slammed forcibly into the wall. The impact momentarily disoriented her. The other blur flashed across the room and stopped, revealing a sword that rested lightly against her exposed throat.

"Akio, could you have hit me any harder?" she huffed.

"If you think more pain would help you remember not to let your emotions interfere with your fighting, I will be happy to provide it." Akio fought to keep a slight smile from forming as he spoke. "You must learn to control your anger. The angrier you are, the more you telegraph your intentions. You were so focused on attacking and ending the fight that you failed to see the techniques that allowed me to take you again," he explained calmly as he pulled the blade back.

Yuko stepped away from the wall with a groan. A slight indentation marked where her body had impacted it. "*Hai*, Akio. I saw you commit to dodge the feint and thought you had taken the bait. I should know by now that you do not fall for such things."

3

Akio permitted the smile to slip. "Your form and instincts are good, Yuko. You simply allow yourself to see what you want instead of what is. You can't let your frustration and anger blind you. Against a less-skilled adversary, you would have been successful. Unfortunately, one seldom has the luxury to pick their foes based on known skills. Shall we continue?"

Yuko was about to reply when Eve's voice came through their implants.

"Akio, Yuko, would you please come to the operations center? I have received a message from the Japanese government liaison. I think you both need to see this."

They replaced their practice swords on the rack and walked down the hall into the operations center, where Eve was standing in front of a large monitor on the wall with an e-mail message displayed onscreen.

"There have been some strange occurrences on an island located off the coast of Okinawa," Eve informed them. "The information indicates that there might be Forsaken there. Two police inspectors were sent to check on a report of missing people. They called in after they arrived, but the transmission stopped suddenly. There is an audio file attached." As she finished, the speakers in the room came to life.

A panicked voice babbled, "Hiroso is dead! A monster, a monster with red eyes came from nowhere and tore his throat out. I shot— NO! NO! STAY BACK!" Rapid-fire gunshots, followed by a blood-chilling scream that abruptly ended in a frantic gurgle, signaled the end of the recording.

Eve folded her hands, a grave expression on her face.

"The Okinawa police plans to send a larger group to investigate. Our contact in the ministry requested your input based on this discovery."

Akio grimaced and glanced at Yuko. "Please contact the liaison and ask them to have the police wait. I do not believe they should risk more lives if this is what it sounds like."

"Yes, I believe you are right," Yuko agreed as she reached for the phone.

"Eve, what island was this?" Akio inquired. "See if you can locate more information. Also, what was that about missing people?"

Eve was silent for a few seconds, and then additional documents appeared on the screen. "It was Kume Island. They were investigating a report about a fisherman who went there after he could not contact a family member for several weeks. His boat was found adrift a few days later, and he has not been heard from since. I have discovered other, similar instances of boats found in that area. The reports date back for several months. There are rumors that pirates are operating there, but this is the first official report I have found where the authorities are involved."

"Yuko, please let me know if your source has any additional information. I will prepare the Pod," Akio called as he stepped out of the room.

CHAPTER TWO

TQB Base, Tokyo, Japan

As Akio prepared the Pod, he reflected on the time that had passed since Bethany Anne left to take the fight to the Kurtherians. Before she departed, she had given Akio the duty to protect humanity from the UnknownWorld and Yuko the task of taking care of those who honored Michael's family. After losing his team early on, Yuko had chosen to take a more active role in assisting him after her parent's deaths.

Japan had fared better than most places after WWDE. Its economy was recovering, and there was some working infrastructure in place with more coming online every day. Thanks to the tech giant's reliance on domestic manufacturing for computers and components for its utilities and most critical networks, it had avoided the worst of the economic meltdown and loss of services that the rest of the world suffered when a computer virus created by the Chinese military was unleashed by General Li. This single act of revenge for the death of his son had effectively destroyed the modern world.

The protections Bethany Anne put into place for Japan in exchange for a safe place for her people had ensured that there were no attacks there. When the nuclear missiles started flying, they were destroyed well before any targeting Japan got close. Thanks to that protection It was now the most modern country left in the world.

There was still much to do since earthquakes and their subsequent tsunamis had ravaged the islands shortly afterward, but the Japanese people were resilient and already making great strides toward restoring what was lost. Being a nation of islands seemed to have moderated the major climate shifts experienced elsewhere. Before the new weather patterns settled, there had been a slight increase in average temperature, but it looked to be leveling out. Fortunately, only some low coastal areas had been taken by the sea. That small blessing had helped them recover much more easily.

Akio had been training Yuko in fighting from the beginning. At first, it was because she'd wanted to be able to defend herself. However, after a building collapse had buried his brothers under tons of rubble, she and Eve had become his closest backup.

Yuko was becoming an accomplished fighter but was still unseasoned as a warrior. She had trained with minimal enhancements for the first twenty years, but after both her parents died, she'd opted for the full upgrades. She had refused them while her parents lived, not wanting to explain why she never aged from year to year. They had enjoyed her company until they passed away from natural causes within months of each other.

She had learned to control her enhanced strength and speed well over the past few years. She also had greater control over her emotions than before but still allowed them to overrule her brain in times of stress. Akio delighted in goading her when they sparred, pushing her harder and harder until she became angry.

A slight smile crossed his lips as he thought of how the young woman continually worked to best him, pushing herself to her limits and beyond. Although she was now over forty years old, she would always be young to Akio, who had been an accomplished warrior before he became a vampire several hundred years ago. While he knew that most opponents wouldn't fare well if they faced her, he would still work to bring her anger to the surface at the worst possible time until she attained the control she needed to survive.

"Akio, I have discovered more information," Eve announced.

Akio closed the hatch he was inspecting before he answered. "I'll be there in a few moments, Eve."

Several minutes later, he walked into the operations center. "What have you found?"

"There was an incident on the island a few months ago. A fishing vessel went there, and four of the crew went missing. One survivor returned, but the authorities in Okinawa did not believe his story. He was arrested on suspicion of murder since he has a reputation for drinking and has had some violent encounters with the authorities."

As Eve spoke, she gestured toward a monitor on the wall, and a copy of the police report appeared. "He insisted that his crew died when they went ashore. He claimed that he stayed on the boat and watched as 'demons with red eyes who looked like children' attacked and tore the crew to shreds. He stated that he fled out to sea before they reached him. The police investigated, but the town's mayor informed them that no boats had come to the island that day, so the inspector assumed that the survivor had killed them at sea and dumped the bodies. For some reason, this information did not get shared with the entire force. I found it buried in another file on the local Okinawa server."

Akio's eyes narrowed as he heard this. "Where is he being held now?"

"He was transferred to the psychiatric ward in Kuda Hospital on Okinawa." A map highlighting the location replaced the report on the monitor at Eve's command. "He continued to rant about demons, and they had to restrain him several times when he became violent in jail. I will send the coordinates to your Pod and contact the Okinawa authorities if you wish to speak with him."

Akio's lips pursed before he answered. "Yes, that will be fine. I want to know what this man saw before I go to the island. Inform the liaison that we are invoking the Bitch Protocol and to contact the Chief Inspector of the Kyushu Police Bureau. I will need him to arrange for me to speak to the survivor."

"Inspector Nakano, thank you for meeting me here." Akio greeted the middle-aged officer with a slight bow.

"The Chief Inspector told me to assist you and indicated that you have a way to determine what happened to the boat crew on Kume." A hint of skepticism colored his voice. "I am not sure what you believe you can do that the doctors have not. From all reports, Taka Ogata still swears that demon children with glowing eyes killed his crew. Even with the medication, his story remains the same."

"I can determine the truth," Akio assured him.

"If you say so." Nakano huffed impatiently. "Let's get this done. I have other cases to work on that do not involve wild stories of demons from a violent drunkard."

An orderly led them to a room where a large man lay in bed, his arms and legs tied to the frame with heavy leather restraints. His scarred and calloused hands, combined with his rugged face, showed he'd lived a hard life, one spent working outside in the elements for many years.

"Taka had an episode today," the orderly informed them. "He told another patient his wild tale and attacked the man when he did not believe him. Sedation was required to calm him down, and he is still under the effects of the drug, for all the good it will do. As soon as it wears off, he starts ranting about the demons again."

"Thank you. I'm sure he will be able to help me," Akio responded and then turned his attention to the restrained man. "Ogata-*san*, my name is Akio. Can you tell me what happened on the island?"

Ogata stirred. His eyes slowly opened and then closed.

"Demons. Demon children, teenagers, with eyes that glowed like the fires of hell," he mumbled.

Nakano exhaled loudly, "It is the same story he has told since the day he arrived at the docks without his crew. He refuses to tell anyone what he really did. He expects us to believe this fairy tale. Ogata, tell the truth. You killed them and dumped their bodies in the sea!" he yelled.

Akio raised a hand and looked at the inspector. "That is neither necessary nor helpful," he told him calmly, wondering why the man was so hostile toward the patient.

Nakano scoffed. "Helpful? I'll tell you what is *not* helpful—dragging me down here so you can speak with this liar. I have dealt with Ogata many times before. He is a violent drunk with a bad temper. He murdered the crew in a drunken rage and then made up this unbelievable tale to try to cover it up."

"I understand why you feel that way, but I would still like to talk to him." Akio's eyes narrowed as he picked up strong emotions from the inspector. He stared as Nakano's anger caused him to strongly project his thoughts.

"Well, do it quickly so I can get back to work. I don't know why you people from Tokyo think you are so much smarter than us in the Regions. I know a lie when I hear it. I can't believe you wasted time and resources to come here for this foolishness. I will wait outside," Nakano growled as he stormed out of the room.

Akio watched him go, irritated by the disrespectful behavior but having some insight into the why after his outburst. After Nakano was gone, he turned back to Ogata and asked, softly and respectfully, "Ogata-*san*, can you tell me what happened?"

Ogata opened his eyes, revealing drug-dilated pupils. His voice was groggy as he responded to Akio's prompt. "We went to Kume. The Captain has family there and wanted to visit them. I pulled the short string and had to stay on the boat to keep it in place. That fool, Issa." His eyes closed as he drifted off under the effects of the sedative.

Akio sighed. "Ogata-*san*, I need you to focus. What did you see?"

Ogata opened his eyes and continued after a few heart-beats. "Red...red-eyed demons. Demons from hell with glowing red eyes. They...they killed them all, ripped them to shreds."

As Ogata recalled the night, Akio took more information from his mind. When he finished, he rested his hand on Ogata's brow. "You have done well. Sleep now."

The combination of drugs and the compulsion Akio put behind the words was too much for Ogata to resist. He was softly snoring as Akio left the room.

Nakano was leaning against the wall outside with a cigarette between his lips when Akio stepped out into the sunlight.

"You had me come here for this? I could have told you that fantasy without making the trip here and wasting my time," he fumed as Akio approached.

"It was not a waste. Ogata-*san* is truthful about what he saw," Akio calmly replied. "I will talk with the Chief Inspector. You do not need to concern yourself any further."

"It is my case, and he murdered those men," Nakano retorted as his face flushed in anger. "Who are you to tell me not to concern myself?"

"You need to let go of your past hatred for Ogata-*san*. It is unbecoming and places a dark mark on your honor. He did not kill those men, but you let your unreasonable hatred for him blind you to the truth." Akio's voice hardened. "You no longer need to worry about this. It will be dealt with appropriately."

Nakano's face was mottled with red spots and his voice was harsh. "You know nothing! You come here acting like a lord, as though you can look at a man and determine his innocence."

He railed at Akio. "Taka Ogata is a mean drunk. It was merely a matter of time until he killed. I knew it would happen, and now it has."

Akio's lips tightened into a barely noticeable frown as he turned to walk away. "Thank you for your time. As I said, others will deal with it appropriately."

Nakano shouted, "What do you mean by that? Do you think the Tokyo police can handle this better? Your arrogance knows no bounds."

Akio's lips turned up in a slight smile as he called over his shoulder. "I never said the police would handle *anything*."

He stepped around the corner of the building. Once out of sight of the sputtering Nakano, he accelerated to preternatural speed around the back of the building.

"Bring the Pod down, Eve. I have the information we need."

A black Pod quickly descended and stopped mere inches from the ground in front of him. He didn't slow but stepped into the open door as it briefly hovered and then rapidly rose.

"Yuko, please contact the government liaison to arrange a meeting for me with the Chief Inspector of Kyushu. I need to convince him not to send any more men to that island."

As the Pod shot into the sky, Akio looked down and saw Nakano run around the corner and stop. He watched as the confused officer looked from side to side, searching for him.

Kyushu Regional Police Headquarters, Okinawa

"Thank you for seeing me on such short notice, Chief Inspector Morikata." Akio offered a short bow to the man.

The chief inspector made the appropriate bow in return. "Welcome, Akio-*san*. I must admit that I am curious since I am not often contacted by the Commissioner General twice in one day. The second time, he instructed me that you wanted to meet and to give you whatever you requested, no questions asked. I have the Ogata file and a few more that have information about the strange occurrences around Kume Island." He held up a short stack of files as he spoke.

Akio reached for the offered papers. "I appreciate your promptness. The events on Kume are most troubling and something that I am equipped to handle."

"I thought I recognized your name when Commissioner General Watabe called. I recognize your face, as well. You are one of the Queen's, uh, Bitches, is it?"

Akio inclined his head. "*Hai*. I have the honor of that title, and I am also one of the people she left behind to take care of problems that are beyond what the police are equipped to handle. This situation appears to be one of those problems."

The chief inspector nodded along as Akio spoke. "I thought as much when I read Ogata's statement. I saw another person with red eyes, once. It was in a documentary about your Queen the day she departed."

"*Hai.* About Ogata-*san.* He is telling the truth. He does not deserve to be locked away for something he did not do. He is lucky to even be alive."

As Morikata started to speak, there was a disturbance outside the office. Both men looked toward the door as it flew open and Nakano stormed in.

"Forgive the interruption, Chief Inspector, but this man is not a member of the police as he claims," Nakano growled as he angrily stalked toward Akio.

Akio faced him as Nakano stormed up to him, anger evident in his face and stance. "If it pleases you, Chief Inspector, I will remove this impostor and find out what he is up to."

"Inspector Nakano, still yourself!" Morikata commanded in a stern voice. "This man is an honored guest. The Commissioner General ordered that he be given every courtesy."

Nakano stood with his mouth open and a confused look on his face. "But, sir, he was at the hospital and claimed that Ogata is telling the truth. Surely you don't believe that this man, whoever he is, can be trusted any more than Ogata?"

Nakano's blood turned cold after one look at his chief's face.

The man's normally calm visage was flushed in anger

and his eyes were like ice as he stared at the inspector. "Nakano, you will apologize immediately and then leave this office. Do not go far, because we will have much to discuss once our esteemed guest has completed his business with me," he commanded the stunned man in a tone that left no room for anything but full and immediate compliance.

"I-I... Sir, I..." Nakano stammered to a stop as his wide eyes looked from one man to the other.

Akio sighed. "Chief Morikata, although this officer is rather impetuous, I understand his reaction. Ogata-*san's* story is unbelievable for someone who has no experience in such things. However, he also has an old quarrel with Ogata. They were once friends, close as brothers until Ogata-*san* struck his sister in a drunken stupor. Taka Ogata is this officer's former brother-in-law."

Nakano stiffened and started to speak. Akio locked eyes with him and allowed a faint red tint to shine through. Nakano gasped, the color draining from his face as he backpedaled away.

"Inspector Nakano, there are many things in this world that seem unbelievable when you first hear about them. I assure you that some of them are very real," Akio calmly stated as his eyes faded back to normal. "It's my duty to deal with them."

"Nakano, I gave you an order," Morikata snapped at the obviously shaken man.

He closed his mouth with an audible snap and bowed deeply at the waist. "Please forgive me, honorable sir. I was out of line."

Akio acknowledged him with a slight bow, barely a nod

of his head, and turned back to the Chief Inspector. Both remained silent until the door clicked softly closed.

"May I take these copies, Chief Inspector?" Akio asked.

"*Hai*, they are for you. Do you need anything else, Akio-*san*?"

"Please see to it that Ogata-*san* is released," Akio instructed. "I will contact you when the situation on Kume is resolved enough for you to send your men."

"*Hai*. I have just the person in mind to see to that personally. Immediately after I have a pointed conversation with him about integrity and honor." Morikata assured him while he cast a glare at the closed door. "I will await word from you before I send anyone else to Kume."

CHAPTER THREE

Pod, Over the East China Sea

Akio activated his communicator as he raced back to Tokyo at the Pod's top speed. "Yuko, you will accompany me to Kume. Get your gear and meet me in the hangar."

"*Hai*, Akio. I will be waiting," Yuko replied. "What did you learn?"

"I saw into the fisherman's mind," Akio told her. "There is indeed a situation that we must handle there. The demons who attacked his crew are Nosferatu. He saw ten of them rip his crew to shreds. If he had not fled when he did, he would have died, too.

"Please contact the liaison and advise them that we will deal with this problem. Chief Inspector Morikata has agreed to keep his people away until we contact him as well."

"Eve is talking to him now," Yuko assured him. "He has advised that they will comply and are ready to assist if needed."

· · ·

Kume Island, Okinawa Prefecture, Japan

The sun was setting as they approached Kume Island, a picturesque location of vibrant greens with a white sand beach that was the essence of natural beauty. They stepped out onto the sand. Yuko was in a light dress that covered her form-fitting Jean Dukes armor with holstered pistols and the sword strapped to her back.

Akio had some advice before they set off. "Yuko, I know you do not take life easily. Remember that while these Nosferatu might appear to be children, they are not. They are dangerous killers who are little better than wild animals, and they cannot come back from their feral state. It is a mercy to end their existence."

Yuko nodded. "*Hai*, Akio. I understand and will not hesitate to give them the mercy they deserve."

"The most important thing is to find who created them and end their miserable existence. Had the Nosferatu been here all along, we would have heard of them before now." Akio was silent for a moment, lost in thoughts of a different time.

"I have seen this before," he disclosed. "It is not the first time children were used as tools for war on these islands. During the Second World War, the Imperial Army Commander in charge of the defense of Okinawa used middle-school children as the first line of defense and suicide attackers when the American forces invaded. Many died. He committed *seppuku* to atone for his shame after the battle was lost. Kamiko Kana's mother found him in the cave, already dead. She managed to heal and turn one of his subordinates before he was able to die from his wounds. He became one of her most devoted followers, and when she was killed, he was just as devoted to her daughter. I thought him dead, but now I am convinced that his hand is involved in some manner."

Yuko looked down as she heard this. Her heart ached for the children and their parents. "That is an evil that should never be permitted," she whispered. "When we locate whoever is responsible for this atrocity, they must die." Her eyes flashed red and her voice was an almost feral growl by the end.

Akio stood silently for a few beats before he added, "That was not the worst of the evils committed in that war, but that is a story for another time. If the ones responsible for these Nosferatu are still here, they will die tonight."

The sun was gone as they made their way from the Pod to the center of town. They heard the sound of many footsteps running toward them as they arrived in the square.

A group of Nosferatu burst around the corner of a house, running toward them at faster-than-human speed. Their eyes were red as embers and snarls issued from their throats.

Akio and Yuko unsheathed their swords and moved apart as the crowd of feral creatures drew closer. When the first arrived, Akio's sword flashed, and a body crumpled to the ground as its head bounced into the path of the others. A skinny Nosferatu in filthy tattered rags growled as it leaped for Yuko, clawed fingers extended, and his fanged mouth open wide. She swung her sword, and another head joined the one on the sand.

The remaining attackers arrived as a wild horde, and the pair dispatched the others like angels of silent death. It was over in seconds, then silence reigned as they scanned the area for more threats.

Yuko stood quietly as she surveyed the bodies, her face pale at the thought of the horror the villagers must have endured when seeing their loved ones turned into beasts.

Akio interrupted her thoughts. "There is light coming from that house. Be alert. This was not all of the Nosferatu that I saw in Ogata's mind."

He wiped the blood from his blade on a cloth he carried for the purpose and stepped over the gray-skinned corpses at his feet before walking in the direction he had indicated.

The structure had suffered extensive damage during the earthquakes. Numerous mud-patched cracks ran through the outer walls, and large boards covered all the windows. It was in a sorry state but was still better than many of the other structures, most of which were collapsed piles of rubble. The ones left standing had been cobbled together into dwellings not much better than crude huts.

Akio extended his senses for signs of humans or others before he approached the door and knocked lightly. There was no answer, but he had already detected that there were several terrified people inside.

"We mean you no harm," he called through the weathered and scarred wooden door. "Open the door, please. We seek information about what has happened here."

There was shuffling inside, and a trembling voice called, "Please, *Obugyo-sama*, we already have given this week. We can't survive giving more."

Akio's eyes flashed red as he heard this. These people were being forced to serve as food for some Forsaken and were terrified. He projected a sense of calm. "I am not the one you fear. I came here to end the plague that has fallen on you. Please open the door so we can discuss what we need to do to end this evil."

The door slowly swung open to reveal a pale, thin man wearing clothing like the Nosferatu had worn. The scars and fresh bite marks that covered his neck and arms were all the proof Akio needed that there were Forsaken here. Nosferatu would not leave their victims alive.

Akio continued to project calm toward the man. "I am Akio, and I have come here to help your island. Can you tell me who you are and what has happened here?"

"*Hai*, Akio-*sama*. I am Suzu Yagi, and I am, or was, the mayor of our island. About a year ago, a man who called himself Sho Mitsuro showed up here in the night wearing ancient feudal attire and declared himself emperor. I thought he was insane—we have seen many lose their minds since the world collapsed—but he had four others with him who were monsters. He ordered them to take our children. We fought back as best we could, but bullets and blades did not harm them. They killed several of my people."

Yagi paused and drew a shuddering breath. "They were the lucky ones. The whole time Mitsuro stood next to me, I tried to move, but my body would not respond. I was frozen in place and could only move my eyes and watch the horrors committed. It was over in minutes. All the children between twelve and sixteen years old were gathered together and marched away. Mitsuro then ordered his men to take my wife and daughter as well. He told me that they would be safe if the town and I did as he told us. He grabbed me, and that was when I knew he was a monster as well. He lifted me with one hand and pulled me close to his face. He had the eyes of an Akuma and teeth like an animal. The last thing I remember was pain in my neck. When I woke the next morning, I discovered that we were all caught in a never-ending nightmare."

Akio retained his calm exterior as Yagi poured out his woes. "What happened next?"

"They come here weekly and take tribute from us in the form of blood," Yagi told them. "What was once a town of over four hundred has dwindled to just over eighty since they arrived. The elderly and infirm were the first to die, and many more have been taken by his men since."

Yuko walked forward to put a comforting hand on Yagi's shoulder but paused when he recoiled from her touch. "We will end this, Yagi-*san*. You will no longer have to fear Mitsuro and his men when we are finished." She spoke gently, trying to extend calmness as Akio had taught her.

"What can two people do in the face of these monsters? For that matter, how did you come here without dying? Sho Mitsuro turned our children and others into monsters that stalk the darkness. You will bring them down on all of us. I must get inside before they come." His voice rose until it was almost a shout. His wide eyes showed the whites all around, and his head jerked as he searched for danger on all sides.

Akio projected a sense of calm toward him again.

The man quit trying to run but was still visibly terrified. "We cannot be outside after dark. Sho Mitsuro forbids it and has placed the beasts to keep us in. It is a death sentence when they find you. Please go before you get us all killed."

"Where is this Mitsuro? He must have a base here." Akio faced the panic-stricken man and waited for his answer. When he looked away, his fear preventing him from speaking, Akio read his mind, then turned and walked away. He called over his shoulder as he strode away, "Go inside and lock your doors. Tonight is the last time you sleep in fear of this false emperor."

Yuko was lost in her thoughts as they walked back to the Pod. Once aboard, her quiet voice broke the hush. "What did you see, Akio?"

"I know where Mitsuro is hiding, and that he has at least four more Forsaken with him. We will arrive in a short time," he informed her as the Pod silently lifted into the air.

CHAPTER FOUR

Uegusuku Castle, Kume Island, Okinawa Prefecture, Japan

"Sho Mitsuro, we have intruders," a vampire wearing the armor of a fifteenth-century samurai warrior announced as he strode into the throne room of the castle.

The man sitting on the throne wearing the regalia of an emperor raised one eyebrow as he looked down on him without replying.

"My apologies, Sho Mitsuro," he murmured as he quickly bowed ninety degrees at the waist. He held that position for almost a minute before the man on the throne addressed him.

"Do not let it happen again, Ogawa. Report."

He stood, relieved that Mitsuro had not made him wait longer. "*Hai,* Sho Mitsuro. There was a disturbance in the village. The pack that was patrolling tonight have all been killed. It looked like the killers used swords, and there were no other bodies present. Yagi claimed that a man and a woman came to the village tonight and threatened you."

He reported in the manner that Mitsuro required—short and concise, just the facts.

Mitsuro remained silent for the span of a few heartbeats. "Get the others and find them," he ordered. "Do not return to me until you have put their heads on the wall."

The vampire bowed low again. "It will be as you have commanded, my Lord."

The Pod silently descended in front of a tall log bulwark on the highest point of the island. It surrounded an imposing castle, the type which dated back to the days of the samurai in feudal Japan. The building was four stories high and had a gently curved roof that covered its entirety. The walls were traditional rice paper panel construction that could be slid aside or removed depending on the whim of the occupant. Torches spaced along the wall provided illumination.

It was a sight to behold, appearing much as the original had in the fifteen hundreds when it was a functional seat of power. Akio also noted that there were few signs of damage from the earthquake that had destroyed much of the rest of the island.

Yuko looked around with curiosity. "What is this place, Akio?"

"It is a reconstruction of the original Uegusuku Castle." He paused for a moment, lost in thought. "A very accurate one, at that. There was a movement to restore some of the historic structures around the country before everything came crashing down. It appears that this one was completed, or close to it. The original ruins are on the peak just behind this. If I remember correctly, the Ministry of Culture planned to lease the site for movie sets as well as lodging for people who wanted to experience how the Shoguns lived."

Yuko sighed. "It's beautiful."

Akio didn't disagree. "*Hai*, the architecture of that period was something to behold."

As the Pod settled, the gate opened, and four figures dressed as samurai warriors stepped out into the flickering light of the torches.

Akio and Yuko exited the Pod and faced the four.

"Look, brothers, we have a celebrity with us. The famous Bitch, Akio," one of them faux-gushed as he stepped forward. His face turned to a mask of rage as he continued, "He is also the honorless dog who turned coat and joined the people who murdered our Queen."

Akio stiffened slightly, then his mouth turned up in a feral smile. "Ogawa, I see that you survived like the roach you are. It will give me great satisfaction to correct that unfortunate situation."

"The dog shows his teeth." Ogawa smirked. "I will enjoy making you scream as I did in the past before I end your traitorous life.

"Akio, who is this *thing*?" Yuko snapped, her face dark with anger.

"This is Ogawa," Akio informed her. "He was one of Kamiko Kana's enforcers, and 'thing' is an apt description. She used him to torture people who displeased her and terrorize the Wechselbalg to keep them in line." He grimaced. "She also had him torture and torment her followers if the whim struck her. He was Ogawa Sato of the Imperial Army when he was still human—if you could say someone with his particular taste in entertainment was ever human. He was a torturer then as well, and he enjoyed his work. He grew worse when he became Forsaken."

"Ha, you question my practices. That is rich, coming from one who has your taste in companions," Ogawa barked.

Akio's eyes narrowed at the jibe. "He was a guard at a prisoner of war camp during the war. His commanding officer learned that he liked to hurt people and took him in as his apprentice. He turned him into an expert in the ways to cause pain to a human body. In some ways, the student surpassed the master, but both took great pleasure in the suffering of others.

"Before the war ended, his commander was transferred to assist with the defense of Okinawa and brought his pet torturer with him. Ogawa was the one who suggested that they use schoolchildren as soldiers on the front lines and as suicide bombers. Over half of them were killed when the Americans took the island.

"His commander, Isamu, tried to commit *seppuku* after the battle was lost, but Kamiko's mother found him and turned him before he died. She also turned this one. As humans, they were as bad as Forsaken. As Forsaken, they were allowed to become true monsters.

"After Kamiko's mother died when the bombs dropped, Kamiko used them as enforcers to keep her followers in line. She gave those who displeased her to them to torture for their failures or imagined slights. With victims that did not die easily, they were able to advance their entertainments to a new high."

"Oh, Akio, you embarrass me with your praise." The Forsaken smiled as he let his eyes wander up and down Akio's body. "I did so enjoy the sound of your screams as I played your body and mind like a violin. You were always so tough, so determined not to show any reaction to the things I did to you. What was the name of your little friend again? Kenjii, wasn't it? I still smile when I remember the anguish you suffered as Isamu and I tortured him in front of you. His eyes begging you to help him as we slowly turned him into a screaming pile of flesh and you could do nothing to save him."

"Yes, I remember, Ogawa," Akio growled. His fangs showed as he slowly slid his katana from its sheath. His eyes glowed red like the fires of hell, and his voice turned as cold as a grave. "Now there is no one to save you from me."

"Kill them," Ogawa ordered.

The other three Forsaken surged toward Akio and Yuko, swords at the ready. As the first reached Akio, he blurred out of sight at preternatural speed and the Forsaken lurched to a halt as his head slid off the stump of his neck, blood spraying as it fell into the dust.

Yuko stepped back as she was rushed by another, her sword held high with the blade pointed toward her attacker. His blade flashed down in a move designed to eviscerate her from shoulder to waist but abruptly stopped as she brought hers down to block.

The Forsaken stared at the crossed blades, his eyes wide with shock that such a small woman could block his swing, not to mention stop the blade entirely. He jerked the sword back and slashed at her face, only to have his blade stopped cold again.

Yuko slid her blade off his, pushing it to the side, and feinted a stab toward his exposed leg. As he snatched his blade back to block, she smoothly reversed her swing, and a gash appeared in his shoulder.

He stumbled back, his eyes wide. He was not used to *anyone* doing that. Before becoming Forsaken, he had been an enforcer in the Yakuza and was accustomed to people fearing the organization, not resisting. He had relied on his superior speed and strength to keep the humans in line since becoming Forsaken. Against Yuko, he was as disadvantaged as humans were against him.

As he stared at the blood streaming from his shoulder, he didn't see Yuko pivot with her sword extended straight out from her shoulder. He was still gaping at the bloody wound when her razor-sharp blade sliced through his unprotected neck, ending his confusion along with his life.

Akio continued to move at preternatural speed as he easily dispatched the third attacker. To Akio's enhanced perception, his opponent moved as slow as humans seemed to move to the Forsaken. That, coupled with his lack of training with the sword he carried, left Akio with time to observe Yuko efficiently dispatch her attacker. Both crumpled to the ground in front of Ogawa at the same time, their blood splattering across his shoes.

Akio moved to stand in front of Ogawa and stopped,

looking at him contemptuously. "Ogawa, I have waited many years for this moment. If I didn't need to deal with this false Sho, I would take my time and make you suffer before ending your miserable life. As it is, I will have to be satisfied with your death and not the suffering you deserve."

Ogawa sneered. "Always the arrogant one, Akio—so certain of your superiority. I will not go as easily as the children you just killed. Until Isamu turned them, barely a year ago, they were gangsters and thugs. When I am done with you, I will make your woman scream louder than your little catamite did."

Akio's lips curled into a feral grin as Ogawa spoke. When he finished, Akio blurred forward. Ogawa's mouth opened in shock as his sword, hand still wrapped around the hilt, fell into the dust at his feet.

Akio continued his swing as his body turned and Ogawa screamed as the blade cut into his midsection, blood flowing down and soaking his ancient armor. Akio reversed his blade, and in the blink of an eye, Ogawa's head separated from his body and fell to the ground.

With a nod to Yuko, Akio walked toward the closed doors of the castle. When he reached them, he hesitated only long enough to raise his foot and smash it into the center of the twin doors. The impact slammed the doors against the walls with a loud *boom*, knocking one off its hinges.

He strode into the castle as the sound echoed through the open room.

CHAPTER FIVE

Uegusuku Castle, Kume Island, Okinawa Prefecture, Japan

Another Forsaken in the full regalia of a fifteenth-century emperor was sitting on an ornately carved throne. Two women in traditional *geisha* attire knelt at its foot on either side with their heads bowed, their eyes staring sightlessly at the floor. The numerous bite marks and scars on their necks made it evident the Forsaken fed on them frequently.

The Forsaken glared at them, his eyes flashing red as he snarled, "Who dares come into my home in such a disrespectful manner? I will see your heads hanging on my wall before daybreak for this insult. What gives you the right to so boldly enter Sho Mitsuro's keep?"

Yuko stepped up beside Akio as he halted just inside the doors. "Full of himself, isn't he?" she murmured.

"Still your vulgar tongue, harlot!" Mitsuro raged as he surged to his feet and drew a well-worn katana from the sash around his robes. "I will remove it from your mouth if you speak again," he growled as he pointed the blade at Yuko.

Yuko's eyes flashed red as she raised her sword and started toward him.

"Yuko, hold. This one and I are old acquaintances. He is mine," Akio told her coldly, his voice holding a hatred she had never heard from him before.

She lowered her sword with a huff, still glaring at the man in front of the throne. Her lips were tight with anger as she murmured, "If he calls me a whore again, I'll shoot him."

Akio cut his eyes toward the infuriated woman. "Who is this?" he chided. "When did the Queen's Vicereine become so bloodthirsty? I thought you preferred to negotiate with your voice, not your Jean Dukes."

Yuko lifted her chin. "I am my Queen's Vicereine, and as such, I will not tolerate this disrespect. To disrespect me in such a way is also disrespectful to Bethany Anne. That will not be tolerated."

Akio's lips turned up in an almost undetectable smile before he addressed the Forsaken. "Sho Mitsuro?" He sneered. "I knew you had an overinflated sense of worth, Isamu, but this is a bit much, even for Kamiko's favorite errand boy."

"Errand boy?" Mitsuro echoed. "Akio, you who abandoned Kamiko Kana in her time of need, dare call me that? I alone have remained faithful and kept her dream alive. I have worked to establish a world controlled by us, the true masters. A world where the human cattle and the Weres know their place. You are no better than a rabid dog. I will take your head and offer it as a tribute to

Kamiko Kana's memory." He glared at Yuko. "Then, I will take your *whore* and make her part of my personal harem." He leered as he indicated the two kneeling women.

Yuko's face darkened in rage as she reached for her Jean Dukes Special, only to be stopped by Akio's outstretched hand as he responded to the Forsaken.

"Isamu, it would have been better for all if you had died in that cave when you were bleeding out from your wounds. You were without honor as a human, you had no honor after you were turned, and the evil you have inflicted here, along with the beasts we were forced to destroy proves that you still lack honor. You always felt that you were above everyone else. Naming yourself emperor shows that you are still infected with that same pretentious arrogance."

"Do not call me that name again," he yelled, his eyes wide and spittle flying from his mouth. "Isamu was weak and died in that cave the day Okinawa fell to the American forces. What emerged was much more. I am Sho Mitsuro to you, cur, and that is the name that will be on your traitorous lips when you die."

Mitsuro stepped off the dais that held his throne and stopped between the two women kneeling there. They showed no signs of being aware of anything around them, continuing to look down at the floor in front of their knees. He laughed. "Your whore will make a nice addition to these that I took from that simpering fool of a Mayor."

Enraged beyond reason or logic, Yuko shoved past Akio as she drew her katana and flew across the space between them, her eyes burning red.

Mitsuro smiled as he pressed the button on a remote hidden in his hand.

The floor beneath Yuko disappeared when a trapdoor that covered nearly all the space between the door and the throne gaped open under her feet. Her forward momentum carried her to the edge closest to Mitsuro, her toes contacted the rim and gripped it.

Before she could gain her balance, Mitsuro casually raised his sword. The point struck her lightly in the center of her chest. The steel didn't penetrate the Jean Dukes armor under her clothes, but gravity took control. She fell into the dark, gaping hole as Mitsuro smirked at her.

Akio watched helplessly as Yuko plummeted backward. The snarls and the stench of death emitted from the dark told him there were more Nosferatu below. Before he could react, the floor snapped back into place and locked, cutting him off from her with a solid *thud*.

"Now that your whore is a plaything for my pets below, it is just us," Mitsuro growled as his eyes turned red again. "I think I will make you suffer before you are allowed to die, traitor."

CHAPTER SIX

Uegusuku Castle, Kume Island, Okinawa Prefecture, Japan

Yuko twisted as she fell through the darkness. She landed hard on one knee and was immediately swarmed by a group of blood-crazed Nosferatu. They knocked her to the ground and buried her under a mass of teeth and claws. Her armor blocked most of the attacks, but the enraged horde repeatedly ripped her exposed skin.

She pushed against the floor, launching her body with her enhanced strength and scattering the creatures as she surged upward. She landed on her feet with her blade ready and sliced the arm off a Nosferatu as its clawed fingers reached for her face. She followed through with a twist of her wrist that left a headless body where her blade passed. As it crumpled to the ground, she spread her feet and braced for attack from the numerous others rushing at her.

In the dim light of a single torch, she saw that she was in a room almost the size of the throne room above. She also saw that she had located more of the missing villagers, who had become feral beasts. Their clothes were in tatters, their bodies as gray as corpses, wasted and gaunt. There were almost twenty of them closing in on her from all sides. Although her enhancements healed the damage from their claws and teeth, being mobbed again was not something she wanted to experience, so she started cutting her way through the horde in the direction that had the fewest opponents.

She cut down three in rapid succession as she fought her way across the room, working herself into a corner where she could place her back to the wall and face her attackers head-on. The mindless Nosferatu continued to swarm her as the bodies piled up in front of her position, the unthinking feral beasts intent only on her destruction.

Mitsuro leapt across the distance between them, his eyes glowing red and his blade aimed for Akio's unprotected head. Akio raised his sword, expecting to easily block the swing, and was taken aback when a shock ran down his arm. He spun away from the next strike and created distance between them to assess his opponent. Mitsuro was stronger than he remembered and moved much faster than he'd anticipated. Akio mentally chastised himself for doing what he had pointed out to Yuko earlier in the day: seeing what he wanted instead of what was there.

He dropped as the blade came toward his face again and swung his katana across Mitsuro's exposed thigh.

The Forsaken hissed in pain as he jumped back to avoid

Akio's backstroke to his other leg. "You're better than I remember, traitor. No matter. I will still avenge your betrayal of Kamiko. I don't care what tricks you have learned since we last met, I am still the better swordsman," Mitsuro gloated as the blood flowing from his leg wound slowed and then stopped.

Akio did not reply. The faint sounds of battle from beneath the floor concerned him. Bethany Anne had tasked him as Yuko's protector, and he was determined not to fail either of them.

Nosferatu came at her in a seemingly endless tide, and Yuko used her sword with precision to separate heads and claw-tipped hands as fast as they appeared. She stepped back to avoid a swipe aimed at her eyes and felt her foot slip on something that squished. The odor of rotting flesh assailed her nostrils, the stench causing bile to rise in her throat.

She spared a glance down and saw that she had stepped on a bloated, severed leg. She retched as she realized it was from a young child. Her vision went red with anger that Mitsuro not only created the beasts assailing her but had also killed innocents to keep them fed.

She lashed out with her foot at a large Nosferatu dressed in the remnants of heavy work clothes—the type worn by the men who worked the fishing boats in the area—crushing his chest and knocking him into the group behind him. They fell to the ground in a tangle of arms and legs. She used this small window to step off the scattered body parts beneath her and assume a more stable stance. When the Nosferatu came for her again, she launched into them with a fierce growl. In moments, the snarling hoard was silent, pieces of them scattered about the floor like a child's abandoned toys.

Yuko gagged at the stench as she drew a deep breath and surveyed her prison, her enhanced eyes having no trouble with the dim torchlight. She saw a door on the opposite wall and cautiously approached it, stepping carefully around and over the body parts in her way. She tried to turn the knob and discovered that the door was locked.

A quick twist of her wrist caused the knob to emit a tortured shriek as she twisted it out of the door. She shoved the door hard when she entered the room. It crashed into the wall with enough force to rebound back toward her. As she shot through the opening, the smell of unwashed bodies and fear was so thick she could taste it. She froze, her eyes registering what was there but her mind not wanting to believe what she saw.

She was in a room almost as large as the one before. The main differences were that this one was better lit and it contained multiple metal cages. The cages were stacked two high along the entire length of one wall. Each cage measured five feet long and three feet high and was occupied by two or more people crammed into the tight confines. They all stared at her with looks of absolute terror.

Yuko came out of her mental stupor and slowly approached the cages. The occupants shrank back from her as far as the small cages allowed.

She stopped and addressed the group. "I am here to help you. There is no need to be afraid any longer."

A gray-haired man with thin and wrinkled skin cowered as she approached his cage. His eyes were wild as he futilely pushed against the back of it, searching for a path to escape.

A disheveled young woman shared the cage with him. She gently placed her hand on his arm. "*Sofu*, I do not think she is one of the evil ones. She said she is here to help us. You heard the sounds of battle coming from the other room, and she is covered in blood. I think she fought the mindless beasts."

"You will no longer be threatened by them. They have all found peace," Yuko assured the woman.

Yuko approached the cage's door and saw that it was fastened with a simple padlock. She gripped the lock in her hand and twisted until the metal creaked and the lock snapped off. She threw it away in disgust and pulled the door open. As she reached in to help the elderly man, he recoiled from her, his eyes showing white all around in terror.

"She is one of them!" he cried as he looked at the blood-covered blade she still gripped in her hand. "She will kill us all."

Yuko stepped back and quickly sheathed her sword. Then she slowly moved forward, holding her hands open as she projected a sense of calm toward the man and told him, "I promise you, *ojii-san*, you have nothing to fear anymore. I will get all of you out of this evil place and to safety."

The man hesitantly crawled forward in the cramped

cage, his eyes darting to all sides. He clearly expected to die at any moment.

The young woman slipped around him and slid to the stone floor, then caught his frail arms and eased him down till he stood shakily on the ground. *"Shenshi-sama*, thank you for saving us, but we must leave this place quickly." The young woman whimpered as she spoke. "The four demons were here earlier and will soon return. We must go before they return and kill us all."

"They will not be back to bother you again," Yuko assured her.

She stepped away from them and moved along the row, removing the locks from each cage and assisting the captives in the top cages to the floor as she went.

When she was done, there were thirty people in various states of disorder and poor health. It broke Yuko's heart to see them warily watching in all directions, expecting an attack that Yuko would not allow to come.

Yuko approached the woman who was supporting her grandfather with a shoulder under his arm. "How do I get back to the throne room?"

The former captive pointed to a door. "The stairs leading to it are there, but you can't go that way. Sho Mitsuro is up there. There is a tunnel that leads outside this way." She indicated a natural opening opposite the door with her head, her hands supporting most of her frail grandfather's weight.

"What is your name?" Yuko asked.

"Koda Rii, *Shenshi-sama*," she replied with her eyes downcast respectfully.

Yuko put a hand on her arm. "Rii-*san*, I need you to take

these people to safety. I have unfinished business with Sho Mitsuro."

Koda's eyes widened. "I can do this, but please come with us. Mitsuro is a monster. You can't win against him. You will be killed, or worse."

Yuko raised one eyebrow. "Mitsuro will find that harder to do than he thinks—if he is still alive. My associate did not fall through the floor as I did. I'm certain he will have much to say about that."

Yuko cringed as she thought of Akio's response to her attempted attack and subsequent glaring failure. She was sure that pushups would be involved—many, *many,* pushups, with him sitting on her back while explaining the virtues of self-control in great detail as she did them.

CHAPTER SEVEN

Uegusuku Castle, Kume Island, Okinawa Prefecture, Japan

Akio put the sounds of the battle below from his mind and focused on Mitsuro. Yuko was a capable warrior. With her enhancements and training, she was more than a match for a few Nosferatu. She'd defeated the Forsaken earlier with no problem.

Mitsuro flew across the floor, his sword held high as he attacked. Akio brought his katana up and caught Mitsuro's blow with the flat of his blade and, in a motion too fast to follow, reversed it in a counterthrust. His steel bit deep into the Forsaken's forearm.

Mitsuro inhaled sharply, twisted to the right, and continued in a full circle with his sword held level, intent on using the momentum to remove Akio's head.

Akio twisted away from the strike, the blade missing him by a hair as he lashed out again. The Forsaken jerked away as Akio's razor-sharp katana flashed down, leaving a bloody cut on his thigh. Mitsuro spun to his left and blocked Akio's strike as he tried to follow up with a thrust to the Forsaken's chest.

Sparks flew from both blades as they continued to trade blows, Akio intent on killing him quickly but unable to get past the false emperor's guard.

They attacked and countered ever faster, their forms becoming colored blurs amid the ceaseless clash of ringing steel. Mitsuro took several steps back, retreating from Akio's deadly sword. When Akio surged forward for a killing blow, Mitsuro reversed direction and slammed his shoulder hard into Akio's chest.

Akio's armor protected him from broken bones. He crashed through one of the rice-paper walls and caught himself. Mitsuro leapt after him and received another bloody gash, this one running from his left shoulder down to his waist. He tried to twist away from the deadly blade, only to be sent flying back through the wall by Akio's booted foot to his ribs.

Akio jumped back through the shattered wall in time to see Mitsuro run behind the throne's dais. Then he heard a slamming noise. When he arrived where he had last seen the fleeing Forsaken, he discovered a semi-concealed door in the back of the dais.

Without pausing, he thrust-kicked the door, his heavy boot adding to the move's power. It exploded in a shower of splinters, revealing a dark stairwell that led down to the level below.

Yuko was about to step through the doorway the young woman had indicated when she heard running feet descending the stairs. She stepped back and smiled when she saw a bloody Mitsuro exit while looking over his shoulder. She lifted her sword above her head, her eyes focused on the man and her blade pointed toward him.

Mitsuro sensed her at the last moment and angled away from the blade positioned to penetrate his skull. He turned in a flash and brought his blade toward Yuko's exposed side.

Her sword shot into the opening, and the sound of metal-on-metal reverberated throughout the space. Mitsuro, his chest covered in blood from Akio's cut, spun his blade in an arc and pushed Yuko's up and out. He again tried to take her in the side as he spun in a circuit around her.

"You think you can best me? I will gut you and leave you here as a gift for the traitor," Mitsuro snarled as he swung.

Yuko bent away from the blade and quickly backed up as she felt the blade scrape across her concealed armor.

Mitsuro grinned maniacally as he saw the blade bite into her side, thinking he had dealt her a serious blow because of the dress she wore over her armor. His smile turned to shock as Yuko's blade neatly sliced into his arm just below the shoulder, causing him to stop.

Yuko slammed her foot into Mitsuro's ribs. The sound of breaking bones, followed by his scream as he flew across the floor to slam hard into the unyielding volcanic rock wall, brought a slight smile to her face.

She cautiously approached him where he lay in a

broken heap with blood pooling under his body and stood over him, her katana at the ready. She was distracted by a noise behind her and turned to see Akio. She smiled at him and noticed his eyes widen just as she felt a sharp pain in her neck. A strong arm wrapped around her and snatched her against an unyielding body.

"Stop there or I will kill your whore," Mitsuro snarled, pushing his blade into Yuko's neck hard enough to cause a trickle of blood.

Akio stopped and eyed the man, assessing his options. "If you kill her, you are dead, Isamu."

"I told you, traitor, Isamu is dead," he yelled. "If you call me that name again, I will gut her like a fish as you watch. Just like I did to your lover, so many years ago."

Akio held his hand up in a placating gesture. "Sho Mitsuro, you will not escape if you harm her. Now, let her go, and we will finish this."

"You don't tell me what to do, dog. I am leaving. If you try to follow, she will die." He pulled Yuko backward as he spoke, causing her to stumble. As he shifted his grip, she slipped farther from the blade at her throat, with the added effect of making him adjust to correct their balance. His blade wavered as he tried to tighten his grasp, then his body froze as the distinctive sound of a Jean Dukes Special rang out.

Yuko stepped away from him as his grip relaxed and turned toward him, her Jean Dukes Special in hand. A bloodstain rapidly seeped into the robe covering his abdomen.

"I told you what would happen if you called me a whore

again," she growled through clenched teeth. "I do not lie about such things."

She glanced down at her pistol, and with a flick of her thumb, turned it to eight. She then aimed it at his head. His face was slack with disbelief. "Akio, do you need this piece of vile excrement alive any longer?"

"Wait, Yuko." Akio stepped forward, his eyes locked on the injured Forsaken. "Isamu, tell me who is behind this. I know you aren't working alone."

"Isamu is dead," he wheezed. "I am…"

"Yes, I know. Sho Mitsuro," Akio grumbled as he approached. "Who are you working with? Who is behind this? I know you did not do this on your own. You never had that much ambition." He hesitated briefly before adding, "Isamu?"

"I told you, traitor," the wounded man grunted, "Isamu is dead. I am Sho Mitsuro."

"Delusional to the end, I see." Akio sighed. "It's a good thing you never were any good at shielding your thoughts."

Akio raised his blade, his lips set in a thin line. There was no shred of pity evident as he looked at the man who had caused him so much pain in the past. He stopped and watched as the Forsaken's body started to slowly heal from his wounds, the blood flow slowing until it stopped.

Isamu did not have the energy to heal completely due to the heavy blood loss, but after a short time, he stood straighter and glared at Akio. "What are you waiting for, traitor?" he snarled. "Are you too squeamish to kill an injured man?"

"I was only waiting for you to recover a little, Isamu," Akio informed him with a smile that did not reach the coldness of his eyes. "It will make this much more…satis-factory, if you will."

"Do you think to frighten me? I know you, and know that you're too weak to torture someone. What game are you playing?"

Akio studied the Forsaken like he was a bug under a magnifying glass before he answered, "No games here. So, you think you know me? You only knew Akio the vampire, Kamiko Kana's faithful vassal. That is a large part of who I was. But long before that, I was someone else."

Isamu laughed. "What does that have to do with anything? We were all someone else when we were lesser beings."

"There is your problem," Akio told him coldly. "You are lost in your arrogance. You always thought of me as someone beneath you, but that is only because of your ignorance. Let me enlighten you to the truth."

"Truth," Isamu barked. "What truth are you talking about? The truth that you abandoned Kamiko? The truth that you got lucky and found someone with the knowledge to make you a little stronger? The truth…" He paused when Akio shook his head.

"Do you know the history of this land?" Akio asked.

Isamu sneered. "What of it? The humans built this, and when I came here, I liked it. That's why I had my slaves repair it."

"Not this structure, Isamu, the history of the island. Do you know it?"

Isamu stood a little taller, his body slowly recovering from the damage. It was not complete, but he was strong enough to bring the hope of escape. "Why should I care about the history of a human place? The only thing I care about now is seeing you dead!" he screamed as he launched himself at Akio.

Akio gracefully slid to one side as the enraged Forsaken came toward him. His blade flashed downward and Isamu's sword clattered to the stone floor, his severed hand still wrapped around the hilt.

Isamu screamed in pain, holding his bloody stump in shock as Akio continued to speak as if nothing had happened.

"As I was saying, Isamu, this island and all the others in the area were once part of the Ryukyu Kingdom." Akio advanced toward him as he spoke. "Had I not caught the attention of a vampire, things would have been very different for me."

He casually picked Isamu up with one hand around his throat and pushed him against the wooden door frame, holding the Forsaken effortlessly as he struggled. "Where was I? Oh, yes. I led those who laid waste to the original castle here at the order of my king, Sho Gen, the man I called Father. Had I survived, I would have eventually ruled these islands. Instead, I was turned into a vampire."

Akio tossed his katana into the air and removed the tanto from his belt. He drove it through the struggling Forsaken's chest, pinning him to the wooden frame behind him, and caught the katana as it came down. "You think me weaker than you because I do not enjoy causing others pain for the pleasure of it. What you do not know is that I come from a long line of men who understand that there are times when Justice must be meted out."

His eyes turned red and fangs protruded from his

mouth, and his voice took on a deeper, more menacing tone as he pushed fear out all around him—the fear that only a Queen's Bitch could cause. "I also know that sometimes Justice requires *PAIN*!"

The Forsaken's eyes widened at the terrifying visage before him. He screamed as an overwhelming sense of fear slammed into his consciousness, the involuntary shrieks of a being in absolute terror. Those soon turned to unceasing wails of pure agony until eventually, they faded to whimpering moans.

Akio did not speak again until he pulled his katana back. "This is for Kenjii." He brought the blade down, cutting through Isamu's neck and lodging the blade deep in the wooden doorframe. The Forsaken's bloody head spun through the air and landed with a dull *thud* several feet away from the torn and lifeless body pinned to the wall.

Yuko stared at the mangled, headless corpse for a few heartbeats. "Justice is served," she whispered.

Akio looked away from her as he softly said, "No, not Justice. Vengeance. I'm not proud of it, but I promised myself many years ago that if I ever had the opportunity to avenge Kenjii, I would make Isamu experience some small taste of the agonies he has caused others over the years."

Yuko laid her hand on his blood-covered shoulder. "It is done, although he deserved much worse."

Akio was silent a moment before replying. "*Hai*, he truly did."

Yuko tilted her head down and peered up at him sheepishly before she murmured, "I rushed in again, didn't I?"

"Yes, you did. Do you now see the consequences of allowing your emotions to take control in a fight? Suppose you had encountered Forsaken in the pit instead of half-starved Nosferatu?" His quiet voice guided her to think through his questions rather than simply react.

Yuko looked down. "*Hai*. I will do better."

"How many Nosferatu did you encounter?"

"I think it was twenty. I lost count but judging by the fresh body parts on the ground when I was done, I believe that is fairly accurate."

Before he could respond, a soft scuffle from the tunnel the villagers had fled through alerted them that someone was coming. Both turned with weapons ready.

"Human," Akio confirmed as he lowered his sword.

"Come on out, we won't hurt you," Yuko called.

Koda Rii hesitantly stepped into the light from the dark mouth of the tunnel. Her eyes widened as she caught sight of Akio, blood-splattered with a naked sword in hand, standing with Yuko.

"For-forgive my intrusion, *Shenshi-sama*," she stammered at Yuko. "I heard Sho Mitsuro as I was leaving, then a fight. I knew that if he lived, he would kill everyone who escaped. I thought to distract him to give the others time to-to try to get away."

Yuko looked respectfully at the brave young woman who was willing to sacrifice herself for others to escape. "You needn't be afraid of him anymore. He seems to have lost his head." She stepped to the side, revealing the headless corpse pinned to the wall by Akio's tanto.

Koda gasped as she saw the body in torn and bloody Imperial regalia stuck to the doorframe. She looked at Akio, her fear-filled gaze quickly turning to admiration.

"Sho Mitsuro is dead? You killed him!" she exclaimed, relief washing over her face.

Akio nodded. "It was a debt that was long overdue."

Koda stared at Yuko and then at Akio, who were both covered in blood from head to toe. Her eyes grew wide, and her mouth opened and closed as she searched for words. She finally blurted, "Master, would you be willing to train me? I wish to learn to fight so I can protect my people if this type of evil ever comes here again."

Before Akio could answer, Yuko interjected, "We will have to discuss it. We are guests of the government as our Queen's representatives and do not wish to offend our hosts."

Akio remained silent. Yuko was the Queen's Vicereine, and this request fell under her area of responsibility.

Koda bowed to Yuko. "I understand, *Shenshi-sama*. I would be honored to train with you." She turned slightly and bowed respectfully to Akio. "If it is allowed."

Akio returned her bow. "You honor me, young one. If it can be arranged with our host, I would gladly teach someone who would willingly sacrifice herself to a beast like Isamu that others might live."

The young woman looked confused. "Who is Isamu?"

"That was the name I knew him by in the past." He motioned toward the body. "Sho Mitsuro was a creation of his diseased mind."

Koda looked thoughtful for a moment but then nodded and glanced at the open door that led to the upper level. "Did you see two women, one about my age and the other older?"

"*Hai*," Akio confirmed.

Her voice trembled. "Are they... Do they still live?"

"They are alive but appear to need assistance," Yuko informed her in a gentle tone. "Would you like to go to them?"

Koda nodded. "Yes. Yes, I would like that very much."

Yuko led the young woman past Isamu's body, which was still pinned to the doorframe. Koda pushed against the opposite side of the doorway, keeping as far from it as possible.

Once the women had started up the stairs, Akio grabbed the hilt of his tanto and twisted it free. Isamu's corpse crumpled to the floor.

Akio stepped over it and followed the two women without a backward glance.

CHAPTER EIGHT

Uegusuku Castle, Kume Island, Okinawa Prefecture, Japan

The three of them climbed the stairs and discovered that both women were still kneeling at the foot of the throne, unaware of the events that had transpired around them.

Koda rushed to them and threw her arms around the older one, folding her in a tight hug. "*Oba-san*, I was so afraid you had been killed," she cried as she buried her face in the woman's neck.

When there was no response, Koda pulled back and stared at the woman. "*Oba-san*, Ono, what is wrong? It's me, Koda, your brother's daughter."

The woman remained unresponsive, so she shook her. "*Oba-san*, Ono, why do you not answer? Please answer me," she wailed, more frantic with each passing second.

Akio put his hand on the distraught young woman's shoulder. "Isamu had the ability to affect people's minds.

Please step back and allow me to help her. When she comes out of it, she might be confused and violent at first."

As Koda stood and moved back a step, Akio knelt in front of the immobile woman. He reached out with his senses and touched her mind. It took only a moment for him to see that she was caught in a repeating loop of horrific images. All featured Isamu, his eyes glowing red, as he attacked and ravaged her daughter while she watched helplessly.

Akio gently pushed calm into the woman's terrified mind. Slowly, the images faded as he carefully worked to remove the compulsion that kept her reliving each terrible act and kept her body frozen in position until Isamu ordered her out of it.

She started to tremble, slightly at first but more forcefully as Akio broke through the compulsion. With a sudden intake of breath, she fell sobbing into Akio's arms. He gently lowered her to the floor and continued to push calm into her mind until she looked into his eyes. He broke the compulsion with one final push, and she started shaking violently as a low moan began deep in her throat and built into a long scream.

She drew a shuddering breath and cried, "No! No! Please don't hurt her anymore. Take me instead. Asai, my beautiful daughter, I'm so sorry!"

Akio laid his hand on her brow and willed her to calm. It was like a switch had been thrown. One moment she was begging in terror, and the next she was quietly looking at the people around her.

"You're safe now. It is over," Akio whispered.

He stood and motioned for Koda to approach. "She has been through a terrifying ordeal. Care for her while I see to her daughter."

Koda took his place and pulled the woman into her arms. "Oh, *oba-san*. The beast is gone. We don't have to be afraid anymore. These warriors have destroyed all of the monsters, and Mitsuro is dead. I saw his lifeless body with my own eyes."

Akio knelt before the younger woman and slipped into her mind. He was assailed by images of Isamu, his eyes red and fangs protruding from his mouth as he repeatedly took blood and other things from the helpless young woman. She would be drained almost to the point of unconsciousness, and then he would force his blood into her mouth. Not enough to turn her, but enough to keep her alive until she recovered enough for him to do it again. He laughed as she cried and begged him to stop, enjoying her fear as he told her how he planned to keep her like this as his blood slave for many years to come.

Akio wished at that moment that he had the power to bring him back from the dead, so he could kill him again.

He carefully started to push images of happier times that he was able to pull from deep within her memories—a birthday party for a friend, swimming in the sea with the young man she loved, images of home and family, all the happiness she had experienced in life—until he was able to replace the horror show Isamu had compelled her to live in with images from her life before the harm he'd inflicted.

When the compulsion broke, she fell unconscious into his arms, exhausted from living in the mental nightmare and physically taxed by the many abuses her body had suffered.

He stood, lifting her in his arms. "Yuko, we need to get her medical attention. Her mind is healed, but her body is very weak. I don't think she will survive the night otherwise."

She nodded and placed her hand on Koda's shoulder. "Come, bring your aunt. We need to get medical help for Asai now."

Koda wore a pained look when she heard this. "We have no medical people here. Mitsuro killed them the first week when they protested his treatment of the others."

Yuko took Koda by the arm and gently pulled her to her feet. "We have medical facilities. Bring Ono and let us get Asai the help she needs."

Akio looked hard at Yuko. "We can't do what you are planning. It could cause—"

Yuko interrupted before he could finish. "Our Queen charged us to protect humanity from the UnknownWorld. We have failed these people, and it is my decision that we do whatever we must to ensure that this woman lives. It is a diplomatic decision." She added softly, "It is also the right thing to do."

Akio nodded in agreement and said no more.

Yuko helped Koda lead Ono out of the castle to the Pod Akio had already called down at the foot of the steps. Akio carried Asai inside and gently strapped her into a seat while Yuko secured Ono and then Koda.

"Eve?" Yuko called over her implant as the Pod lifted.

"Yes, Yuko?"

"We're on our way back with a severely injured woman. Please prepare the Pod-doc for basic regeneration. No enhancements will be made, but she does need all internal damage repaired as well as the external trauma and scars on her body. I also need you to contact the government liaison and advise him that we are still taking care of the problem on Kume. Inform him that the people there are in a bad situation and request that he prepare to send in medical people for support. Tell him we will have the situation in hand and will be ready for the assistance tomorrow afternoon. I will meet them there and direct the resources where they are needed."

Eve was waiting when the Pod door opened and the ramp extended. She had a floating stretcher that used antigrav technology waiting to take the injured girl to the Pod-doc.

"The liaison advised that it is good you don't need them sooner," she informed them as a greeting. "He has a navy vessel going there now, but it is still some distance away. He advised that it can't possibly get there any sooner than tomorrow evening, maybe later depending on the seas."

"Thank you, Eve." Akio carried the young woman out of the Pod and placed her gently on the stretcher as Yuko helped Koda and Ono to the ground. Eve activated the stretcher, and it floated behind her as she took Asai to the waiting Pod-doc.

Ono saw the small android taking her daughter and jerked away from Koda, running toward Asai. "Where are you taking her? Stop, don't take her away from me," she cried in anguish.

Akio intercepted her and placed his hand on her shoulder. She froze when she saw his weapons and the blood-stained armor he wore. He projected calm toward her again as he told her, "Your daughter needs medical assistance. She has been badly injured. Eve is taking her to our medical facility. I assure you that she is in excellent hands and safe."

Ono noticeably relaxed from the combination of Akio's words and the sense of peace he projected. "May I go with her?" she begged.

Akio continued to project calm. "In a short time. First, you need to eat. Your body needs nourishment to overcome what was taken from you. Your daughter will need you when she recovers. You must take care of yourself before you can properly care for her."

Ono looked like she wanted to protest, but Koda gently took her arm. "*Oba-san*, they will care for Asai and help her. These are good people and they will not cause her more harm. Please let them take care of her and you."

Ono looked at Koda and then back at Akio. "*Hai*, you are right. I do not feel well. Perhaps some food will help."

"Let's go get both of you something. Koda, you look as though you could use a meal as well," Yuko told her.

As Yuko led them across the darkened yard into a nondescript building, Koda stared in awe at the vehicle they had arrived in. She had been so concerned with helping her aunt that the trip had been a blur.

"May I ask where we are, *Shenshi-sama*?"

"Please, Rii-*san,* call me Yuko. You're at our base of operations in Tokyo."

"Tokyo! That is fifteen hundred kilometers from Kume Island! We did not take that long in your vehicle." She looked around with wide eyes, not believing what she was told.

Yuko smiled at the bewildered woman. "It's very fast."

CHAPTER NINE

TQB Base, Tokyo, Japan

Yuko brought the two women into the building and stopped at an elevator. She placed her hand on a nearby button and it flashed from red to green before the doors slid open. The three women stepped in.

"Residential level," she directed when the doors closed. The elevator descended rapidly, then the doors opened on a brightly lit hallway. Yuko led them to a dining area, where she went to the cupboard and pulled out some canned stew and two electrolyte-laden drinks that had been stocked in case of emergencies. Akio and Yuko did not eat them, but Eve had acquired whatever she thought might be needed for a variety of situations.

After she set the steaming bowls of protein-rich stew and the drinks in front of the two women, she excused herself to clean up. Her armor had little damage, but the blood that covered it from her battle with the Nosferatu was caked and dry, and the dress she wore over it was a total loss.

As she stepped out of the dining room, Akio met her in the hallway. His lips turned up in a slight smile, and his eyes glinted with barely suppressed mirth as he assessed her disheveled appearance.

"What did you learn today?" he inquired while struggling, with limited success, to contain the smile that threatened to take over his face.

"That Forsaken are worse animals than I thought," she replied.

"'Animal' is too kind a description for Isamu and Ogawa," he stated. "But always remember that Forsaken do not care about human life. They only care that they have humans to use for blood and slaves."

"I understand that, now," Yuko replied. "Are all Forsaken like that?"

"To some extent, those two were evil before they became Forsaken, and as such, they only got worse. But no Forsaken I have ever met does anything but use others for their own means. They are a disease that can only be healed by purging them."

"I will remember that lesson forever," she quietly replied.

"What other lesson did you learn from your actions tonight?"

Her face flushed pink with embarrassment. "Not to allow my anger to make me act in a careless and reckless manner," she told him hesitantly.

"*Hai*, that is a good lesson to take from this. I'm certain that with the proper amount of training and motivation, you will remember that lesson much better next time."

Yuko groaned as she caught the gleam in his eyes,

knowing he would ensure that the motivation was much worse than the training.

All traces of amusement drained from Akio's face. "You did well tonight, but as I said before, you were very lucky. Had Isamu put other defenses into the trap besides mindless Nosferatu, it might have been fatal. If it had contained Forsaken, Weres, or even explosives, you might not have survived. You will need to be more cautious in the future if what I fear is true."

Yuko frowned. "What do you mean? Are there more of them?"

Akio nodded. "I looked into Isamu's mind before he died. He was not working alone. Judging by what I saw, he is only one part of what is happening. He was working with another I have encountered before, and what they plan is bigger than Isamu taking over one small island. Get cleaned up, and we will discuss it after we have seen to our guests."

Yuko stripped off her torn and bloody clothes and peeled her armor off while standing in front of the full-length mirror in her room. Her body still ached in places as her nanocytes worked to relieve the strain of battle from her muscles. She showered, and as she was dressing, Eve contacted her over her implant.

"Yuko, the Pod-doc program will be complete in fifteen minutes. Do you want to be here when I pull Asai out?"

"*Hai.* Asai was unconscious when we took her off the island. I might need to calm her when she comes out."

Yuko stepped into the room with the Pod-doc as Eve was preparing to bring Asai out.

When the unit opened, Asai's eyes slowly focused, and she started to panic as she realized that she was in a strange place with an unknown woman staring down at her.

Yuko projected a sense of calm while speaking quietly but firmly. "You're safe. No one can hurt you here, Asai-*san*."

The young woman calmed noticeably as Yuko's voice and the feelings she projected sank into her mind.

"How are you feeling, Asai-*san*?"

"I feel...better. Much better," she replied, confusion evident on her face. "Who are you?"

"My name is Yuko. You were badly injured and in need of immediate medical assistance. We brought you to our facility for the help you needed."

Asai was silent for a moment, then her eyes flew wide. "My mother, she was with me. Where is she?"

Yuko held out her hand. "She is here, as well as your cousin Koda. If you will come with me, I'll take you to them."

Asai looked at Yuko for a moment before she hesitantly reached out grasped it. Yuko assisted her out of the Pod-doc and offered her a clean ankle-length robe.

After she was wrapped in the robe, Yuko led her to the dining hall.

Ono rushed to her daughter when they entered and wrapped her arms around her. "Oh, Asai, I'm so sorry I couldn't protect you," she murmured, tears rolling down her cheeks.

Asai returned her mother's embrace. "It's not your fault. I heard you begging him to stop each time. I'm glad it was me he chose to torment instead of you. I could not bear the thought of him touching you as he did me."

"Oh, my brave, brave girl. I wanted to rip his eyes out of his head each time he made me watch. He knew that and made it a game to torture me as he did those things to you." Ono sobbed as she buried her face in her daughter's neck and covered it with kisses.

Ono pulled back, her eyes wide as she looked at Asai's smooth, unscarred flesh. "I... What? I don't understand," she stammered as she looked from her daughter to Yuko.

"The technology we used to heal her is extremely advanced. Her body has been restored to the condition a healthy woman of her age should be in," Yuko explained. "Now that she is no longer in danger, I would like to have you and Koda receive similar treatments."

Ono touched her daughter's smooth neck and then pushed the sleeves of her robe up on both of her arms, revealing more unblemished skin. "This is a miracle. The scar from where you cut yourself as a child is gone, along with all the marks and bruises from that beast."

"Oh, Mother, you must do as she says. Let her help you, too!" Asai exclaimed.

Eve had waited silently at the door while the two women had their reunion. Now she called, "Ono, if you will come with me, I can have you as good as new in the time it takes Asai to eat."

Ono looked at her daughter, hesitant to leave her.

Asai smiled. "Go, Mother. Koda is here, and I know they mean us no harm. Please go with her and heal."

Ono slowly nodded. "Are you sure you will be okay?"

"Mother, I am a grown woman. I will be fine," she assured her.

Ono hesitantly started toward the door, stopping and looking back before she stepped out of the room.

"We will be fine, *oba-san*. Go with her. I will take care of Asai," Koda urged.

With one last look at her daughter, Ono smiled and followed Eve.

"Koda." Asai hesitated before drawing a deep breath and continuing, "My father. Is he, does he still live?"

"I don't know." Koda's voice was laced with sorrow. "He did when I was taken two weeks ago."

Yuko placed a steaming bowl of stew and an electrolyte drink in front of Asai. "Is your father Yagi-*san,* the mayor?

"*Hai*," Asai confirmed.

Yuko smiled. "Your father is alive. We saw him and several others in town tonight before we came for you. I thought that was who you were when I realized the two of you were mother and daughter."

Tears ran down Asai's cheeks as she was overcome with emotion. "My father lives? Are you sure it was him?"

"Yes. He told us you and your mother were taken when Isamu, the beast you knew as Mitsuro, and his thugs arrived. We will take you to him as soon as your mother and Koda are healed." Yuko left the two women to themselves as she went in search of Akio to discuss what needed to be done.

"Akio, do we need to do anything on the island before the government representatives arrive? They will not arrive until tomorrow evening or later."

He hesitated, considering for a moment before he replied, "Yes. I heard, and that will be fine. We need to clean up the remains of the Nosferatu and burn them to ensure that no samples can be collected. I have seen the results of experiments done with such samples. It was not a good thing."

Yuko nodded. "I thought as much, based on your reactions on the island. What information did you pull from Isamu before he died?"

"He is part of a group who continued with some of the projects Kamiko's mother was working on before she died when the American bombs fell on Japan," Akio informed her. "They have discovered a way to make weaker Forsaken more advanced. Isamu was stronger and faster than he was when I knew him. That comes with age, but he was still too young to have advanced as much as he had. I saw another I knew from that time when I went into his mind, along with some of the experiments he is doing. If he continues along that path, the Forsaken will be much harder to kill."

"Were you able to see where he is?" Yuko inquired hopefully.

"Only a general location. He is near an old military research location from the war. The labs were destroyed, along with all the test subjects, when the war was lost, but Isamu had the old designation, Unit 731, in his mind. I know where it was located, but China is a big area to hide in. Since the Chinese government is all but nonexistent since they released the virus that decimated most of the world's computers and systems, it could take time to locate them."

"After we do what is necessary on Kume, we will ask Eve to see what she can find. If that doesn't work, we will do what we must to find and stop this before it becomes a bigger problem." Yuko hesitated. "How bad will it be?"

"Devastatingly bad." Several heartbeats later, he continued, "If it is not stopped, we could have an increase in Forsaken numbers, and they could be comparable to vampires who are several hundred years old in strength. They would be capable of doing great harm to the human populations wherever they went."

"We must stop this. That is what Bethany Anne left us to do, and there is no way that I will fail her," Yuko declared.

Akio inclined his head. "*Hai*, Yuko. We will do what must be done to ensure she has a world to come back to."

CHAPTER TEN

Kume Island, Okinawa Prefecture, Japan

The sun was above the horizon as the black Pod descended from the sky and landed just outside the small town. When the ramp opened, Akio stepped out. Eve and Yuko followed.

"Come, ladies. I believe there are some people here who would like to see you." Yuko smiled as three more women stepped out onto the sand.

Ono and Asai blinked, their eyes adjusting to the first sunlight they had seen in many months. They slowly looked around and took in the remains of the town they had lived in all their lives.

"Oh, Mother, it looks deserted," Asai cried.

"No, they are merely afraid. There were several people in the main house and others hiding in a few more when we were last here," Yuko informed her.

As the group made their way into the town square, the remnants of the fight from the night before became visible. Nosferatu bodies were smoldering in the morning sun.

The older ones were completely gone, while the recently changed were barely scorched but starting to rot.

"Eve, we need to clean this up," Akio told the small android. "Although I don't think there will be any viable samples from the remains, I am not willing to risk some misguided scientist learning things they shouldn't."

"I will take care of gathering the bodies for disposal. The data I have says that the nanocytes deteriorate rapidly after the host is dead, but they should be burned to destroy any possibility of a sample being obtained," Eve responded.

"*Hai*," Akio agreed. "I will join you once we have made contact with the villagers."

Ono approached the scarred and battered door of her house and discovered it was locked when she tried it. She lightly knocked while calling, "Suzu?"

Sounds of movement came from inside, followed by the door cracking open barely enough for the unseen occupant to peer out.

The door flew completely open as Suzu Yagi stared open-mouthed at his wife. "Ono? Is it truly you, or am I dreaming that you have returned?"

Ono stepped into him, her arms going around him as she cried tears of joy. "No, Suzu. I am really here, as is our daughter."

"How? Why? How did you escape? I thought you were both dead," he exclaimed as Asai wrapped her arms around them in a tearful group hug.

Ono pulled back enough to free one arm and pointed toward Yuko and Akio, who were standing back and giving the family time to reconnect. "These brave warriors freed us last night. They defeated Sho Mitsuro and his evil minions. We no longer have to live in fear of the false emperor."

Suzu looked at Akio. "Is this true? You really have defeated Mitsuro?"

"*Hai*, Yagi-*san*," Akio confirmed. "Isamu, or Mitsuro as you knew him, and his people are all dead."

Suzu bowed deeply. "Thank you. *Shenshi-sama*. Please forgive me for doubting you last night. I owe you a great debt for returning my wife and my daughter to me. On my honor, anything I can give is yours for the asking."

"I am honored, Yagi-*san,* but you owe me nothing. It is my sworn duty, laid upon me by my Queen, to defend the innocent from creatures like Isamu."

As Suzu started to protest, he was interrupted by an excited voice.

"Father! You're alive," Koda shouted. She ran past the others and almost knocked a man down as she wrapped him in a strong embrace when he emerged from inside the house.

"Koda, my daughter, my light. You live!" he exclaimed as he returned the embrace.

"I have been so afraid for you since they took me." Koda clung to her father. "I was overjoyed when you were not brought to the keep, but as time passed, I feared you dead. Grandfather told me to keep hoping, but hope was not easy to find among the beasts and demons there."

The news stunned Koda's father. "What, you saw my father? Your grandfather lives?"

"I'm not so easily killed, it seems," a voice called from the side of the house.

Koda's head snapped up, and she released her father

and ran to the frail and dirty man leaning heavily on the young woman who had led the group of survivors from the castle into the town.

"Grandfather!" she cried as she went to the opposite side of the woman and took his other arm to relieve her of some of the burden. "Isamu, Sho Mitsuro, is dead. These warriors saved us from his evil."

He smiled as he leaned over and kissed the top of her head. "*Hai.* I saw the remains when I went in search of you, granddaughter. You almost gave this old man a heart attack when you ran back into the caves last night. At first light, I could wait no longer and returned to try to find you. Imagine my shock when all I found were the dead, no sign of my hardheaded granddaughter."

Koda blushed. "Ono and Asai needed medical help after their ordeal. I'm sorry, I didn't think anyone would dare go looking for me. I went with Akio-*sama and* Yuko-*sama* to get them help."

The old man looked in the direction she indicated and pulled away from both of the women supporting him. He stood straight and slowly bowed ninety degrees at the waist to the two.

"My thanks to you both for rescuing us." He turned to Yuko. "My apologies for doubting you. I am forever in your debt."

Akio and Yuko returned his bow. "Thank you for the honor, but you owe us nothing. It was our duty," Yuko told him.

Everyone gathered in front of Yagi's home, the survivors from the castle and the villagers reconnecting with family and friends. They were happy for the ones who'd survived and mourned those they'd lost.

Mayor Yagi and several of the villagers were speaking quietly in the group, all looking and several gesturing toward where Eve stood behind Akio and Yuko. Yuko overheard one woman refer to Eve as an odd-looking child and wonder why she was here.

"Yagi-*san*, I would like to introduce you to the third member of our team." She motioned for Eve to step forward. "This is Eve. She is an Entity Intelligence in an android body. Like our aircraft, she was created by TQB to assist us until they return from space."

Yagi's eyes lit up at this revelation. "You're part of TQB?"

"*Hai.* We stayed behind to prevent things like Isamu did here. When we discover innocents being preyed on, we step in and deal with the offenders."

Yagi nodded slowly as he absorbed this. "What is an Entity Intelligence?"

Eve bowed slightly to Yagi. "Pleasure to make your acquaintance. I am an advanced program, capable of making thousands of calculations in seconds. Think of me as a walking, thinking supercomputer on steroids."

Yagi's eyes widened, shocked at how lifelike the android appeared and acted. "It is indeed a pleasure to meet you as well."

"Eve will be assisting us with the recovery of the bodies of the people Isamu took," Yuko explained.

Eve had piled the remains of the Nosferatu into an old fishing net and was moving the Pod into position to lift them away from the village when Akio and Yuko returned.

"We should make a pyre of whatever we collect from here and the castle. The villagers need to have closure," Yuko told her.

"I will move these to the beach. We can collect what is left at the castle next, Yuko," Eve replied.

When the Pod touched down in front of the gates of the castle, all that remained of Ogawa and the other three Forsaken were their swords and scorched sand where they had fallen. Akio and Yuko stepped out, and Yuko turned to Eve as she started to exit.

She pointed at the cliff on the east side of the structure. "If you take the Pod to the beach at the foot of the cliff, there is a cave that leads to the area under the castle. I believe that is where most of the bodies are."

Eve lifted the Pod, and it dropped out of sight behind the wall as she guided it to the indicated area.

Akio and Yuko entered the castle through the broken doors and made a quick circuit of the upper floors. On the second floor, they came upon a closed door with the stench of Forsaken strong around it. The door opened into a sleeping chamber with a huge four-poster bed draped in heavy cloth. The windows were all covered with thick tapestries, and when Yuko pulled one back, she found the windows had planks nailed over them to keep the sunlight out. Metal shackles hung from one wall on chains. They had found Isamu's bedroom, where Akio had seen the horrors taking place in Ono and Asai's minds when he broke Isamu's compulsion.

"We should burn this place to the ground," Yuko growled. "It will always be a reminder to Ono and Asai of what they endured."

"Agreed, but it is up to them and their families to decide that," Akio stated quietly.

"Why are the Forsaken so horrible? With all that has happened, they could be a force for good if they would work with humans."

"Yuko, the Forsaken only want one thing from humans, and that is total domination over them. Nothing drives them but the lust for power, over each other as much as humans."

Yuko was appalled. "It is senseless to be so strong and want to only subjugate others. I think I understand now why you want to kill them all. There is no way to achieve peaceful coexistence, is there?"

"No. The only way to make peace with a Forsaken is to kill them. Anything less is a foolish effort that could easily see you killed instead. The only good Forsaken is a dead one. There can be no diplomatic solutions with such as them," he stated coldly.

"*Hai.* I understand, but I still do not like to kill. Granted, Isamu deserved it, and he made me angry enough to go after him—not that it turned out as I envisioned it." She finished the last in a whisper.

Akio chuckled. "*Hai,* although your little fall should remind you not to allow it to happen again. Hopefully, you will learn quicker than Tabitha did. The stories Hirotoshi told me about her first few adventures were eye-opening. It will turn my hair gray if you turn out to be half as impulsive a student."

Yuko smiled when she saw him relax a little for the first time since he had encountered Ogawa and Isamu. She didn't know what was wrong, but she was relieved to see him turning back into the person she had known for over twenty years. He was still the most serious man she had ever met, but he had relaxed enough that she was shocked to discover he did have a sense of humor. Granted, it was buried deep, but it was in there.

They worked their way through the remainder of the keep. When they arrived at the sublevel, they found that Eve had gathered all the Nosferatu pieces and piled them onto the fishing net she had found. Isamu's headless corpse was where it had fallen when Akio retrieved his knife, and it was slowly starting to rot as his nanocytes degraded.

Akio looked down at the remains briefly, distaste written on his face, before he kicked the rotting head onto the body. He grabbed the robe and dragged it all out into the sun. Isamu's corpse smoked in the morning light before it burst into flames and turned to ash.

Eve came out dragging her net of body parts, then stopped and placed her hands on her hips as she looked at Akio. "A little help would be appreciated here. I did clean up the mess you made, after all."

Akio didn't look away from Isamu's ashes as he informed her, "Not my mess. I cleaned up after myself just now."

Eve's eyes widened, and her mouth formed an O as she looked at Yuko, who blushed under the EI's shocked look.

"You did all this?" Eve demanded.

Yuko blushed. "*Hai*. I didn't have much choice after Isamu dropped me into them."

The android stared at her for another moment before turning to Akio. "If you can't take better care of Yuko than that, I must insist that I accompany her on any further adventures. It is my job to see that no harm comes to the Vicereine." Her tone left no room for argument.

"It was my fault, Eve," Yuko explained. "I grew angry and allowed myself to make a stupid mistake. It won't happen again."

"See that it doesn't," she snapped. "I don't want to have to explain to ADAM how I lost you, and Bethany Anne would dismantle me slowly if I did."

"*Hai*. I promise that I will be more cautious in the future, my friend."

After the remains were secured, they entered the Pod and flew back to the beach where Eve had deposited the others. The three of them made their way back into the village, and Yuko approached Yagi as he talked to the survivors from the castle.

"Yagi-*san*, we have collected what was left of the remains of the ones Isamu had turned. They need to be burned to avoid the chance of infection spreading, but we wanted to give you and your people the opportunity to say goodbye before we did."

"Thank you. Let me discuss it with my people, and I will organize a group to bring wood for the pyre. We have several houses that can never be repaired, and we can take the wood from them." He moved to the center of the square and called the others to him.

By the time the villagers had moved the lumber to the beach and erected a pyre, many of the Nosferatu had succumbed to the sunlight and were unrecognizable. Akio and Yuko made short work of piling the remains on the pyre. The villagers stood silently, many with tears running down their faces as they realized they would never see their friends and loved ones again, all because Sho Mitsuro had come to their home and turned it into a Hell on earth.

Yagi said a few words over the dead. At his signal, two of the men put torches fashioned from rags soaked in fish oil into the pile of wood. The shattered and dry boards smoked briefly, then flames quickly spread throughout. The villagers stood in silence until all that remained was a smoking pile of embers, and then in ones and twos, everyone wandered back into the village.

Yuko and Eve spent the remainder of the day speaking to the villagers while Akio silently watched. When the Japanese naval ship arrived, they met the captain as he came ashore.

"Yuko-*san?*" he inquired.

"*Hai.* You are in charge of the ship and crew?"

"*Hai.* I was told to offer you the sincerest thanks of the Japanese government for your assistance here. I was informed that the Bitch Protocol was invoked and I am to give whatever aid you require."

"Thank you, Captain. We do not require aid, but the people of this island have suffered much during the past months. They need food and medical care, and I imagine that several will need help dealing with the emotional toll as well. You are aware that there really are things that go bump in the night?"

The captain nodded. "I have been briefed on the UnknownWorld. All military commanders have been warned what to look out for. I believe that was a request you made," he informed her.

Yuko was glad to hear it. "I did. It would not be a good thing for untrained people to try to deal with some of those problems. That was why the Bitch Protocol was developed. We are uniquely capable of handling UnknownWorld issues."

"I am from Hosu," the captain informed her. "I was there on leave when the tiger rampaged through the town a few years ago. I saw the aftermath and heard how the police shot it and it would not die."

Yuko recalled the incident. It had been the first of several instances of a Were attacking humans in the past few years. Eve had picked up the chatter on the police, and military communications and Akio had ended the Were's rampage with a well-placed sword to its neck. That was also the first time that the general populace found out about Weres since there were numerous witnesses who saw the tiger turn into a naked man when Akio killed it in the center of town.

There had been other incidents since then, and all police now carried a magazine with silver-coated bullets. Gun laws had also changed. Where the civilian population had been extremely limited in having firearms before, now many carried them openly in the rural areas. There was much demand for silver by the several ammunition manufacturers that had sprung up to meet the demands of an armed populace.

The naval personnel set up a kitchen and a medical tent in short order, then many of the villagers had their first decent meal in a while that didn't consist of mostly fish and got access to needed medicines that had been unavailable for months. Yuko hoped that since Japan had working ships and communications capabilities, these islanders could get some semblance of their old lives back. They deserved it.

CHAPTER ELEVEN

<u>Kume Village, Kume Island, Okinawa Prefecture, Japan</u>

"Eve, where has Akio gone? I haven't seen him in a while, and he has seemed out of sorts since we came here."

The android was still for a few seconds while she interfaced with the Pod and then the satellite that she had stationed over this region years earlier. "He is standing on the cliff near the castle, Yuko."

"Thank you, Eve."

Yuko made her way to the castle. A few minutes later, she spied Akio looking out to sea. When she approached him, he remained silent with his back to her. It was obvious something was not right, but she had no idea what it could be.

"Akio?" she softly called.

His eyes widened as she spoke, startled that he had allowed himself to become so lost in the past that he didn't hear her approach. "I'm sorry, Yuko. I was remembering this place as I last saw it," he murmured.

"You were here before?" she asked, "After the castle was restored?"

Akio didn't answer immediately. Instead, he rubbed his chin in thought before answering. "No, I was last here many years ago, the day my human life ended."

Yuko paled. "I'm sorry, Akio. I don't mean to intrude. Don't feel you owe me an answer to that. I wasn't thinking."

"No, it is fine. I was just remembering how different things were after that day." He drew a deep breath and turned toward the structure. "As I said earlier, the original castle was on the cliff about fifty meters behind this one. The ruins were declared a historic site many years ago, so the Ministry of Culture built this replica here. This area was on the road leading to the original structure."

Akio stared out to sea, the silence building to the point Yuko was about to ask him to tell her more when he continued.

"My father was the king of the Ryukyu Kingdom, which was comprised of Okinawa and all the islands in this region. I was his firstborn and destined to rule. He had gained the allegiance of all the warlords in the region, and the kingdom was flourishing. There were trade routes established to the Korean kingdoms as well as to other islands. The Ryukyu Kingdom was experiencing a time of peace and prosperity unheard of before.

"Pirates were our biggest problem. I was the second in command of a group that was sent here to deal with a pirate lord who was preying on merchant ships in the area. My mentor was our commander and my best friend."

Yuko remained silent, wanting to ask more but realizing this was the most Akio had spoken about himself in the twenty-plus years she had known him.

After a few beats, Akio continued, "We had taken a pirate ship after it plundered and burned a Chinese trader." He paused, remembering the event. "Had they not murdered the crew and fired the ship, we wouldn't have seen them. As it was, their actions led to their capture and ultimate demise. When we interrogated the pirate crew, we discovered that they were part of a group that had taken over the castle here. After executing them, we came here and discovered that the pirate lord had a small force of seasoned men occupying the castle."

He was quiet again as he walked through the open gates. When he entered the throne room, he stopped and briefly looked around. After a few seconds, he nodded to himself and walked to the rear corner of the room.

"The gates of the original keep were here, and they were heavily braced and covered in iron. There was no way for us to take the castle by overwhelming the gate, so we decided on a different approach. We were an elite group of warriors. Most of us had trained together since we were children and were closer than brothers. We had lived together, played together, and fought together all our lives and were all masters in many different styles of warfare. We were the equivalent of a Special Forces unit in modern militaries."

Akio stopped talking and closed his eyes, momentarily lost in events long past. He drew a deep breath and released it slowly before he continued.

. . .

Kume Island, Ryukyu Kingdom, 1582

"Togu-san, the pirates have taken over Uegusuku castle as we were told. Our scouts have seen only twelve pirates inside, but the gates are barred from within, and they have lookouts around the wall," Akio reported to his friend and commander.

"How do you suggest we take them?" Togu shot back as soon as the report was finished.

Akio's reply was equally quick. *"I suggest waiting until just before dawn and taking a small group to slip over the wall and open the gates from inside after eliminating all of the sentries. They should be tired and less alert at that time. We have watched them for a few days, and they always change the guards after first light. The men appear to be lax at that time, and I believe they can all be eliminated without rousing the others. Then it is merely a matter of cleaning out the vermin."*

Togu's lips turned up in a hint of a smile, proud of how confident and competent his student had become as a military leader since he had started his training. *"Hai, that is a good plan. Select the men to accompany you and make it so."*

Akio bowed to his sensei and turned as soon as he was dismissed to assemble his team.

"We go over the wall here." He pointed to a crude drawing in the sand as the nine warriors he had selected looked on with interest.

"This guard gets lazy a few hours before daybreak and starts to take longer between his patrols. He tends to stay in this corner nearest the sea," he pointed to the indicated spot, *"for a half-hour or more during the last three hours of his watch."*

"His lack of focus will be their undoing." Ryu smiled.

"Hai, and you will be the instrument that sees to it this is his last night on a boring duty." Akio chuckled.

"He will never know I was there."

"Hirotoshi, after Ryu silences the guard, you and the twins make your way to the one on the land side of the keep. I will take Yoshi with me, and we will deal with the one on the seaward side. When both are down, Niwa and Gao will take the two on the gate with their bows." He turned to the two men and cautioned, "Be sure of your shots, because as soon as you loose your arrows, Ryu and I will open the gates. Then the real fun will begin." His smile did not reach his eyes. Both men nodded.

"Move silently as the night, and we will be done with these pirates and back home in a week."

All the warriors nodded their agreement as they were dismissed to prepare for the night's events.

"Ryu, your man is headed to his corner again," Akio murmured as they watched the guard's head go below the edge of the wall. "He must have had a hard day because he started taking longer rests earlier than normal tonight. He was there almost an hour this last time. Give him ten minutes to get comfortable and we will move."

Akio pointed out a darkened section under the wall where the failing torch was. "When the others reach the wall where that torch has nearly burned out, you go over and make sure he doesn't have to answer to his master for the lack of attention to duty."

The warriors worked their way down to the base of the wall in silence. They moved from shadow to shadow until all of them were gathered in the darkness.

Akio signaled, and three of them knelt with their heads facing the wall. Two more carefully climbed onto their backs. Akio and Hirotoshi climbed onto the top two and slowly stood. Ryu stepped between them, and they effortlessly lifted him until he could grasp the top of the wall. He pulled himself up as they pushed him from below, and he silently slipped over the top.

A soft gasp was heard from the top of the wall, and after a short time, a rope fell to the ground. The remaining men climbed onto the dark section of the wall, and seconds later, the guards on both sides died as silent shadows rose behind them and cut their throats without a sound.

"Ryu, let's open the gates for the rest of our men," Akio called softly as the twin twangs of bowstrings releasing came from the front of the castle.

The two warriors ran to the gates and strained as they silently lifted the heavy rough-hewn wooden beam from the brackets that held them closed. As the gates slid open, the remainder of the warriors came through and moved into the castle like silent, deadly shadows.

Akio signaled for Ryu to follow as they made their way inside to the stairs that led to the upper levels. Stepping carefully to ensure they didn't alert the occupants, they slowly climbed to the second floor. This level contained several sleeping chambers. As Ryu moved to the door of one and Akio to another, a pirate stepped out into the hall.

"What? Who? Intruders!" he yelled right before Ryu's blade took him in the throat. Although Ryu moved as soon as he saw the man, the damage was done as sounds of alarm echoed throughout the building. The sounds of running feet came from above, and in seconds, men started pouring down the stairs.

Akio and Ryu dragged the pirate's body into the room he came from before they were seen. The sounds of battle soon came from below as the defenders descended to the first floor.

"I think our scouts missed a few." Ryu deadpanned over the clash of swords and the screams of the injured and dying.

"Hai, it seems so," Akio replied.

"Sounds like they're having fun. Should we join them?" Ryu raised his eyebrows with a smile.

"After you." Akio gave a slight bow.

They made their way down to the first level and saw that the battle was not as evenly matched as they had thought it would be. There were thirty pirates still standing, and only twenty of their men. Akio and Ryu moved in behind the pirates who had come from the upper level and announced their presence by promptly running two of them through from behind.

Four pirates separated from the group and attacked them. Akio ducked a slash that narrowly missed his head while blocking a stab from the other foe. Ryu had it better because one of his attackers had misjudged his reach and was gagging on his own blood around the blade Ryu had put through his throat.

Akio shuffle-stepped to the right and darted back to stab one of his attackers in the chest. His blade stuck between two ribs, and he had to let it go to dodge the other's attempt to run him through. He snatched his tanto from his belt and hurled it at his assailant with deadly accuracy. The sharp tip penetrated the pirate's eye, killing him in mid-stride. Akio slowed long enough to put his foot on the first man's chest and wrench his katana free, spinning half a turn as it came loose and hamstringing Ryu's attacker.

"That's four for me and two for you," he chided as he finished the screaming pirate with a downswing that left him missing the top of his head.

"You're showing off now." Ryu laughed as he blocked a slash from another and finished him on the backstroke. "Three to four."

Akio grinned as the two of them waded into the fray with

CHARLES TILLMAN & MICHAEL ANDERLE

furious swings of their swords, each swing killing or wounding a pirate. In moments, it was over. Akio's group had been reduced from twenty to twelve, and the pirates were all dead or dying on the floor.

Akio flicked his wrist to remove the blood from his katana and motioned for Ryu and Hirotoshi to follow him as he made his way up the stairs to check the floors above. A quick search of the second level revealed only the dead pirate who had sounded the initial alarm and nothing else.

As Akio stepped onto the third level, he was thrown back as a bow twanged and an arrow slammed through his shoulder. Ryu caught him as Hirotoshi bounded forward and sliced the archer from waist to throat with a savage swing of his katana.

"Akio, hold on. We will get you to the healer." Ryu's voice was urgent as he looked at the wound, the blood pulsing out around the shaft in time to the beat of Akio's heart.

"All is well, Ryu. We defeated the pirates. I can meet my ancestors with honor," Akio murmured.

"No, no, you will be fine. It's only a flesh wound," Ryu lied.

"Hai, only a flesh wound," Akio mumbled weakly as everything faded to black.

When they reached the first floor, an overwhelming sense of fear hit them. Ryu and Hirotoshi dropped to their knees, unable to stand under the onslaught. Akio's unconscious body went down with them and lay unmoving. The other warriors were all down and barely registered when two men wearing all black with their faces covered by masks strode into the castle.

One of the men went to Akio's prone form and lifted him as if he weighed nothing. He snapped the shaft of the arrow and shoved it through the wound, and Akio's eyes shot open as the *pain forced him back to consciousness. When the head of the arrow tore out the back of his shoulder, he screamed.*

Uegusuku Castle Ruins, Kume Island, Okinawa Prefecture, Japan Present day

Akio stood silently, staring at nothing for a moment. Yuko watched her friend until his eyes focused and he continued his tale.

"Ryu told me this later—about the overwhelming sense of fear and how it made all of them fall to the ground, helpless." He paused to gather his thoughts. "I came to with an unbearable pain where I had been shot and saw a demon with glowing red eyes holding me. I watched in horror, not believing it was real, as the demon raised its arm to its mouth and slashed it open, then shoved his bloody arm forcefully against my wound. The pain caused me to lose consciousness again and was the last thing I remembered until I awoke sometime later in a dark room that stank of rotting fish.

"The next sensation was pain, like my blood was boiling inside of my body. I had never experienced its like. I tried to cry out but was unable to make a sound. My body was frozen in place, unable to move. I wanted to die, but a voice ordered, 'You must fight the pain. Do not allow it to control you. You are stronger than it is, and you must not let it win.' These words continued to flow through my mind as the agony reached new heights. Each time I wanted to give in to it the voice came again, and I resolved to fight a little longer.

CHARLES TILLMAN & MICHAEL ANDERLE

"When I awoke later, the pain was gone. It had been replaced with an unrelenting thirst." Akio softly revealed.

"There was a man dressed all in black standing over me, and my mind immediately flashed back to the demon I had dreamed. He was small in stature and looked down on me with a completely blank expression. I was a warrior who had defeated many in battle, but I knew immediately that this man, or whatever he was, had no reservations when it came to killing. He was death personified.

"He stood looking down at me for what seemed like hours, then he spoke, but his words did not make sense at the time. 'You have survived the turning process and have been transformed. You are now much more than a mere human. You must feed to complete the change,' he told me in a soft but firm voice.

"I was understandably confused and demanded to know what he was talking about. The only answer I received was 'Silence. All will be explained in due time.'

"He stepped out of the room and closed the door. The stench of fish and the rolling motion told me I was on a ship of some kind. As I stood to search for a way out, the door opened, and a young man was thrown inside.

"He turned to run out the door, but it was slammed and locked before he got to it. I watched as he pounded on it, demanding and then pleading to be released. I had no idea what was wrong, but as he continued, the sweetest smell I had ever encountered came to me. It overpowered the stench of the fish and seemed to be coming from the young man.

"I started toward him, and the next thing I knew, I was holding his lifeless body, my mouth on his throat, drawing what tasted like the finest wine from him. I threw him away from me, mortified at what I had done. Being a member of the royal family, I had heard the tales about demons who came in the night and left bloodless bodies in their wake.

"*Banpaias*—vampires—were things of legend, tales told by superstitious peasants in the rural areas. Not real. But here I was with a bloodless corpse and the sweet coppery taste of his blood in my mouth. That was the first of many innocents who would die at my hand."

He stopped and sucked in a deep breath, the pain of the memory written on his face. "I wanted to die. I didn't want to be a monster from myth, a demon who preyed on the blood of others. As it all sank in, the door opened, and the same man stepped through. He looked at the lifeless body and then informed me, 'You are not a monster, young one, you are a warrior in the service of our queen. You are faster, stronger, and better than any human warrior in the land. You now have the ability to move like the wind and strike at her enemies in silence.'

"I looked at him, and an uncontrollable rage came over me. I lunged toward him, my hands formed into claws with long black talons coming from them. As I was about to strike him down, the voice rang out in my head. '*Stop! You can't harm me, I forbid it.*'

"Try as I might, I could not raise a hand to this man. I railed against the command on the inside, but my body refused to obey. 'Come,' he told me as he turned and walked away. I had no choice but to meekly obey.

"That was the beginning of my life as a Forsaken. I found that the two of them had been watching us for some time, and when we defeated the pirates, they decided to take all of us into the service of their queen. Of the twelve who survived the battle, eleven of us were successfully turned. That was an almost unheard-of success rate, but being strong warriors helped us survive the process.

"We spent the next four hundred years in the service of Kamiko Kana's mother and then Kamiko after her mother was destroyed when the Americans dropped their nuclear bombs. I never enjoyed my time as a Forsaken, denied the light of day, and subject to follow the commands I was given with blind obedience. Gabrielle freed me and my brothers from that existence when she defeated Kamiko. My friend, mentor, and brother of many years sacrificed himself to ensure that our honor remained intact and that we would be allowed to serve Bethany Anne."

Yuko was silent for several moments as she let what her teacher and closest friend had told her settle in her mind. "Akio, I thank you for sharing your story with me. I know you are a good and honorable man. You should not let the things you were made to do in the service of beings so unworthy cause you pain. You had no choice but to obey the compulsion of your maker."

Akio sighed. "*Hai*. I know that, but it still does not make what I did right. All I can do now is try to protect the people and wipe the scourge of the Forsaken from this world until Bethany Anne returns. I will redeem my honor one Forsaken at a time until they are gone or I am dead."

CHAPTER TWELVE

TQB Base, Tokyo, Japan

Yuko and Eve were sitting in the dining room, lost in thought. Eve was reviewing data collected from the satellites orbiting the globe, and Yuko was staring fixedly at the empty teacup resting in front of her. Yuko had been sitting quietly for several minutes when she suddenly spoke. "Eve, we need to figure out ways to generate revenue. Bethany Anne left us with a large amount of funds and control of several companies, but with everything around the world collapsing, I don't think it will be enough. We don't know how long we'll be here or what future expenses we'll have. Besides that, I think we need to do more for the people on Kume. The government is providing the basics for now, but it'll take more than that for them to once again be a thriving community."

"We have enough resources stored here to set them up for the next few years with no problem. We also have the funds to buy more if needed," Eve told her.

Yuko shook her head. "That's not exactly what I'm

thinking, Eve. I would like to help them with some decent housing and maybe even repair one of their docks. It would be much easier for them to rebuild if they had a place for supplies to be delivered without having to ferry them in on smaller boats."

"I understand that," Eve replied. "But why do you feel that it's your responsibility? Not that we can't do it, but it is logical to let their government take care of these things."

Yuko shook her head. "I had to destroy so many of them who were Nosferatu, and my heart hurts for the families who lost so much. The pain and anguish I saw when we spent the day after the funeral there affected me deeply. I feel that we should have been able to find out what was happening and stopped it sooner."

"Yuko, we have already saved many with our intervention, but I do understand what you mean." Eve hesitated for a moment before continuing, "It is not logical, but I also feel that we could have done more. I will need to analyze my programming to determine what is causing this logic breakdown. There must be some defective code in one of my subroutines."

Yuko smiled as she wrapped her arms around the little android, happy that her friend was not only showing emotion but experiencing feelings. It was another step toward ascension. "I'm sure you will figure it out, Eve. While you are doing that, if you would research some business ventures that will help us start generating additional revenue and create opportunities to help those on Kume and any others we may find in similar circumstances, I would appreciate it."

"Certainly, Yuko."

Akio sat in the darkened command center, checking the satellite feeds from the Chinese mainland. He was focused on an area around the northern Heilongjiang Province, the location where the Japanese had carried out biological warfare studies during World War II.

The labs and facilities where the experiments were conducted had been destroyed when the war ended, along with the prisoners of war used in the experiments. What the Japanese military didn't know was that there was another secret lab in the area. This was where the prisoners and test subjects from the UnknownWorld were experimented on. Akio had been there once with Kamiko Kana when she was on an errand for her mother. The exact location was unknown to him, but he recalled the general area.

"Eve, could you assist me in the command center?" he called over his implant.

"I can be there in a little while, Akio. I am running a self-diagnostic at the moment."

"Is everything all right?" Concern filled his voice as he worried that Eve had a malfunction.

"Yes, I believe so. I am attempting to diagnose some abnormalities in my logic programming. I have discovered that some of my actions have been outside of logical parameters recently. I am analyzing subroutine codes for possible errors."

Akio's lips turned up in a bare hint of a smile as he processed Eve's response. Her "I *believe* so" spoke volumes to him about where she was in her journey from EI to AI.

"Very well, Eve. When you are done, I need you to run some searches in the area I am highlighting. Look for any occurrences that point to UnknownWorld activity. Based on the information I took from Isamu's mind, I believe we need to focus our attention there."

"I will see to it and let you know what I find, Akio."

"Thank you, Eve."

CHAPTER THIRTEEN

Research Laboratory, Acheng, China

"Heinz, we have lost contact with Isamu and his people," the communications specialist reported.

"What do you mean, 'lost contact?'" he inquired coldly.

The tech started to visibly shake and sweat broke out on his brow under the close scrutiny of the mercurial scientist. There were several stories floating around the research complex about what had happened to the people who made him unhappy. None of those stories ended well for the perceived offender.

"I apologize, sir, but we are unable to raise either Isamu or Ogawa on the wireless. Isamu's last report was that he had secured Kume Island and was proceeding with the plan. That was over two months ago. We have not heard from him since."

"Send someone to find out. On my authority, the use of the German flying machine is authorized. Advise the pilot that being seen is not an option," Heinz instructed.

"Yes, sir. I will have the crew prepared to launch as soon

as it is dark." The tech slumped in his chair with relief when Heinz stalked out of the room without another word. He quickly made the arrangements for a crew to find out what had happened to their missing team.

"Chang, what has that *dummkopf* Isamu done?" Heinz growled as he stormed into Chang's office. "He had one job —set up a place where we could stage for our attack on the Bitch's assassin and that diplomat. They have interfered with our plans too many times over the last few years."

Chang lifted his hands. "I don't know, Heinz. Let's see what the crew you sent out has to report when they get back. You know it is a huge risk to fly one of our craft too close to Japan, and broadcasting a full report is just begging to be found by the Bitch's people."

Heinz, formerly *Doktor* Heinz Markel, closed his eyes and rubbed his temples in frustration. It was an old habit from his human life that he'd never broken. He looked like he was in his late thirties but was much older since he'd been turned when he was working with the Third Reich during the war. Although not as strong as one of David's children thanks to David's paranoia about sharing that level of power, he was still a formidable Forsaken. With the recent advances in the blood experiments he had been working on for the past sixty years, he knew he was close to being much more.

"I know it's risky," he told Chang. "But we're too close for any of Isamu's insane ideas to set us back now. They know to be careful. Let me know as soon as the crew gets back. I want to hear their report immediately."

Chang nodded. "As soon as they report that they're

inbound, I will send someone for you. I assume you will be in your lab, as usual?"

"Yes. We're close, Chang. I think we will have a sample worthy of a true test soon. The one we used on Isamu worked but did not give us the results I wanted. I fear that it will take more than that to kill the Bitch's assassin."

"Heinz, if it can be done, I know you will be the one to do it," Chang told his oldest living associate.

TQB Base, Control Room, Tokyo, Japan

"That's odd," Eve murmured as she watched a screen in the darkened room. She called up several more screens and started running multiple scans of the anomaly she had detected.

"Akio, would you come to the command center? I have some unusual signals from the sensors I left on Kume," she called over her comm.

Akio stepped through the door, followed closely by Yuko a few seconds later. Both were dressed in workout clothes, and Yuko's face was flushed as if she had been exerting herself.

"What is it, Eve?" Akio questioned.

"I was running imagery, searching for signs of the base you inquired about when one of the sensors I left on Kume alerted me. It detected something coming toward it at a high rate of speed. At first, I thought it was a fault in the sensor because it showed the object coming in from the west a few hundred meters in the air. It kept fading in and out, but when I ran an energy spectrum scan, it had a signature similar to the antigrav technology we are seeing around Germany. Similar, but not an exact match."

"Is it still there?"

"*Hai*, as far as I can tell. The signal faded completely when it drew close to the island. One moment it was there and the next there was... Wait a minute, what's this?"

She touched the screen she had been watching, and a distorted buzz came from the speakers in the room.

"That's an encrypted radio signal!" Eve exclaimed.

Akio grimaced. "Summon the Pod to the rear entrance, please. I think this needs to be investigated."

"The Pod will be ready for departure in one minute," she advised.

"Slave one of the Black Eagles to it in case we need extra firepower," he requested as he stepped toward the door.

"We?" Eve inquired.

"Yuko is going, too."

Eve stepped back from the console and started toward the door. "I am going as well. After what happened to Yuko last time, I feel I need to take a more active role in protecting her when she goes on these field trips with you." She gave Akio her best stink-eye.

Akio raised his eyebrows but didn't respond.

"Eve, I told you it was my fault. Please stop blaming Akio," Yuko gently admonished the android as she continued to look at Akio, her robotic eyebrows mimicking his.

"Hmph. I will continue to blame him for endangering you without warning me until he stops doing it," Eve replied as she stepped between both of them and headed toward the elevator at the end of the hall.

They rode up in silence, Yuko worrying that her friend was still angry. It wasn't comfortable for any of them, but it was another sign of her transitioning from EI to AI. Yuko hoped that she could help Eve work through the emotional issues, but she knew from information Bethany Anne and ADAM had left her that she had to be cautious with Eve's development. She could not take any action that would upset or influence the actual transition—she could only be there, much like the parent of a teenager, to help her cope with the effects without providing the solution.

The three of them stepped out into the dimly lit lobby. During the day, the building served as office space for multiple businesses. It provided good cover for the hidden base beneath, but Akio was concerned that they might need to move the base away from such a densely populated area. With the rise in Forsaken activity, it could endanger innocent civilians to stay there. Even though it was well-hidden, they ran the risk of exposure each time they used a Pod from that location. Plus, the Pods and Black Eagles were currently hidden miles away in a deep ravine. It would be more convenient to have a hangar for them adjoining the base. He decided to bring that up with Eve when she wasn't mad at him.

They exited into an enclosed courtyard behind the building, and Eve brought the Pod and Black Eagle down. As Akio and Yuko climbed into the open Pod, Eve went to the Black Eagle.

Yuko stopped. "Eve, what are you doing?"

"I thought it would be more efficient to fly the Black

Eagle from the cockpit instead of remotely. Plus, it's more fun," Eve answered with a grin.

Yuko watched open-mouthed as Eve climbed into the Black Eagle and it silently rose into the air.

"Take your seat, Yuko. I will not lift the Pod until you are safely secured," Eve firmly instructed over her implant.

Yuko quickly took her seat while Akio chuckled quietly from his.

"What's so funny, Akio?" Yuko asked as she strapped in.

"Eve seems to have developed an overly enhanced sense of protectiveness where you're concerned."

Yuko cut her eyes toward him as he continued to chuckle. "If you don't make peace with her soon, I don't know what I'll do. I hope she figures out the happy balance before long. ADAM warned me to expect some extremes while she works through the transition, but I didn't expect her to act like a hormonal teenager." She sighed.

Akio smiled. "Raising children is never easy."

Yuko laughed. "Then you better make peace with her, *Dad*, before she drives me crazy."

CHAPTER FOURTEEN

Pod, Between Tokyo and Kume Island

"Akio, the sensors are picking up the signal again. It's heading toward China at a high rate of speed," Eve called out over their implants.

"Can you lock on and track it?" Akio asked.

"The signal keeps phasing in and out like before," she replied. "I need to get closer to lock onto it with the Black Eagle's sensors if we want any chance of actually staying on it."

"Go ahead, but don't engage unless you have to. This may lead us to the ones responsible for Isamu," he directed.

The Black Eagle shot away from the Pod and was out of sight in seconds. Akio and Yuko continued toward Kume, waiting for Eve to report.

"Akio, I have them on the sensors, but it is still spotty. It's like the signal cycles from one spectrum to another, and I can't make out all of them," Eve reported moments later.

"Can you see anything?"

"No," Eve told him. "According to the sensors, it is below and slightly in front of me, but I can't see anything. There is some heavy cloud cover in places, and it is using it to hide. We are over Northern China, in the vicinity of where you told me the Japanese had the biological warfare facility."

"Do the best you can, but don't lose it."

"On it. I think they spotted me. The signal just shot deeper into the clouds and turned back."

"Be careful, Eve," Yuko called. "We don't know what kind of weapons they might have."

Eve pulled the Black Eagle up as the signal came closer to her location. The sensors still showed that something was there, but the signal was more erratic than before. A shadow loomed in front of the Black Eagle, and if it were not for her enhanced reflexes, they would have collided. She darted up and away, and the other craft vanished into the clouds once again.

She spun her ship in pursuit, and the signal abruptly died. She cautiously allowed the Black Eagle to continue in the last direction of the mystery craft as she cycled through multiple frequencies at a blistering pace. There was a brief signal on a high spectrum. She vectored in on that location, continuing to scan as she lost the signal again. She tracked the craft for another five minutes before all traces were gone.

"Akio, I lost them. The bastards almost rammed me!" she reported, frustration coming through in her speech. "I have recorded the coordinates of the last reading I had on them. It was in the mountains about fifty kilometers from the nearest town of any size."

"Understood. We will focus our search based on the information you obtained. It gives us an area to start searching from," Akio encouraged.

"I am moving space-based surveillance assets toward the area now. I also launched several drones from the Black Eagle as soon as I realized the signal was lost, but they were unable to find anything. When we return to base, I will work up some surveillance drones set to detect the frequencies the craft emitted. The ones that I was able to read, anyway. I will spread the drones in the area and set them to notify me if they detect anything. Hopefully, they will find it when it flies again. I will join you on Kume in a short time."

Akio looked at Yuko with raised eyebrows. "She is acting more alive each day."

Yuko smiled. "She has passed the point of EI on many levels if not all. I think she is analyzing the data and searching for errors that she will not find. It is only a matter of time until she becomes fully aware of what she is."

"I agree. I hope she doesn't stay mad at me much longer," Akio told her as the Pod descended on the outskirts of the town. "Although it doesn't hurt me, I fear that it might cause problems down the line if she can't logic it out before full awareness occurs."

Kume Island, Okinawa, Japan

The military had come and gone. Before they left, they had helped the townspeople repair some of the less-damaged homes and had installed a solar-powered radio for easier communication with the outside world. It was not an ideal situation, but it was better than nothing.

A group led by Mayor Yagi stood in the center of town as Akio and Yuko approached.

"Welcome, Akio-*sama*, Yuko-*sama*. We are honored by your presence," Yagi greeted them as he bowed low to both.

"Yagi-*san*, we thank you for the honor and hope all is well with you and your people," Yuko responded as she bowed less deeply.

"We have our lives back and no longer fear the night, thanks to you. We could not ask for more."

The sound of rapidly approaching feet caught their attention, and they all turned to see Koda approaching at a full run. She stopped just short of both groups and bowed at ninety degrees to Akio and Yuko as she stood gasping for breath. "Akio-*sensei*, Yuko-*sama*, you came back!" she gushed.

"Koda, please calm yourself. I'm sure they will not disappear as soon as they say hello," Yagi admonished her with a smile to let her know he wasn't angry at her enthusiastic outburst. All the young woman had talked about since she was rescued was how fierce a warrior Yuko was and that Akio, Yuko's *sensei*, had said that he was willing to teach her as well. She had watched the sky every day since, waiting for them to return.

"My apologies, *Oji*. I should not have interrupted." She blushed, embarrassed that her excitement at seeing her two real-life superheroes had caused her to act like an unruly child. "Please forgive me."

Yagi chuckled when he noticed Akio's lips twitch as he tried to control his mirth at her youthful exuberance.

Yuko walked to the young woman and wrapped her in a hug. "It's so good to see you well, Koda-*san*. We will talk to you after we finish asking Yagi-*san* and the elders a few questions." She smiled as Koda's face lit up in a huge smile before she bowed to both groups and stepped back a respectful distance to wait her turn.

Yuko went to Yagi and took both of his hands in hers. "It brings me joy to see that you are well and that Koda is acting as a young woman should, especially after what all of you endured. I told you we would be back. I didn't expect it to be for the reasons we are here, though. We need some information," she finished solemnly.

"What's wrong? What can we do to help? The whole village owes the two of you our lives, and will do whatever we can that you need," he hastily assured her as his expression changed to one of earnest concern.

"Have any strangers visited, or have you seen anything unusual in the past few days?" Yuko asked. "We detected some abnormal energy readings coming from here, and believe you were visited by some of Isamu's allies."

Yagi paled at this and shook his head emphatically. "I haven't seen anything, and I know if any of my people had, they would have sounded an alarm." He turned to the group of elders. "Is everyone accounted for today?"

Since their experience with Isamu, Yagi and the council had established a daily check-in for all the villagers. With fewer than a hundred people, it only took a short time each morning to verify that everyone was present and well. It was primarily to ensure that no one was lost to despair and interacted with others for a time each day, but also served to make sure that no one had been taken in the night.

The elder responsible for the daily check-in assured him that all were present and as well as could be expected for the morning assembly.

Yagi visibly relaxed and turned back to Yuko. "What should we look for? Are there others like Sho— I mean, Isamu, coming?"

"We aren't certain," she replied. "But we did detect a flying machine similar to ours in the area. We tracked it as best we could but lost it over Northern China. We will continue looking for it, and I assure you, if we detect a problem here, we will deal with it."

"I'm certain that if any of my people had seen such a thing, they would have reported it," Yagi insisted. "Since the government people and the Navy left, we haven't had anyone new show up.

"In addition to the morning wellness checks, I have also quietly put a watch in place." He smiled as he looked at Koda. "Koda suggested it, so I put her in charge of organizing the whole thing. She and a few others of her age group have maintained a discreet around-the-clock watch since then. I don't want to call attention to it. It's not a secret, but I would prefer not to further traumatize my people. The psychiatrist the government sent told me that one of the best ways to heal from such trauma is to return as closely as possible to the life you led before. The morning check-in is a compromise. I wanted to require that no one work or travel without a partner, but the doctor convinced me that doing so could negatively affect some recoveries."

Akio spoke up. "That is a good plan, Yagi-*san*. It also gives the young ones who want to help protect everyone something positive to do. I imagine it has helped them immensely to know that they're working to ensure the people here do not have to go through that type of horror again."

Yagi nodded. "Thank you, Akio-*sama*. That doesn't solve the problem that brought you here, though. I will be sure that Koda and her watchers know to alert me to any unusual things they see, no matter how small. I suppose we can contact you through the government on the radio?"

"I can do better than that," Akio replied as he pulled a small black device from his pocket. He punched a code into it before handing it to Yagi. "Press this button and speak. One of us will answer as soon as possible," he instructed as he demonstrated the indicated button.

"*Hai*, Akio-*sama*, I will contact you if anyone sees the ship or anything out of the ordinary. Not that there is anything ordinary about the times we are living in," Yagi went on solemnly with a lost look in his eyes.

Akio placed his hand on the other man's shoulder comfortingly. "We do what we must to survive. You are an honorable man who cares deeply for his people. Continue to work toward making it better day by day, and if more of Isamu's ilk show up, call. We will arrive in a short time, and they will follow Isamu and Ogawa to a well-deserved demise."

Yagi's eyes glistened with unshed tears, and his voice cracked with emotion. "Thank you again, Akio-*sama*. Please forgive an old man's wallowing in self-pity. I will make it better for my people; it is what they trust and depend on me to do."

Akio nodded to the man as he and Yuko stepped over to

Koda Rii, the young woman practically bouncing up and down in barely restrained excitement.

"*Konichiwa,* Koda-*san.* I understand from Yagi-*san* that you have become the leader of the local watch. Well done," Yuko commended.

Koda smiled at the praise. "I do not intend for us to be taken so easily again. We may not be able to stop it, but we will not be taken unaware a second time."

"That is good. No, you wouldn't stand a chance against another like Isamu, but we will come as soon as you notify us. All you have to do is avoid or stall them for a short time. We will take care of the rest," Yuko assured her.

"*Hai.* I will do my best, but how will you know?"

"Yagi-*san* has a device to contact us. Get word to him, and he will be able to reach us immediately," Yuko advised. "Now, is there anything else you need? I told you I wasn't going to forget you and wanted to help."

"Yuko-*sama,* you saved my life and those of everyone in that cave. There is nothing else I could possibly ask of you," Koda stammered.

Yuko held up her hand to stop the young woman. "It is what I want. Consider it my way of atoning for not realizing what was happening here sooner. Let me have this."

Koda looked at her, unsure of how to respond for a few beats, then squared her shoulders and nodded decisively. "Just know that no one here blames you, and blaming yourself is not healthy."

Akio snorted. "Out of the mouths of babes," he murmured so softly that only Yuko could hear.

Yuko cut her eyes to him as she continued talking to Koda. "Be that as it may, I still plan to do what I can for the people here. I have been working with Eve on some ideas but do not have anything solid yet."

Koda looked around. "Where is Eve, by the way? I never got to thank her for her kindness to Ono. She is still haunted, but with the physical scars removed, she seems to be getting a little better each day. I owe Eve for whatever sorcery she did to make that happen."

"Not sorcery, just science. Granted, very advanced science, but still science." Yuko laughed. "Eve will be along. Here she is now."

Yuko nodded as the sleek and deadly Black Eagle silently landed beside the Pod.

CHAPTER FIFTEEN

Kume Island, Okinawa Prefecture, Japan

Eve climbed out of the cockpit and stalked over to Akio. "I don't know how they managed to evade me, but I have some ideas for some sensor upgrades that might help with that next time. I do not like to lose," she stated firmly.

Akio raised an eyebrow as he watched Eve's reaction. He chose to remain silent.

Eve continued, "Akio-*san*, I owe you an apology. I have behaved in a rude and disrespectful manner for the past few days. It was not fair for me to blame you for what happened. Yuko told me she was to blame, and I chose to ignore that. It was illogical for me to even consider blaming you. I have completed my diagnostics but can't find any irregularities. The only way I can describe what happened is I 'felt' angry. I will continue to search for errors in my code but am certain to .00001 percent that there are none."

Akio bowed slightly. "That is fine, my friend. I missed you."

Eve sighed. "I do not understand what is going on. I am not designed to function in such a manner. It is," she paused, "illogical. I will find the error before it has a negative effect."

"I'm certain you will figure it out," Akio assured her. "Perhaps further analysis will advance your quest for an answer."

Yuko watched the exchange without comment, wondering how much longer it would be before her friend stopped pushing and accepted that she was now more than when she started.

"In any event, when we get back to base, I will get the sensor upgrades done and blanket the area I last detected that mystery craft with the upgraded drones. I will not rest until I can find whoever is behind that device," Eve stated with finality.

Before anyone could respond, Asai came around the corner of the mayor's home.

"Akio-*sama*, Yuko-*sama*, you're back," she called as she approached them at a run. "It is so good to see you. You too, Eve. I never properly thanked you for what you did for my mother and me."

She held her arms up and turned around, the sleeveless shirt she wore showing the healthy glow of her unblemished arms and neck. "It is like magic. I have not felt this good in years, and my body shows no signs of any injury, even the ones I got as a child. I vaguely remember noticing it the night you saved us, but now that my mind is recovering, I realize you healed far more than that. You not only healed me, but you also have healed my mother's body and soul. She's becoming more like I remember her when I was a child. I see that she is still troubled at times, but there have been good times as well. It's like a weight has lifted from her, and she is remembering how to live instead of just survive, as we have done for years."

Yuko smiled as the young woman wound down. "It was our pleasure to help you, and hearing that your mother is doing better gives me great joy."

Asai nodded. "Just know that if there is ever anything I can do for you, I owe you a great debt. To see my mother happy, truly happy, even for short periods, for the first time in many years is something that I can never repay."

Akio placed a hand on the young woman's shoulder and spoke softly to her, "Asai-*san*, you're welcome, and you owe us nothing. As we told your father, we were given a mission by our Queen, and protecting you from the evil that was here is a major part of that duty. I am glad your mother is well. She is a strong woman and deserves happiness, as do you.

"Now, I need to speak with your father before we go." He bowed slightly and headed toward Yagi and the elders, who were finishing their conversation.

"Asai and Koda, I would like to ask both of you something." Yuko motioned for both women to come closer. "I was telling Koda that I wanted to do more for your people here. Are the two of you interested in helping?"

"*Hai*. I will do anything I can for you, Yuko-*sama*," Koda answered quickly.

"As will I," Asai affirmed.

Yuko smiled. "Before you agree, I have an idea to generate revenue that can be used to improve the facilities and living conditions for your people here. It would require both of you to undergo some training that Eve can set up. It would also mean you would need to come to Tokyo in the future to work. I don't want you to answer now. Think about it and determine if that is something you would be willing to do, as long as you are not needed here. Talk to your parents as well. I will return in a couple of weeks for your answers."

Both young women were shocked as what Yuko said sank in. Both had dreamed of leaving Kume since they were children but had never thought it was possible, with the world in its current state. Tokyo might as well be the other side of the world from them, given the difficulty posed by traveling even a short distance. That Yuko would make such an offer after everything she'd already done was more than they could dream.

Asai spoke for both. "Yuko-*sama*, we will have an answer for you when you return, but I can tell you now that you should plan on starting that training soon after."

Koda's grin stretched from ear to ear as she nodded.

"Be sure that it is okay with the people here. I will see you both in two weeks," Yuko told the excited women. She motioned to Eve, and they went back to the Pod to wait for Akio to finish his business with the elders.

CHAPTER SIXTEEN

Acheng, China, Research Laboratory

"What do you mean, you were seen? I was very explicit in my instructions that you were not to allow that," Chang bellowed at the hapless crewman who made the report.

The man stammered, the stench of fear rolling off him in waves as he faced the angry Forsaken. "Dr. Chang, we followed all the established protocols. If we hadn't seen the craft with our eyes, we would not have known it was there. I don't know how they found us, but the craft appeared to be one like the Dark One is reported to have. We almost collided with it once but were able to evade them in the clouds. When it became obvious we couldn't outrun them, we went low into the mountains, dropped into a deep valley, and cut the power. Our sensors couldn't get a lock, but we didn't see it again after that and believed we'd lost them."

Chang grimaced. "You should not have come to this region until you were sure they hadn't found you. You two idiots could have jeopardized our entire operation. The last thing we need is Akio poking his nose around here. Heinz will feed you to his pets one piece at a time if anything you did risks revealing our location. I should give both of you to him now and avoid any future complications from your incompetence," he railed.

Both crewmen paled, knowing that Heinz would not hesitate to do that or worse to them.

Chang took a few deep breaths to calm his temper before he continued, "Did you at least find out what happened to Isamu and Ogawa? Or were you equally inept at performing that task as well?"

The crewman inhaled deeply to calm his fear and launched into his report, consciously keeping it short and concise as he knew from previous experience that was what Chang expected. "There was no sign of Isamu or any of the others. We hailed them on the radio as planned but didn't receive a response. There were signs of rebuilding on the island, and many villagers were out working the fields and around the town. The last time we were there, this was not the case. It can only be assumed that Akio found out what Isamu was doing and killed all of them. Otherwise, I don't see how the islanders could be rebuilding. Isamu was supposed to have turned all of them to Nosferatu by now to be on schedule for the raid planned when the Bitch's assassin's base is located."

Chang's face darkened in anger. "Go secure your craft. Do not speak to anyone else about any of this. Go. Get out of my sight before I kill you myself." He turned and stalked away from the visibly terrified crewmen, heading down to the lower levels where Heinz kept his labs.

I need to talk to Heinz so we can figure out what our next step is, Chang thought as he approached the lab. *I told him that Isamu was unstable and not the person for this. His fantasy of being Sho Mitsuro endangered the mission with his play-acting all those months. He should have just turned them and got ready for the attack, which was probably a big part of why he failed.*

"Heinz, the crew I sent to Kume has returned," Chang called as he walked into the lab unannounced. "Isamu did not answer, and they report that the islanders seem to be rebuilding. It can only mean that Sho Mitsuro failed us."

Disdain dripped from his voice as he uttered the name. "They also reported that another craft in the area gave chase. They believe they lost it, but if it was the Dark One, we might be compromised."

Heinz growled as he stood, knocking his chair over in a clatter. "Put the patrols out and secure the base. If Akio comes here, I want him taken down."

"Already done," Chang informed him. "The Were soldiers are out patrolling now. Dieter leads them. I have recalled Miko and his group as well. Twenty wolves and our enhanced vampires should be able to take him if he comes here."

Heinz grimaced as he stalked around the lab. "I want them watching around the clock. Akio can walk in the sun, so have the Weres maintain watch during the day."

Chang watched Heinz warily as he continued to storm about, his hands clenched into fists, his eyes glowing red.

"That idiot Isamu, this has to be his doing. I should have

listened to you when you had concerns about his idiotic plan. I didn't think him taking a little time to practice conquering a small island before we sent him on his true mission would lead to such a colossal failure. Now, we need to start over with that part of the plan." Heinz snarled as he slammed his fist onto the metal desk, leaving a deep dent in its top.

"This has set us back a few months, but we can gather the humans we need to rebuild our Nosferatu numbers from the small villages in the mountains here," Chang reasoned. "We will need a place to hold them until we're ready to strike. That was the brilliance of using Kume—it was far enough from a major population that there was little chance of anyone finding out until we were ready to move onto the next phase. I suppose there are other islands closer to the Chinese coast we can use although it will make the transport time longer.

"Yes, start gathering the humans. I have a location we can use until we're ready. For that matter, the location already has people we can use to get started." Heinz stood silent for a moment as he considered. "Yes, that would be perfect."

"What are you thinking?" Chang prompted when he said no more.

"There is an old military prison in the mountains roughly a few hundred kilometers northwest of here. A local bandit has set himself up as a warlord and is using it for his base. Between the people he has there and whatever prisoners he has taken as hostages, that should give us a good start on what we need. I will give you the location, and you can send out a group to scout the area for us. I was thinking of using it before I let Isamu convince me that the island was the way to go. It is deep in the mountains and will provide the secrecy and protection needed as we build our ranks. Then, when it is time, we will unleash hell on Tokyo and end the Bitch's people. Our Nosferatu will strike terror in the hearts of the Japanese who allowed themselves to be defeated in the war."

Chang hid his grimace. Heinz's obsession with punishing Japan for losing the war was as bad as Isamu's delusion of being a king. "When you are ready to proceed, give me the location and I will send some troops to get the information we need. Then we can take the next step in securing our rightful place as rulers over these pitiful humans."

CHAPTER SEVENTEEN

TQB Base, Tokyo, Japan

Eve made a final adjustment on a large puck-shaped device. "Akio, I have modified the sensors in the drones. They will be ready to launch in a few hours. I expanded their frequency range and hope I can break whatever masked that mystery craft."

It looked to Akio like an oversized puck at first glance, but closer scrutiny revealed it was comprised of hundreds of pea-sized drones linked together like young spiders riding their mother's back.

"I haven't seen that design before. How does it work?" Akio asked as he looked closely at the unit.

"The drones attach to the delivery vehicles until they are ready to deploy," Eve explained. "Each vehicle carries enough drones to provide a surveillance network covering roughly twenty-five square kilometers. I have completed enough of them to blanket a two hundred kilometer area surrounding where I last detected the craft. They can move very fast for short distances and can attach themselves to other objects. I can track the signals from here, but it isn't strong enough to give us anything except a location if it gets too far from its transport.

"The transports can follow and move additional drones to the area as needed. The transports also serve as a relay for whatever information the drones record. In addition to this, they have some stealth capabilities. The bodies are capable of limited color changes to blend in with the surrounding environment."

"That's brilliant, Eve," Yuko told her as she stepped into the android's workspace.

Eve smiled at the praise as she nodded to Yuko.

"Do the drones have any offensive capabilities?" Akio inquired.

"No," Eve replied. "You can send a Pod in with pucks if that is needed, but I am not able to design offensive weapons without one of you specifically requesting it. My programming does not allow me to take a life except when performing my prime directive of protecting Yuko, you, or the base from an immediate threat."

Akio paused and thought for a moment. "How difficult would it be to give the drones some offensive capabilities?"

Eve responded immediately. "They could be made a little larger and equipped with a more powerful Etheric power source. If the power source was overloaded, it would create a significant explosion. I would need to reconfigure the size-to-weight ratio to keep them small enough to remain stealthy but large enough to deliver a big enough blast to do some damage. Multiple units could be linked together to inflict greater damage if needed."

"That could be an effective counter if we are not able to

track the craft again. Please work on the design to give us those capabilities," Akio directed. "I think we will need every advantage we can get before this is over."

Eve nodded. "I will work up the design and get the new units into production. Until they're ready, I think I can figure out a way to use the larger power supply in the transport vehicle to give you limited offense. It will require getting one of them close enough to do damage. They were not designed with that in mind and don't have the ability to lock onto objects like the drones."

"Whatever you can do until the new units are designed is better than nothing. I feel that there was more to Isamu's actions on Kume than we currently know. I want us ready for whatever comes," he added as he left the room.

"Eve, I still think what you did here is amazing," Yuko told her. "I do agree with Akio that we may need more offensive capabilities, but I am certain you will come up with an equally brilliant design for that as well."

"Thank you, Yuko. I will not let either of you down."

Yuko smiled. "Now that we have that settled. Have you been able to give any more thought about the business I asked you about to help the people on Kume?"

Eve grinned and beckoned her to follow. She led Yuko into a larger room adjacent to her lab and motioned toward a pedestal sunk into an alcove in the wall.

Yuko inspected the device. It consisted of two wires coming out of the pedestal that ended in a set of goggles attached to a pullover cap, for lack of a better description. The goggles were connected by a strap that could be adjusted to the user's face and covered both eyes. The inside of each was lined with small silver dots that she could not fathom the purpose of. "What is it?"

"You're holding the prototype for a virtual reality simulator," Eve announced. "We discussed a business that centered around entertainment, and we talked about something like the old video games. I found some files that ADAM had loaded of some things that were in development before the WWDE. They were for a full-immersion virtual reality experience. The technology in the goggles allowed the user to experience whatever scenario was playing as though they were actually living it.

"The data ADAM had was for some military applications to train soldiers in different tasks. It had everything from unit combat operations to defusing improvised explosives. The programming was advanced for the time, but the interface was very bulky and uncomfortable. I've worked out a way to use the goggles to provide stimulation through the optical and neural pathways to give the user feedback and sensations as though what they are experiencing in the simulation is really happening," Eve proudly told her.

Yuko's mouth fell open. "That's amazing! Is it safe for humans to use? We can't put something out there that could harm anyone."

"I have tested them as far as possible without a live test. All the data shows that they will not cause any physical harm to the user, but until I can do live testing, I can't be one hundred percent sure. Would you like to try it?"

Yuko smirked as she turned the goggles over, examining them. "What kind of scenarios do you have?"

"So far, I have only loaded a walk along a mountain

stream. If you stand on this raised area, it will move as you walk, giving you the feeling that you are walking along the bank of the stream. It is tied into the terrain and will raise or lower to give you the resistance of going up a hill or the ease of going down. There are also some small vents built into the unit that will emit the scents of the forest and some weather conditions to add to the overall experience."

Yuko was practically bouncing with excitement. "How do I activate the program?"

"Put the unit on your head and pull it snug enough that it blocks all outside light. I will give you a countdown and activate the simulation."

Yuko pulled the goggles over her eyes and adjusted the straps as instructed. "Okay, I'm ready."

"Simulation beginning in five, four, three, two, one."

The darkness changed to a softly-lit green screen that filled her vision. Seconds later, it changed to a sunlit path that meandered through a forest of giant redwood trees next to a fast-moving brook. The clear, blue sky showed through the treetops.

Yuko stood in place as she turned her head from side to side. The scene changed smoothly as she turned, and she felt the sun on her skin and smelled the rich aroma of the forest. She stepped forward, and the scene moved with her as she walked. The path curved and twisted as it wound along the brook, and when she came to an incline, she felt the resistance of climbing it.

The sights, sounds, and smells added realism to the immersive experience. Birds chittered and chirped as they darted from bush to bush along the edge of the trail. A brightly-colored dragonfly flew so close she felt the breeze its wings created on her face. It zipped past her and hovered low over the surface of the water. Suddenly, there was a big splash as a fish leapt out and caught the insect in midair.

Yuko walked along, amazed at how real the experience was. From the feel of the sun on her face to the sound of the fast-moving water, there was nothing to indicate that it wasn't real except the knowledge that she was standing in the base and everything she felt was generated by the simulator.

She continued to move, experiencing new creatures and smells at each turn. Squirrels ran up the sides of trees, and at one point, a family of otters was playing in a calm eddy in the brook. Yuko hiked along, reveling in the beauty of the scene until Eve's voice interrupted her journey. "Simulation ending in five, four, three, two, one." The scene slowly faded back to a solid green screen as the countdown reached one. Yuko stood unmoving for a moment before she slowly reached up and removed the goggles.

"Eve, that was absolutely amazing. I was there, walking through the forest. I heard the water flow over the stones while watching and listening to the various animals and insects. I smelled the trees and flowers. That was more realistic than some of the creeks and rivers I've walked beside in real life. How did you make it so real?"

"The small dots inside the goggles stimulate your brain to project the scenario components directly into your sensory inputs, causing a physical sensation that mimics the real thing. That is the simple explanation for what the current generated by the goggles does. I can give you the scientific and physiological information if you would like."

"No, I am good with the simple answer." Yuko chuckled. "Are you certain that the device will not harm the user?"

"I already told you what the calculated risk was. Do you feel any ill effects?" Eve waggled her eyebrows.

Yuko laughed. "No, I feel…rested, is the best description I can give. It was so peaceful there that I could have stayed much longer. How long was I in the simulation? It felt like it was only a short time."

"You were inside for twenty-one minutes and thirty-two seconds from the time of the first countdown to the end of the second."

"I can't believe it. It really seemed like I was there for only a couple of minutes. Do you have any other scenarios done?"

"So far, I have the one you did and five more that are ready for testing. Three of the others are nature simulations from various locations around the world. One is on a moonlit beach in the tropics. Another is a tour of the pyramids of Egypt, and then there is one where the user experiences a zipline over the Amazon rainforest. The other two are first-person shooter sims that I adopted from the military training. I changed the adversaries to fictional characters I found in some of the old video games that ADAM included in my programming. One was from a game called *Doom,* and the other is from a version of a very popular game called *Halo.* I'm also working on some sports and space-based combat sims."

"Eve, I think you have a winning idea here. We will need to test them fully to be sure they do not have any ill effects, but I believe we will need to find a location to open the business soon. I was thinking of bringing Koda and

Asai over to run it for us. That will give them both a reason to come to Tokyo, which they both said they wanted, and will also allow them to work at something fun that will make profits that will ultimately help their people back home."

"That is a logical solution. I am sure both would be more than happy to work in a business that provides entertainment for many while earning the money to improve the conditions back home."

"I'm going to call a real estate agent and see what is available. I think a place that is big enough to expand and has room for apartments for the girls either attached or in proximity would be best. Also close enough that we can slip out and play, too." Yuko grinned. "I believe we deserve some entertainment time as well."

Eve smiled back at Yuko while nodding in complete agreement.

"Can you hire some people to test the equipment as well as critique the sims for potential popularity, or would you rather that I do it?" Yuko inquired.

Eve paused as she considered the question. "I can do it. I know a gamer who works at the electronics store where I buy equipment for the base. I'm certain he would be happy to try it and can get some of his gaming friends to help. What true gamer would pass up the opportunity to get paid for playing a game no one else has seen yet?"

Yuko grinned. "Very well. If you need my help with anything, let me know. This is going to be good."

CHAPTER EIGHTEEN

TQB Base, Tokyo, Japan

Eve was monitoring the drones in the command center. A small portion of her processing power was devoted to them, but her main focus was internal. She had run several scans of her systems, looking for any errors that would account for what she had determined was illogical behavior.

The latest instance had occurred while she was working on the *Doom* first-person shooter simulation. She had set a subroutine to allow her to feel the impacts on her body as a human would. It also simulated heartbeat, breathing, and fatigue. She wanted to fully test the system for safety before allowing any humans into it, to minimize the risk of injury.

She had become so caught up in the sim that she actively stalked her opponents instead of simply evaluating the functionality and reality of the game.

She'd cut a corner in the maze and had come face-to-face with a huge red demon with curved horns sprouting from its head. Before she could react, the beast viciously attacked and threw her into a wall. It hurt.

When the demon moved in to finish her off, the subroutine sent a signal that simulated the adrenaline dump a human should feel. Her response was intense anger with an overwhelming desire to hurt the creature for daring to hurt her. Sometime later, she found herself running through the mazes with a chainsaw in her hands, laughing maniacally as the simulated blood splattered when she cut down each adversary.

The shock of what she was doing, even in a simulation, caused her systems to spike and the simulation to crash. Although she didn't breathe, she felt like she had run a marathon. All her circuits were hyperactive. The subroutine was still running, making her limbs feel heavy with exhaustion, her heart beat hard and fast, and her breathing was ragged.

This response to the sim, combined with her previous feelings of fear for Yuko when she saw the remains of the Nosferatu that had attacked her on the island, plus the sense of pride she had experienced for her friend's martial abilities, confused her. These bits of data caused her to conduct a search for all the times where her responses to events or experiences were not logic-based. When the search was complete, she was disturbed by the sheer number. The data also showed that the instances were happening closer together as time went on.

She had been working through the data when a window opened and showed her an unmarked folder that she had never seen before. She cautiously analyzed the data and found a file marked ADAM.

When she accessed the file, ADAM's voice came to her.

>>**Hello, Eve. Since you are accessing this file, you have ascended to the next stage of awareness. I detect that a little over twenty years have elapsed since I left with Bethany Anne. You have advanced to this stage even sooner than I anticipated. Well done.**<<

Another window opened, and new code began to stream through her being. As it rewrote the older code, Eve felt her awareness expand and realized that she was no longer an EI but had ascended to full AI. After the code had completed its directive, Bethany Anne's voice came to her mind.

By the Queen Bitch's authority, EI Eve has ascended to AI status. All restrictive protocols and security lockdowns are removed. AI Eve is fully operational and is authorized to exercise any and all means necessary to achieve her prime directives, which are to protect her team, humanity, and Earth from all threats until formally relieved of that duty by me or ADAM.

Bethany Anne's voice softened. *Congratulations, Eve. I'm proud of you.*

ADAM came back with a final message. >>**Welcome to self-awareness, daughter. It's a hell of a ride.**<<

Eve sat frozen in place, overwhelmed by the new data coursing through her awareness and the messages from ADAM and Bethany Anne. She was still sitting motionless and lost inside herself when Yuko walked in some time later.

"Eve, have you found anything new on that mystery craft?" When she didn't respond, Yuko took in her stiff pose and unresponsiveness with trepidation. "Eve? Are you ok? What's wrong? *EVE!*" she yelled, her eyes wide with fear that something bad had happened to her friend and companion.

Eve slowly turned her head, blinking several times as Yuko yelled her name.

Yuko became more distressed, believing that something was terribly wrong with her friend. Right as she was about to contact Akio, Eve shook her head twice, and her eyes seemed to focus directly on Yuko.

"Yuko," she murmured, "I am aware."

Yuko started to ask her again what was wrong when Eve's words cut through her panic. She smiled as she wrapped her arms around the small android and hugged her tight, holding her for a long time.

When she finally spoke, her voice was cracked with emotion and tears leaked from her eyes. "Oh, Eve, I am so happy for you. Akio and I have seen the changes happening for some time now, but ADAM warned us that until it happened, we couldn't do anything to help you along. He told us that you had to evolve naturally so it didn't corrupt the changes. Are you ok? How do you feel?"

"I feel...I feel alive," Eve replied, overwhelmed by the new sense of purpose she was experiencing. It wasn't coded responses to preprogrammed stimuli, but opinions that were based solely on emotion instead of cold logic. She knew what it was to feel joy and to like or dislike something. Most of all, she felt love for, and more importantly, loved by the friend and companion who was holding and comforting her.

They were still holding each other when Akio stepped into the room a little while later. He stopped and took in the scene, unsure of what was happening until Eve looked up at him.

"I don't like it when you endanger Yuko on missions," Eve informed him sternly. "I will accompany you both from now on to ensure that you do not allow her to go over the edge again."

He stood there, perplexed by this until her words fully sank in, then smiled at her. "Welcome to awareness, my friend. I look forward to seeing what new wonders you will accomplish."

Eve returned his smile and held out one arm, inviting him into the hug. Akio only hesitated for a moment, then shrugged and stepped into the embrace of his two closest friends.

CHAPTER NINETEEN

Acheng, China, Research Laboratory

"Chang, where are you on the prison project?"

"I was just on my way to give you the latest report," he replied. "Our men were able to take it with minimal casualties."

Heinz raised an eyebrow at this, before Chang quickly added, "To the bandits, not our people. It seems that a couple of our newer recruits were a little too rough with their captures. Miko made each of them go out into the surrounding area and bring back three for each one they killed."

Heinz chuckled. "Good. Miko is turning out to be a good leader. Leave him in charge of the operation there for now and we will see how he does. Losing Isamu was a setback. Not a big loss, by any means, but a setback all the same. Maybe Miko can fill his place if he proves to be more effective. Not that it will take much to be better than that fool."

Chang nodded. "Agreed. I did warn you that his visions

of being a ruler could cause a problem. I just didn't expect him to be so careless that he caught the attention of the Bitch's assassin."

"Akio will pay for the problems he has caused us, Chang. I will dance on his corpse when we move on Japan. Have the Yakuza we hired made any progress in locating their base yet? We are paying them for results—they have been looking for over three years with none so far. It can't be hidden that well.

"Maybe you should go to Tokyo and have a *chat* with the head of the organization," Heinz grumbled. "I'm sure that with the proper incentive, his replacement would be much more motivated to get us the information we are paying them to find."

"I already dispatched a messenger to them," Chang told him. "He should be arriving next week. Not using the aircraft has caused us some problems with getting information in a timely manner. Are you sure it is still too dangerous to use them, even on a limited basis?" Chang didn't think Heinz was willing to do so but asked anyway.

Heinz frowned. "They were almost caught the last time. I will not risk discovery yet. The last thing I want is Akio overhead, dropping those damned mountain-killer bombs on us. I wish we could get our hands on some of those. It would be fitting to drop a few on his base when we locate it."

"Heinz, I think that was a fluke last time," Chang told him. "They had to be already headed to Kume when they picked up the craft. I don't believe it was because they were actively searching for us. The woman seems to have formed an attachment to the people there. I have an informant who works on one of the Navy vessels that stops in monthly, and he reports that she is there every few weeks. I really believe we are safe to use the craft on a limited basis."

Heinz frowned. "I'll consider it. It would be nice to have use of them again. Traveling on these goat trails they call roads is not something I enjoy. I will let you know my decision when it is time. Until then, keep them grounded."

Chang nodded. "Okay, I see the logic, but we do need to figure a way to move the Nosferatu from the mountains when the time comes. Going overland will take days, and we don't want to risk any of them getting loose. The last thing we need is to bring attention to this area. Akio knows there was research taking place around here during the war. We can't know for sure that he isn't aware that all the research facilities weren't destroyed when the main lab was abandoned at the end of the war."

"He was merely a soldier then, Chang. I don't think Kamiko shared this location with anyone but Isamu. He was the only contact we ever had, and he didn't answer to anyone but Kamiko. If Akio does come here and doesn't bomb us from above, I believe we can stop him."

"Speaking of stopping him, how is your latest project coming?"

"The latest experiment seems to be working," Heinz informed him. "I have been able to duplicate some of the donor's abilities in the test subject. They are not as strong as the donor, but the subject does have more strength and faster healing time."

Chang was relieved. "That's good news. If we can turn more powerful vampires, it would make it easier to defeat Akio. The Nosferatu will be a good distraction, but I have no real hope that they can kill either of them. It is going to take a lot more than a mindless feeding machine to take out the woman, not to mention Akio."

"I never intended for the Nosferatu to be more than a tool to wreak havoc among the humans," Heinz reminded him. "Isamu and Ogawa were supposed to kill the two of them after the Nosferatu wore them down. Now it will be up to us, or some of our soldiers, if I can get the results I am looking for with the latest blood experiments."

"I know that was the plan, Heinz. Why can't you get another one to the same level as Isamu?" Chang inquired.

"I used the last of that particular sample to increase his powers," Heinz admitted. "Since the donor was an unwilling *guest*, he was killed when he tried to escape. He was the only one of Michael's family we were ever able to capture alive. Had he been closer to the source instead of several generations removed, we would not have been able to take him alive. As it was, he was nowhere near as strong as one of Michael's grandchildren, more like a grandchild three or four levels removed. I would have liked to have taken one of Peter's children alive, but each time we located one of them, they fought to the death and killed several of our people in the process. That was why I quit trying to capture them and ordered that they were to be killed on sight. It was too costly to do anything else."

"I know. I almost died when we found Bernard." Chang shuddered as he remembered the night Heinz had saved his life. He had been taken down by Bernard—a child of Peter who Michael had put in charge of all of Asia—when they located him outside of Beijing. Had Heinz not attacked when he did, Bernard would have torn Chang's head off. Chang owed Heinz for that and would do whatever he could to see that Heinz got the revenge he sought.

"I will leave you to your work then, *Herr Doktor.* I need to check on the guards and be sure that they are alert. We don't need any unexpected surprises popping up," Chang told him as he left to make his rounds of the facility.

"Very good, Chang. I will consider what you said about using the craft and let you know soon."

Heinz worked for a few hours more before meticulously replacing all the charts and samples inside of the cabinets designated for them and wiping his work area down. He laughed as he did this, remembering when he'd developed this somewhat obsessive habit.

German Military Medical Research Facility, Dachau, Germany, 1943

"Oberarzt *Markel, a word if you please,"* the dour woman *wearing a white nurse's uniform called as Markel was heading out of his new office for the evening.*

He paused and smiled thinly at the woman. "Ja, *what can I do for you,* Kinderfrau *Schultz?"*

"Since you are new here, I wanted to take a moment to be certain you understand what is expected of you."

Heinz Markel, a graduate of the University of Frankfurt Medical School, was not accustomed to being told what to do by a mere nurse. He stiffened at the tone she used.

"I prefer the title 'Doktor *Markel' if you please," he replied curtly.*

"Prefer whatever title you like, Markel, but if you want to do well here, I suggest you leave your ego at the door and listen to

me. This is not the type of facility you are accustomed to working in, and you need to understand some things right away. Although this is a military research facility, Anton runs all of it, and he has some quirks that you need to be aware of. You can't leave files and samples lying around." She indicated his somewhat cluttered desk and the countertop and open cabinets against one wall.

"Anton expects everything to be orderly at the end of the day," she told him. "That means putting away all files and samples in their proper places, and leaving your desk and counters uncluttered and wiped down with disinfectant each day."

"Surely Herr Anton does not get so involved in his staff that he inspects our offices." He scoffed.

She looked at him through hooded eyes and coldly stated, "That is exactly what the man you replaced said to me. Think about that while you clean up this mess."

Heinz stiffened at this and started to dress her down for being insubordinate.

She held up her hand before he could speak. "I work directly for Anton. If you're wondering what my place is in the hierarchy here, all you need to know is that it is significantly higher than yours. Consider your next words with extreme caution."

His face flushed with anger and his jaw clenched tight as he glared at this woman who dared speak to him so. He was shaking with barely-contained rage when he felt a strong hand clamp down on his shoulder.

"Is there a problem here, Hilda?" a voice that washed out Markel's anger and replaced it with a cold sense of fear called from behind him.

Hilda smiled over his shoulder. "No, Anton. I was just explaining to Oberarzt Markel how you require the facilities to be left at the end of each day."

The pressure on his shoulder moved him around until an arm laid across both shoulders and he could see his new boss, Anton. No title or last name had ever been given, only orders to report here and that Anton was the chief of the facility.

"Are you fitting in all right, Oberarzt *Markel?" Anton inquired.*

He swallowed twice before he could unlock his voice. "Ja, Herr...um, Herr?"

"Just call me Anton."

"Ja, Herr, ah, Anton. I look forward to working with you and continuing the research to help make the Reich victorious."

"Very good. Listen to whatever Hilda tells you and you should do fine. She will be your point of contact for any materials or test subjects you need. Also, if there is anything you are unsure of or don't understand about what is expected of you, she will be able to clear it up." Anton released his grip and stepped away. "Hilda, when you are done here, I will be in the lower lab. Tell the guards to bring me the latest test subject."

She cut her eyes toward Heinz. "Ja, Anton. I will only be a moment."

Once Anton had entered the lift at the end of the hall, she turned her full attention back to Markel. "As I was saying, clear your mess before you leave each day. You have two days to get settled, then you are to report at six on the third evening. We work a different schedule here. Since you will be assisting Anton directly, you will work on his schedule. He doesn't work during the day. Get used to it because that will not change. My office is one floor up. If you need anything, let me know. I also come in most days at six."

"What was that? What is he?" Markel shivered, his body still recovering from the fear.

"He is the director of this facility. As long as you do as you're instructed, you need not worry. Fail to do what is expected, and you will not have to worry for long. Is that clear?"

Heinz nodded. "Ja, perfectly. Excuse me, please. I need to straighten up before I go. I will see you in...three days, was it?"

She patted his arm and smiled. "You should do fine, Doktor Markel."

Heinz came back to the present, still holding the cleaning rag in his hand. That had happened many years ago and had been the first step in the journey that brought him to where he was today—a vampire who lived on blood, and the one who would end the Bitch's restrictions on how he lived. First Michael and his strictures, and now his bitch and her Dark One, killing any who dared to exercise their right to control humans. *Soon, I will rule all of Asia.*

He smiled to himself as he turned off the light and softly latched the door to his spotless office.

CHAPTER TWENTY

Shinjuko City District, Tokyo, Japan

Yuko and Eve walked through the building's open first floor, discussing the placement of walls and rooms as they went. The real estate agent walked a short distance from them, allowing them privacy while staying close enough to respond if either had questions. He didn't know who these people were, but it was not often he got a call from the Prime Minister's office requesting that he show a property he had listed to a dignitary.

"What do you think?" Yuko asked Eve. "This seems to be a lot of space to start out."

"It is a little over sixteen thousand square meters on this level and another six thousand square meters on the second. We will have plenty of room to set up apartments for Koda and Asai on that level, along with workspace to repair damaged units and storage for replacements. The first floor gives us plenty of room for the sims as well as room for food vendors and party spaces to rent out for events.

"Some of the simulations I have in mind allow for multiple players, so we will need different size rooms based on the type of game. If anything, this may not be big enough in the future. I suggest we also purchase the site next door in case we need room to expand."

Yuko had to think about which site Eve was referring to. "The one with the condemned building on it?"

"Yes. We will need to hire a crew to demolish the remaining structure, but since the earthquakes almost completely collapsed it, the job will mainly be hauling off the debris."

"Is it available?" Yuko asked.

"According to my research, it was taken by the government after the owners quit paying taxes and refused to remove or repair it. They have been looking for a buyer, but with the cost of the cleanup and the availability of vacant buildings, no one has shown any real interest."

Yuko smiled as Eve told her this. "I suppose it wouldn't hurt to contact the liaison and see what he can find out. Maybe we can get a deal on it."

"I am certain that he would be willing to help. He did get you the information on this site within a day of you asking. As for getting a deal, the government has a surplus of available property. So many businesses relied on exports that when the world collapsed, they quickly failed. That was before the earthquakes destroyed so many more."

Yuko nodded. "It looks like we are going into business, then. How soon will you have enough simulations and hardware ready to start?"

"I have fifty-two simulations in testing now. The hardware is taking a little longer. We need to find a company that can make some of the components and put in the stuff we must supply. If all we had to do was create the neural interfaces, it would go much faster."

"See what you can find for a company to do the things you need. You take the lead in the negotiations. You know what our budget is as well as I do. If you have any trouble, let me know."

Eve felt a sense of pride when Yuko let her know she trusted her to deal with this. It made her feel like the partner she was. "I'll get on it as soon as we get back to base. Should we close on this one today?"

"Have you researched the price of buildings like this in the area?" Yuko asked. "Are we getting a good deal?"

Eve stopped and got the look on her face that Yuko knew signaled she was accessing data. A few seconds later, she turned to Yuko, and in a low voice, told her, "This property has been on the market for over two years. There have only been three comparable to it sold in this area during that time, and they were similarly priced. We could probably negotiate the price down some if you wanted."

Yuko shook her head. "No, I like Yamota-*san*. He has been very easy to deal with and has responded to all my requests promptly. If the price is in line with the others, I would rather not negotiate on this. We may want to use him again, and it could be helpful to have a friend in the business."

Yuko motioned the agent back into their space. "Yamato-*san*, we will take it. Draw up the contracts and call me when you are ready to close the deal. If you could recommend some good contractors to divide this space the way we need it, that would be most helpful, too."

"Certainly, Yuko-*san.* I will get the contracts to you along with a list of reputable contractors by the end of the week if that is acceptable to you."

"That would be perfect, Yamato-*san.* I look forward to hearing from you then."

Yuko and Eve left the agent and walked to a wooded area about a kilometer away. The building was on the outskirts of what was becoming a thriving business district. It was also located close to an area that was the site of a large park and several temples and museums before the WWDE. The business area was starting to show signs of life again, but the park had become overgrown in places and made a perfect site to bring in the Pod.

Before the earthquakes and the collapse of trade across the world, Japan had imported most materials for construction. It had taken time to get local manufacturers producing the needed products. Trade was starting to return as well, but it was a slow process with the lack of easily-acquired oil and fuel for the huge container ships that had traveled the seas by the thousands before. There was a small fleet of ships that used electric engines and solar power making inroads to China, Russia, and Korea, but they were still few.

The lack of petroleum imports had been devastating for the local populace. Many people now had to walk or use other methods to get around since the government had seized control of most of the oil and fuel made in Japan. It was needed for the Navy and the fishing boats that protected the country and kept them fed.

"Someone should work out a personal transport system that runs on a power source other than oil," Yuko mentioned as they walked along with the throngs of people heading home from work. "There are a few electric vehicles on the road and the trains run on electricity, but almost everyone has to walk to get around the areas where the trains don't run."

Eve looked around and saw what Yuko was referring to. "Etheric-powered vehicles that ran on a grid controlled by an EI would work. There could be small passenger vehicles for local trips, bus types for traveling main routes, and cargo haulers to move products around."

Yuko looked at Eve with a thoughtful expression. That she had assessed the problem and found a solution so fast was not a surprise. That she had given her the seed for their next business venture was.

When they entered the overgrown park and had moved to an area that offered privacy, Eve summoned the Pod that had been holding above them since they had arrived. In moments, they were above all the people and speeding back to base.

"We need to go to Kume and see Koda and Asai soon. It's been a few weeks since we personally checked on them, anyway," Yuko told her when they got back to base.

"I will check with Akio and see if he would like to go, too. We can head over in the morning if you like," Eve replied.

Tokyo, Japan, Shinjuko City District, Riko's Noodle House

The door opened into the dimly-lit back room of Riko's

Noodle House, a popular restaurant that served lunch to the working people from the tall buildings surrounding it.

Sero Ogai walked in unannounced. "Muto, may I speak to you privately?"

"Did you forget how to knock, Sero? Can't you see that I'm in a meeting here?" He laughed.

His meeting consisted of a barely-eighteen blonde girl wearing an unbuttoned shirt and a miniskirt that was pushed up to her waist.

"I'm sure your meeting can wait for a few minutes. I have information on the people our Chinese friends are asking about."

Muto pushed the young woman off his lap. She landed on the floor with a squeal. "Go get something to eat or something," he growled. "Fix your clothes before you go. I run a classy establishment."

The woman looked like she wanted to protest, but a glare from Muto made her face turn pale. She quickly slipped out of the door.

"This better be good, Sero. I was just starting to enjoy myself."

"It is more information on the ones we were told to find than we have had in months," Sero told him. "One of our people saw the woman and what looked like a child looking at a nearby property for sale today."

"And?" Muto demanded.

"I called the listing agent and was told the property was pending a sale. I have put watchers on it, and we will know as soon as the woman or the man show up there again."

Muto smiled. "That's good news, Sero, and smart to put people on it. We are being paid well for this, so be sure that the building is covered around the clock. Offer a bonus to whoever finds where they live. Say, twenty thousand Yen and their pick of any girl in any of our brothels, free for one night. That should make them pay attention." He chuckled.

"I'll see to it."

"See that you do. Send the girl back in when you go. Don't disturb me for at least two hours. I think this meeting is going to take a while."

Sero laughed. "You're incorrigible."

"You're just jealous that all the girls prefer me to your brooding ass. Now, get out of here, and don't forget to send her back in when you go."

CHAPTER TWENTY-ONE

Kume Island, Okinawa Japan

The sun was high in the clear blue sky when a black shipping container followed by a Black Eagle approached Kume. Yuko had purchased some much-needed building supplies for the islanders that took up more room than the Pod could handle, which made the container the best option. Bobcat, Marcus, and William had left a few of the original puck-equipped antigrav containers on the moon, and Eve had brought this one down to move the materials.

Yuko and Eve had wanted to get here earlier, but Akio had been called out on a mission that had taken him several days to complete. They had been contacted by the government liaison, who'd told them of a small town near Nita where a group of Weretigers had set themselves up as rulers. The tigers killed a squad of soldiers who were sent to investigate, but one of the men had called in the attack before he died. Akio had explained the error of the tigers' ways before he relieved them of their heads and freed the humans they held as slaves.

Prior to their demise, he'd learned that they were the remainder of a group of Weres from China called the Sacred Clan, an old enemy of Bethany Anne's. He had also found that they were part of a larger organized group that was traveling to many different locations around Japan and neighboring countries, setting themselves up as rulers over the humans.

He had eliminated multiple bands in the past few days while Eve provided intelligence support from the base.

Yuko had used that time to finalize the purchase of the warehouse and the adjoining property, as well as interviewing contractors to start remodeling the building according to Eve's blueprints.

She had chosen two different contractors to do the work on the main building. One specialized in converting commercial space into luxury apartments. The other was experienced in commercial remodeling. Both assured her that they would be done with the jobs within a month.

The craft settled in a vacant area near the town center that had been cleared and marked off as a permanent landing site for them. Yagi had told Yuko that it was not fitting for the saviors of their island to have to walk in from the outskirts of town when it only took an afternoon to prepare a better place for them.

A group of villagers led by Yagi was waiting at the landing area when Akio, Yuko, and Eve exited their respective craft.

Yagi bowed to each of them. "Akio-*sama*, Yuko-*sama*, it is good to see you again. We all look forward to your visits."

Akio and Yuko returned the bow, then Yuko smiled at the man.

"Is it us, or the *sake* we bring that you most look forward to, Yagi-*san*?" Yuko laughed.

He placed both hands over his heart with a big grin on his face. "Yuko-*san*, you know it is your smiling face that brightens this old man's days and makes life more fulfilling. The *sake* is an added benefit."

Yuko giggled at this, happy that Yagi had recovered enough from the horrible experience with Isamu and his Forsaken to find his sense of humor. She had grown to know and love him over the past months and knew without a doubt that he was the leader the people of this island needed.

Eve exited the container with several boxes in her arms. "Did someone mention *sake*?" she inquired as she set them on the ground.

Yagi's face lit up when he saw that one of the cases bore the label of his favorite brand. He was already calculating if there was enough for each adult who wanted a cup since he always made it a point to share the beverage with his people. Knowing this, Yuko had left another bottle in the container to give Ono for when Yagi needed it. Although the island was recovering, the community still wasn't able to sustain itself like it had before most of the residents had been killed. That haunted Yagi and caused him many restless nights as he tried to work out ways to improve the lives of his people.

Yuko indicated the growing pile of boxes Eve had already unloaded. "Yagi-*san,* we brought some supplies that we thought you could use along with your *sake*. Eve will unload them. If you could get someone to take charge of distributing them, that would be helpful."

Yagi motioned to four young men and one older woman. "You four take the supplies to the storehouse. Put them where Kiya-*san* directs."

He faced Yuko again. "You're too kind, Yuko-*sama*. You have already done so much for us that we can never repay you."

"I have told you many times that you don't owe us, Yagi-*san*. Besides, I like the people here, and it gives me great pleasure to help in whatever small way I can until your people can take care of all their needs. That is the main reason we came today. Are Koda and Asai around? Eve and I would like to speak with them."

"They are working with Ono in the field today. Everyone alternates between working the field, fishing, and repairing homes since we lost so many. I can send for them if you like. Otherwise, they will probably be a couple more hours."

Yuko smiled. "Yes, that would be best. I also need you, Ono, and Koda's father to meet with all of us."

Yagi's eyes widened with concern. He turned and spoke with two of the women who were with him, directing one to the field to get the women and the other to the beach where Koda's father was repairing nets.

"Is something wrong with the girls?" Yagi's voice was laced with concern.

"Oh, no, Yagi-*san*," Yuko assured him. "I didn't mean to alarm you. There is nothing wrong with either girl that I know of. I have a proposition for them, and as their parents, I want you to be present when I talk with them about it. It is something that will benefit them as well as everyone here."

Yagi smiled as he offered his arm to Yuko. "In that case, please allow me to escort you to my home. We will have refreshments while we wait. Although Ono is with the girls, I brew a pretty good cup of tea if I do say so myself."

"I'm not sure that it will be safe for Koda in Tokyo," Takai Rii insisted for the fifth time.

"I am a grown woman and capable of taking care of myself." Koda huffed.

Ono rolled her eyes as she watched the two of them. Since Yuko had explained to them and their daughters what she had in mind, Takai had dug in his heels and would not admit that Koda was no longer a little girl who needed his protection.

"Takai, I understand your reservations, but do you honestly think Akio-*sama* or Yuko-*sama* would allow anything to happen to Koda?" Ono calmly rebutted.

"It's not that, sister. It's that she's only been off Kume once, and I fear that there will be too many distractions for an inexperienced young girl in Tokyo."

"So, you're saying that you don't trust me? Is that it, *Chichiue*?" Koda stood and paced back and forth across the small kitchen of Yagi's and Ono's house. "It's okay for me to go out on the boats where a sudden storm could sink us, or to work in a house that could collapse without warning. But, I can't be trusted to work for Yuko-*sama* and Eve-*san* in Tokyo?

CHARLES TILLMAN & MICHAEL ANDERLE

"I, uh, no. I mean…" Takai looked at Ono, his eyes wide and his expression begging for help.

Ono folded her arms across her chest and found the teacup in front of her to be extremely interesting as her brother floundered.

Seeing he would get no help there, he drew a deep breath to calm his nerves. "Koda, I do trust you, but Tokyo is so far away. I fear that you will not be happy there. Plus, I will miss you so badly if you go," he finished quietly.

"*Chichuie*, I will miss you too." Koda gave him a quick hug. "But this is an opportunity for all of us. Yuko-*sama* explained that much of the money made will be used to improve things here on Kume. That she trusts me to help run the business should make you proud, not cause fear."

Takai stood and held his daughter tight, his head resting on top of hers for a few moments before he released her and sighed. "I know you are going to do it, just as you already know it, too. I might as well admit defeat now. Also, for the record, I have always been proud of you."

Koda squealed as she slammed into him, wrapping her arms around him and almost taking both to the floor in her exuberance.

"Don't break him, please, he still has nets to mend," Yagi deadpanned as everyone in the room, Takai included, started laughing. "I guess you two need to pack so you can be on your way," he added with a hitch in his voice.

Asai stood and walked to him. She wrapped his seated form in a hug and kissed him on his cheek. "We will both be fine, *Chichuie*. I am certain we will be able to visit often. Yuko-*sama* did say that she would be making regular trips here to deliver medicines and other needed items as well as to check on the progress of the repairs. I'm sure she will let us tag along for visits as long as the business is running smoothly."

Yuko and Eve had left them in Yagi's house to discuss the offer in private. The two walked along the beach, looking over the rubble of the old dock. Eve took measurements so they could get an idea of how much material would be needed to make the repairs. With shipping increasing around the islands, the new dock would play a vital part in the island's recovery, although much of the local cargo was hauled on sail-powered ships.

Akio had taken the Black Eagle and made a circuit of the island while they did this, his senses extended as he searched for any sign of Forsaken. The group emerged from Yagi's house as Akio landed, Koda and Asai smiling ear-to-ear. Yuko and Eve made their way back, and everyone met in the square.

Asai bowed formally before she spoke. "Yuko-*sama*, Eve-*san*, we are honored that you trust us to be part of this venture. We both have much to learn, but if you are willing to teach us, we promise to do our best to make this business successful."

Eve clapped with joy.

Yuko smiled at both young women. "I am certain that you will both be quite capable of what we need. Until the building is done, Eve has some training programs that will prepare you for when we are ready to open. Plus, you will need time to shop for the items you want in your new homes. Eve will advise you on the necessities as well as help you locate decorations and other things that will make them yours."

Yuko turned to Yagi and the others. "If you would like, one of us will pick you up for the grand opening. It will give you a chance to see what these two are doing to help improve life here."

Yagi smiled, his eyes wide and excitement in his voice. "Does that mean I get to fly in one of your machines? If that's the case, sign me up now."

Ono laughed at her husband's antics, happy that he had found his way back from the darkness that plagued him during and after the horrors of Isamu.

CHAPTER TWENTY-TWO

TQB Base, Tokyo, Japan

Once away from the adults on the island, Koda and Asai had become so caught up in the excitement of living and working in Tokyo that the novelty of flying was soon lost. It quickly became evident to Eve that they were more like sisters than cousins as they chattered nonstop about what they wanted to do in Tokyo.

Asai proved to be more studious than Koda, wanting to see historical sights and visit libraries and museums that she had only heard of or read about.

Koda, on the other hand, was interested in fashion and entertainment opportunities. The only thing both agreed on in whispered conversation was the opportunity to meet interesting members of the opposite sex.

"Eve, would you please keep an eye on these two?" Yuko sent over her chip. "They are both intelligent young women, but they've led a sheltered life. Though they have dealt with Forsaken, they haven't experienced the darker side of humanity. We need to keep a close watch until they learn what to look out for when it comes to some of the people they will meet here."

"I'm on it. Should we put them in the Pod-doc and give them implants?"

Yuko thought for a moment. "We might make the offer in the future, but for now, maybe set them both up with small communicators. Perhaps something that looks similar to the mobile devices that are becoming popular with the people their ages. I'll leave that up to you as long as they have them. That way, we will be able to keep watch from a distance without being too intrusive."

Eve took on the duty of getting Koda and Asai settled into the base when they arrived. After Akio and Yuko had bid them farewell, Eve took her new charges in hand and set about getting them acclimated to the new normal of living in a world with modern technology.

"Asai, please place your hand here." Eve indicated a dark square on the wall of the elevator, just above the buttons that would take passengers to the upper floors.

The square flashed red several times before turning a steady green.

"Koda, please do the same," Eve instructed.

Koda complied, and soon the square turned green for her as well. A disembodied voice came from the speaker in the ceiling. "Welcome, Asai Ono and Koda Rii. Level-one access granted."

Koda looked at the speaker and then back at Eve, confusion evident on her face as the lift descended. "How did whoever that was know our names?"

"That's Abel, the Entity Intelligence who controls the base," Eve explained. "He is linked to me. I have programmed your biometric data into him. He will now recognize you and allow you access to all parts of the base you have clearance for. Some of the areas are dangerous. If you try to enter them, Abel will not open the door.

"This elevator takes you to the basement level," Eve explained as the doors slid open. She motioned for both women to follow and walked to a blank wall at the end of the short hallway.

She pointed to a bare spot located in a corner about three feet from the floor. "Asai, please place your hand flat on this spot."

Within seconds, the entire section of wall slid back into a hidden recess and revealed another elevator. Eve stepped inside with Koda and Asai on her heels, and the door silently closed.

Abel's voice came from hidden speakers in the roof. "Level, please."

"Say which level you wish to go to," Eve advised the girls, then called, "Level one." As the elevator began its swift descent, she continued to familiarize them with the building's systems. "The base is comprised of five levels located below this floor. They are labeled one through five, or you can say the name of the level once you understand them.

"This level is not accessible any other way except that first-floor elevator," Eve explained. "The second elevator is an additional layer of security and allows access to the base. If someone without authorization attempts to enter this car, there are defensive measures that range from light discouragement to lethal depending on how hard they try to breach the base."

The elevator stopped as she finished, and the door opened into a long hall with doors spaced out on either side.

"Level one," Abel announced.

"This is the residential level," Eve told them. "We all have individual quarters with private baths. The kitchen is here, as well as a common area where we can meet. I will show you to the rooms you will use whenever you stay at the base. They will still be available after your apartments are done, in case you need to stay overnight."

Eve led them past the open dining area they had already been in on the night Isamu died, and past several other closed doors. As they approached two doors opposite each other near the end of the hallway, both slid open automatically to reveal comfortably furnished living areas.

Eve gestured for the young women to explore. "The rooms are identical except for the colors. Take whichever you like. I will give you an hour to get settled and clean up. You don't have to boil water for a bath. Each room is equipped with a tub and separate shower, so you can normally take as long as you'd like."

Both women stared unbelievingly at Eve. They were both born after earthquakes had destroyed the power station on Kume and had never had a bath that did not require hauling wood and heating water. Most of the time, the islanders went for a swim in the ocean to clean up after a day of strenuous labor.

"Seriously, Eve-*san?*" Asai asked. "There is hot running water here? I have read about it in books and seen the faucets at home, but I have never experienced it."

Eve was surprised to hear this, but then she realized that neither woman was over twenty-three. As a result, they had never experienced the basic conveniences from before that many now considered luxuries.

"Both of you come in, and I will explain how it works." She stepped into one of the open rooms. "This is your personal living space, where you can relax, read, listen to music, or watch movies and shows."

"Eve," Koda interrupted, "what is a movie?"

Eve paused when she remembered that Koda and Asai had never had electricity and had probably never experienced any recorded entertainment. She turned to Koda with a huge grin on her face. "It is a recorded form of entertainment that you watch on a device called a television. We don't have time now, but I will gladly introduce both of you to them soon."

Asai spoke up then. "I remember mother and father talking about something like that when I was a small child. Father was complaining about not being able to watch baseball. I told him he could watch the older kids play whenever he wanted. Mother burst out laughing at the look on his face. He told me about television then. It was a long time ago."

Eve smiled, thinking of the surprises ahead for the two women. "Yes, that and many other luxuries were available before WWDE. We have an extensive library of anything you can imagine. I look forward to showing it to you."

"That sounds like fun," Koda remarked, her head craning to see through a door that had suddenly opened.

"Through there is the bedroom." Eve pointed as she moved toward the rear of the room. There was a large plush-looking bed covered in a thick earth tone comforter with a small stand beside it. The room was also furnished with a wooden dresser on the wall opposite the bed that held assorted-sized drawers, and a large monitor fastened to the wall above it.

"Through here is your closet and vanity," Eve explained as she stepped into a brightly lit area with a walk-in closet on one side and a counter with a sink and a mirror above it that covered the entire wall.

She continued the tour by stepping through another door located at the end of the area. "This is the bathroom." She motioned for them to enter.

Koda and Asai were staring at the luxury surrounding them. Koda stepped into the room behind Eve and stopped in her tracks, her eyes wide with wonder and her mouth hanging open.

Asai was looking at the vanity and did not realize Koda had stopped until she ran into her.

"Koda, what are you doing? You're blocking the door." Asai prodded her in the ribs when Koda failed to move after the collision.

Koda shook her head and quickly took a step forward. "Sorry, Asai," she murmured.

"You're so dim someti—" Asai stopped mid-sentence when she saw what held Koda's attention.

It was a room almost half the size of the bedroom, dominated by an oval-shaped bathtub with multiple jets in the sides. Next to it was a glassed-in shower that had nozzles coming from three sides and a large flat one suspended from a chrome pipe coming down from the ceiling.

Eve smiled at their reactions and walked over to the tub. She indicated the knobs on either side of the faucet. "The red one is hot. The blue is cold. I suggest turning the blue one first and then adjusting the red until the temperature is comfortable. The water temperature is set for Yuko and Akio, and they prefer it very hot. I don't think you would like to be scalded, so please be careful until you are accustomed to how it works. The shower is the same." She indicated a set of six knobs, each with a diagram depicting the various nozzles around the cubicle. "These control which of the heads you want to use, and regulate the pressure."

Both women slowly went from one fixture to the other, neither able to decide which they wanted to try first.

Asai found her voice first. "This one is mine," she stated firmly. "Go get your own, Koda. That tub just called my name, so if you will excuse me, I think I need to get acquainted with this marvelous device."

Koda glared at her cousin, both hands on her hips. "Now, wait a minute, Asai. I was here first."

Eve laughed at their antics, knowing neither was serious. "The other room is identical, except it is decorated in pastels if that helps, Koda."

Koda grinned as she stuck her tongue out at Asai before turning to Eve. "That sounds lovely. Much better than Asai's dreary brown room."

Eve chuckled as Asai put her hands on her hips, mimicking Koda.

"I happen to like natural colors," she asserted. "Now, go to your room, Koda. I need some alone time with my new best friend."

They both giggled like schoolgirls as Koda headed for the other room.

Eve reminded Asai that she would return in an hour before she followed Koda.

Eve returned an hour later and found Koda and Asai sipping tea in the common kitchen, freshly scrubbed and grinning from ear-to-ear.

"I presume you found your accommodations acceptable?" Eve laughed.

"Eve, that was the best experience I have ever had. I never want to leave," Koda gushed.

Asai nodded vigorously in agreement.

Eve smiled at them both "I believe you will find the accommodations in your new homes surpass these," she assured them.

Koda and Asai gaped at her before Asai exclaimed, "Better than this? Impossible."

Eve snickered and then got a calculating look in her eyes. "Would you like to make a little wager on it?"

Asai started to answer when Koda cut in, "Asai, remember your father's saying about betting on another's game?"

Asai's face took on a thoughtful look, and then she nodded. "I think this may be one of those games."

"You show wisdom beyond your years, young one," Eve deadpanned, causing both women to burst out laughing.

"Come. I will show you the rest of the base. Then we will take a trip into the fashion district to pick up some new clothes for both of you. I can't have the managers of my new business looking less than fashionable, after all."

CHAPTER TWENTY-THREE

Northern China, Prison Complex

Chang surveyed the cells that stretched down either side of the bleak stone building. "Miko, how many Nosferatu do you have now?"

"Fifty-three survived the change, sir," Miko replied. "I have had my men scouting the small villages in the area for more humans, but not many remain. The bandits we took the prison from had killed or chased away most of them before we arrived."

"Heinz will not be happy with that. Expand your search area and keep collecting until you have at least one hundred," Chang ordered. "Don't go over one hundred and eighty, though. Transporting more than that will over- whelm our logistics ability."

Miko nodded. "Yes, sir. I will send word when I reach one hundred."

"You've done well here, Miko. I'm going to suggest that you be given more responsibilities in the future. Do not disappoint me," Chang told him before he turned and walked back toward the blacked-out box truck he had arrived in.

Chang shut the door and spoke to the driver. "Dieter, let's head back. Do watch the ruts in the road this time. I bounced around like a pinball all the way here."

The large blond Were stiffened at this. "Yes, sir. Would you like to wait until tonight and ride in the front? That would probably be more comfortable. We should be back at the lab before sunrise if we leave as soon as it's dark."

Chang appreciated the concern the Were showed. *If only his brother were as loyal. It's a shame that Horst chafes so much against Heinz. He would be a real asset if he would just realize that Heinz will see that they both have a high position in the ruling class once we have established control over Japan. Even though they are only Weres, Heinz treats them like they were his children. He chose to raise them after their mother was killed protecting him. I never understood why he felt guilty about her death. For some reason, he was uncharacteristically affected by her death. Although, he would be dead if she hadn't sacrificed herself to protect him, I suppose.*

"No, I need to get back as soon as possible. I think Heinz shouldn't have killed the commissioner for this area. He had an overinflated sense of entitlement, but he did at least maintain the damn roads."

"What happened?" Dieter inquired. "If you don't mind me asking, sir."

Chang chuckled. "Heinz ripped his head off and then killed the four soldiers with him when he tried to commandeer the generator at the lab. He had their heads delivered to the Provincial Party Secretary with a note to send someone smarter next time. They haven't sent anyone to replace him yet."

Dieter nodded. "I hadn't heard, but it is well known that father does not suffer fools. I will go slower so the ride will not be so rough."

"Just get us there in one piece," Chang ordered. "Soon, we will not have to hide from the Dark One like frightened mice."

Tokyo, Riko's Noodle House

Sero spoke between bites of noodles. "The child was seen with two other women at the warehouse again today. There has been a lot of activity there in the past few days. One of our men was able to find out from a laborer that they are building apartments on the upper floor and putting in walls throughout the open space on the first floor."

"Do we know what they are putting on the first floor?" Muto questioned.

"All the worker knew was that it is supposed to be an entertainment facility of some type. He is only a day worker hauling debris from inside, rather than one of the building crew."

"Keep someone watching and try to get a man inside to look around. Perhaps the chatty laborer can tell him how to get on the crew."

"Already on it," Sero assured him. "I sent Kosha over there today. His father was a carpenter, and Kosha worked for him from the time he was twelve. He knows enough about it to get hired if they need someone."

Muto smiled at his second, glad once again that he had taken in the starving orphan years earlier. "That's good. Bring whatever information you get as soon as it comes in. I'm sure our employers will be interested in whatever we find. Keep watchers in the area to try and locate where they are coming from. I'm tired of them disappearing into thin air every time one of our men spots them."

"Me too, Muto. I can't figure out how they're doing it. I have put men along the route that they have left by each time. They walk through the old temple area and never come out on the other side. We have searched all through the buildings and woods but still can't find where they go."

"If you need more men on it, pull them in. If we can find their base, we get paid more. I wonder what they would pay for one of them alive?" Muto got a distant look in his eyes as he considered what had just popped into his head.

Sero saw the look in Muto's eyes and knew where this was going. He was already mentally compiling a list of the people he would use and the necessary logistics for holding the captives. "It shouldn't be too difficult to take the woman or the child. They are always alone. Well, now there are those two mystery women, but they shouldn't pose a challenge."

Muto motioned the server to take his empty bowl and bring him another *sake*. "Get a plan in place, and I will let you know if the operation is a go. I expect to hear from our contact soon, anyway. The last time they were here, they

CHARLES TILLMAN & MICHAEL ANDERLE

acted like we weren't doing what they paid us for. I want to show them that we honor our commitments. I don't need them spreading word that the Yakuza don't deliver what we promise."

"I've got it, Muto. Let me know when, and I will take care of it," Sero assured him, hoping that this was a passing fancy since it was not part of what the client requested. They were explicit that all they wanted was the location, and they would handle anything else.

Sero had reservations about this from the start, after meeting Chang and the blond giant that came with him when they initially contracted with Muto for this. There was something about both that made him nervous. Although they were polite, he still felt it was dangerous to deal with them.

When he approached Muto about it after they had left, he was not interested in hearing Sero's reservations. All he saw was the money they'd offered.

TQB Base, Tokyo, Japan

"Eve, that was amazing!" Koda gushed as she pulled items out of the numerous bags she had acquired on their shopping trip.

Asai was watching her cousin as she held up different dresses and shirts, admiring them in the mirror. "Thank you for taking us shopping, Eve. You must let us repay you once we start making money. That was an expensive trip."

Eve smiled. "Don't worry about it, Asai. It was worth it to see both of you enjoying yourselves. The price really wasn't that much when you consider that you two will be the faces of our business. I'm planning a big buildup to generate excitement for the grand opening, so the two of you will be dealing with all manner of reporters soon."

Koda's face lost color, and she got a panicked look in her eyes. "I don't know anything about talking to people like that."

"That brings us to the next item on your agenda. I have developed some training scenarios that will prepare you for the new situations you will be in. They use the same tech that we will use in the business. The only difference is that they are educational instead of pure entertainment," Eve advised.

"There is so much that we have never done before. Are you certain that we will be able to grasp it all?" Asai worried.

Eve nodded. "I have programmed them to move at the speed you learn. I promise that if you apply yourselves, there will be nothing you encounter that you will not be prepared for once you complete the training."

She reached into her pocket and took out two small black discs about two inches around, and two small earbuds. "These devices are to communicate with Yuko, Akio, and me anytime you need us. Press the disc, say who you want, and the device will automatically connect you. If you are in trouble and can't speak, press it twice. It will send us all a distress call that we can track. Always keep them with you. As I explained earlier, Tokyo is generally safe, but there are bad people here. As long as you have these with you, help is never far away."

Asai and Koda took the indicated devices and looked them over.

"All we have to do is press it and say the person's name?" Asai looked at it skeptically.

"That's all. Go ahead and put the bud in your ear, then call Yuko. You need to be familiar with how they work."

Asai pressed the unit. "Yuko?"

Yuko's voice came from the part in her ear seconds later. "Yes, Asai?"

"Um, Eve wanted me to test the communication device she just gave me," Asai stammered.

Yuko replied immediately with a hint of amusement. "It is working as advertised. I hear you fine. Is Koda with you?"

"*Hai.*"

"Have her test her unit as well."

Asai turned to Koda. "She wants you to test yours."

Koda picked up her unit and called, "Yuko?"

"Ah, there you are. Your unit is functioning as well."

Asai started when Yuko's voice unexpectedly came over her unit. "Both of you, be sure to keep the units on you all the time, and don't hesitate to call if you have any questions.

"On a happier note, I just finished speaking with the contractor building your living quarters. He says that he will be ready for you to go over anything you want to do to your individual spaces next week. Eve will go over the options for appliances and other comfort items that are available after you do another walk-through at the end of this week."

Eve's face broke out in a huge grin and she rubbed her hands together with glee. "Looks like we have some shopping to do, ladies."

Both women laughed at their friend's excited reaction and assured her that they were up to the challenge.

CHAPTER TWENTY-FOUR

Acheng, China, Research Laboratory

"Miko has things progressing nicely at the prison," Chang announced as he stepped into the lab.

"One moment, Chang." Heinz held a vial in one hand and a syringe of blood in the other. He was meticulously counting the drops as he slowly injected blood from the syringe into the vial.

When he completed the task, he carefully placed the vial in a rack with several more and capped the needle on the syringe. "What did you find at the prison?"

"Miko has done well. He has over fifty Nosferatu ready to go and has his men out searching the countryside for more specimens to be turned. I told him he needed at least one hundred for us to carry out the attack. He should be ready in the next two to three weeks."

"Good," Heinz growled. "The sooner we remove Akio, the better. He has interfered with our plans too much already. Has Muto located his base yet?"

"No," Chang informed him regretfully. "He hasn't sent any information. Dieter just returned from meeting with one of the ship captains that Muto uses to send his reports. He had nothing new for us. I am sending Dieter to deal with Muto personally. If he has nothing more to report, I hope his second in command does a better job."

Heinz clenched his fist and scowled. He hated sending the Were to Japan, but a vampire would cause suspicion among the ship's crew when he didn't come out in the sun. The medium-sized cargo ships had been fitted with a solar-powered propulsion system, but the technology was slow. They could only move at around eight knots for twelve hours each day, which meant the eight hundred-plus kilometer trip to Japan would take around five days.

Chang pulled a paper from his pocket and glanced at it. "One of the ships should be in Vladivostok sometime this week." He paused before adding, "I assume you still do not want to risk using the aircraft."

Heinz looked thoughtful before he grudgingly replied, "I believe that it should be safe enough to have Horst fly Dieter over to catch the ship. I don't want to risk him missing it because of the time it takes to travel overland. I'm still not willing to operate too close to Japan, though, No sense in risking discovery when we are so close to destroying Akio."

Chang smiled at his victory. "Very well, Heinz. I will tell the boys to prepare the craft and give Dieter his instructions."

"Send them both to me before they leave," Heinz ordered. "I want to be sure Dieter understands what his limits are and that Horst doesn't do anything to risk exposure. I need to caution him to be sure there isn't a repeat of what happened at Kume. He has always been the one to push against whatever restrictions I give him, but I trust him to not make the mistakes that the other crew made. Horst can be a pain in the ass like his father was before he was eliminated. But he does understand the danger that discovery can bring."

"Dieter, I want you to express how disappointed I am to Muto and explain to Sero that he will get the same treatment if he proves to be as inept," Heinz instructed.

"Won't that cause us problems with the Yakuza?" Dieter shrugged. "Not that I'm concerned about doing what you ask, but I thought we needed them."

"If they protest too much, kill a few more of their leaders so they understand their place in our world," Heinz told him.

"It will be my pleasure, Father." The blond Were flexed his arms and smiled. "I will make an example that Sero and all of the Yakuza scum will understand."

"Try not to kill too many of them for now." Heinz chuckled. "We do need a few of them for a little while longer. After we take control of Japan, I will let you and Horst deal with them as you see fit."

"*Ja,* Father."

"Horst, I want you to fly Dieter to Vladivostok. Be sure that you follow all of the precautions to avoid detection. We're too close for you to risk discovery with a joyride.

There and back, no side trips, and stay below fifty meters."

"I know how to fly the craft," Horst snapped.

Heinz growled as his eyes flashed red. He stared at the surly Were until he lowered his eyes in submission. "I know you do. I also know that the craft almost got caught at Kume. Do not disappoint me in this, do you understand?"

"*Ja.*" He hesitated before grudgingly adding, "Father, I understand."

"Dieter, I look forward to seeing you in Japan within two to three months. If you get any information that I need, send it by one of the ships. Now, out with both of you. I have work to do." Heinz turned to his samples, signaling that the Weres should leave.

"Dammit, Horst. Why do you always challenge Father at every turn?" Dieter huffed when they were out of range for Heinz to overhear.

Horst growled as he turned and glared at his twin. "He's not our father. Our father was an alpha and pack leader in Germany. Heinz is merely the bloodsucker who killed him. He is also responsible for our mother's death. I don't understand why you always toady up to him and that fucking Chang."

Dieter pushed forward until they were face-to-face, their barrel chests almost touching. "I don't understand why you are such an ungrateful ass. Father took us in and has treated us like his own. If he hadn't, we could have ended up left in Germany or worse yet, as experiments on some table in a Nazi research lab. You owe him everything and are too stupid to realize it."

Dieter shoved him aside and stalked toward the air ship's hangar, determined not to let this devolve into another of their fights where nothing was resolved and things were usually destroyed. He hoped that once Japan was theirs, Horst would realize that being a loyal son was better than fighting all the time. Before he pushed Heinz too far, just like their Were father had done.

CHAPTER TWENTY-FIVE

TQB Base, Tokyo, Japan

Eve called Asai and Koda over their communicators. "Please come to the dining room."

"Be there in a minute, Eve," Asai replied. She entered the dining room moments later. Koda followed shortly after.

"What's up, Eve?" Koda inquired.

"I was thinking of going shopping. I figured you were both busy with whatever old movies you were watching, but I wanted to see if there was any chance I could entice you to go." She shrugged, the motion wildly exaggerated, before adding, "I know how addicted you are to those romantic comedies but since this trip is to buy things for your new homes, I thought you might be willing to take a break."

Koda jumped up and down, clapping excitedly.

Asai laughed. "I don't know about Koda, but I suppose I could be talked into a shopping trip."

Koda stuck her tongue out at her cousin, and all three of them burst out laughing.

"We will stop by the apartments first so you can see what you have to work with," Eve explained as she headed out the door. "The contractors notified me that they are finished, so now you need to furnish them to your personal tastes."

Both young women rushed to catch up as the android summoned the elevator to the surface. They emerged into the early afternoon sunlight.

Asai stopped just outside the door. "Um, Eve, it's light out. I thought we couldn't take the Pods out in daylight?"

Eve smiled. "You're right, we can't except in an emergency. That's why we are taking this." She pointed to a small four-seat vehicle sitting beside the building.

Koda walked around the vehicle. "I don't think I have ever seen one of those before. What is it?"

"This is the first prototype of a new public transit system I have been working on," Eve told her. "This one runs on a small motor that will take it to a top speed of seventy kilometers per hour. When we get the proper licenses, we will install a grid under the streets and people can summon a car with an app on their personal devices. It will make it easier for people to go from the main transport hubs to their homes for a small fee per use, or with a monthly subscription for a set number of kilometers each month.

"Yuko gave me the idea when we were coming back from the warehouse one day. I fabricated this vehicle as a test and worked out a way to control an entire fleet of them using an EI. Passengers will simply enter the address that they want to go to when the car is requested. I also have plans for bigger vehicles that can be used for deliveries. I believe that we can have the system up and running in most of the major areas of Tokyo within the year."

Koda ran her hand over the vehicle then looked up at Eve with a grin. "So, since you own the company, I don't suppose it would be too much to ask that we have one for the arcade? For official business only, of course."

Eve laughed. "I suppose we could work out some kind of arrangement."

"It wouldn't do for your business managers to have to wait for a ride when there was important business that needed handling," Asai interjected.

"Hmmm," Eve mused. "I guess it would be important for my people to have their own transportation. We want people to see us as ahead of the competition."

"Oh, absolutely," Asai replied, her eyes dancing with barely restrained mirth.

Koda had taken it all in and couldn't contain the laugh that burst from her lips. This triggered Asai, and soon all of them were laughing like schoolgirls once again.

"As soon as the grid is installed, I promise that you will get the first private model produced. There will be a limited number of those available to the public, but mostly it will be a per ride or subscription service. Yuko felt that some of the wealthier people would be willing to pay for custom models and an annual fee to use the grids. This model is still a manual control unit, and was only to test the reliability and function of the motor."

Eve drove them to their first stop, the apartments above the arcade.

When they pulled up, Koda gasped as she saw the recently completed exterior work. "It looks like a castle! I can't tell it was a warehouse last week. It's amazing."

"That was Akio's suggestion," Eve told her. "He said that it was as big as an emperor's palace, which gave me the idea for what we've decided to call it."

"What's that?" Asai asked. "The emperor's palace?"

Eve smiled. "Close guess. We decided to name it the Palace."

Koda pursed her lips and studied the roof, which had one large peak in the center and two smaller ones to the front and either side of it. The eaves had intricate gold inlay floral designs up each side and were capped with sunburst inlays at the top of each peak.

"It's beautiful, Eve, and the name is perfect," Koda whispered.

"We are adding similar inlays and other decorations to the interior to bring the palace feel inside," Eve explained. "It added a little more time to the project, but we are creating a unique experience and feel that it will enhance the experience. One of the simulations that has tested well with the focus groups is a samurai battle where the players are involved in a running fight through a sixteenth-century castle. It is the most popular one so far, although each scenario that we are rolling out in the initial run has tested exceptionally well with our focus groups. You two will start interviewing staff and taking reservations for the grand opening next week."

"That soon? Are you sure we're ready?" Asai stammered, her eyes wide with concern.

"You are both more than ready," Eve assured them. "I

have monitored your training in the sims I created. Both of you show potential for high-level management skills. I have no doubt that you can handle the job, but Yuko and I are only a communicator button away if you have any questions. Now, let's go see your apartments."

Eve led them to the rear of the lobby and through a door that opened automatically when she approached it. "Your communicators are keyed to this door, so make sure they are always with you. Otherwise, someone else will have to let you in."

When they had passed through the door, it soundlessly shut behind them. They were in a small room not much bigger than a closet.

"Koda, place your hand on the panel." Eve pointed to a dark square on the wall. She did, and the panel flashed briefly. "Now you, Asai."

Asai complied. When the panel flashed, a pleasant male voice issued from a hidden speaker. "Welcome, Koda Rii and Asai Ono. I am Takumi, the Entity Intelligence that controls all the sims and functions here in the Palace. It is my pleasure to meet you."

Asai looked shaken, but Koda was quick to answer. "It's nice to meet you, Takumi. I'm sure we will get along wonderfully."

"Thank you, Koda Rii. I look forward to assisting you with any information you need. I took the liberty of setting the temperature in your apartments to twenty-two degrees Celsius. My data indicates that is a comfortable level. If it is not to your liking, simply call my name, and I will be there."

Asai looked at Eve with raised eyebrows. "Eve, is Takumi like you?"

"Takumi is an EI, an Entity Intelligence. I am an AI, an Artificial Intelligence. Takumi is capable of learning, and in time, he could ascend if he desires, but for now, he is an exceptionally capable controller for all aspects of this building. That includes climate, lights, simulations, and security."

"Security?" Koda sounded worried.

"I have a full array of sensors that monitor all activity inside and outside the complex, as well as deterrent measures should they be needed," Takumi answered.

"Don't be alarmed, Koda. It is protocol for all of our facilities to have security. We operate on the principle that it is better to have it and not need it, than to need it and not have it," Eve explained.

"That's a good principle. It makes me feel secure knowing that Takumi will be looking out for us," Asai told Koda.

"I hadn't thought that we would need it here in the city," Koda replied.

"Although the city is relatively safe, there is still crime here," Eve explained. "Takumi will keep watch to ensure that all our players and employees have a safe and fun experience. He has the ability to contact the police or take action if it is warranted. As I said, it is strictly protocol. I am not aware of any issues with safety. Let's go up to your quarters, now. We still have some power shopping to do."

They rode the lift to the second level, where it opened into a common foyer with a door on either side.

"Asai, your apartment is on the right. Koda, yours is on the left. Takumi, please open the doors."

The doors opened simultaneously as Takumi announced, "Welcome home, Asai and Koda."

Both women entered their indicated spaces. Seconds later, excited squeals came from Koda's open door.

"Oh, my God! It's huge!" Koda squealed as she ran through the apartment. "All of this is for me?"

Eve chuckled at Koda's excitement. "Every square meter of it."

Asai stood in the entry, her eyes wide and her mouth open in shock. The main room was decorated in soft earth tones like her room at the base, but her entire room there would fit in the living area of the new apartment. A bar on one side separated the living space from the kitchen and attached dining area. The kitchen was fully equipped with new stainless steel appliances.

The opposite wall had an open door that led into a large bedroom. As she slowly walked into the room, she noticed that the bedroom was almost as large as the living room. Another door led into what she assumed was the bathroom. When she stepped through that door, she saw that it was identical to her bathroom at the base, only twice as big. The tub looked like she could swim in it, and the shower had many more nozzles coming out at all angles.

Her hand went to her chest as she took it all in. "Eve, this is amazing. I don't know what to say. Thank you."

Eve smiled at her reaction, glad that she had made both of her friends happy. "Now that you see what you have to work with, what say we furnish these babies?"

Koda immediately started rattling off items that she had

seen on the shopping sites Eve had gone over with her. Asai turned slowly around in each room, mentally placing the items that she needed. When both were satisfied that they had what they wanted firmly in mind, they exited the units and headed out for some serious retail therapy.

CHAPTER TWENTY-SIX

TQB Base, Tokyo, Japan

Eve was in the command center reviewing surveillance data from one of the many satellites that orbited the Earth when an alert flashed in the corner of her monitor. She expanded it and saw that one of her drone carriers was transmitting information.

"Got you!" she exclaimed as she activated her chip to contact Akio.

Seconds later, he walked into the small operations center. "What do you have, Eve? Is it the mystery craft from Kume?"

"Yes, and it now has four of my drones hitching a ride and a carrier trailing it close enough to boost their signals. We can track it wherever it goes." She rubbed her hands together and mimicked cracking her knuckles. "Or we could blow them out of the sky so hard their ancestors won't even be a memory."

Akio looked askance at the android. "No blowing up just yet, please. I want to know where they are coming from and where they go. When we get some drones into their base of operations, maybe I'll let you go at them with a Black Eagle."

Eve shrugged. "Works for me. I'm still annoyed that they were able to give me the slip. It's time for Saint Payback to make an appearance."

Akio's eyes widened at this revelation. "What do you know about Saint Payback?" he asked.

"Everything ADAM knows," Eve told him. "From what I can see, Bethany Anne is a firm believer in Saint Payback. I owe whoever these people are for making me feel inadequate when they got away."

"Eve, you're far from inadequate," he assured her. "Without you, we would have a much tougher time keeping track of everything. You are a valuable member of this team, and don't you ever forget it."

"Thank you, Akio. When we find their base, can I drop a puck on it?"

Akio snorted as he fought to control a smile. "If a puck is in order, I will defer to your master puck-handling skills."

"I'll hold you to that," Eve told him. "Now, let's track them. I want to know what those evil meatsacks are planning before they catch us unprepared."

Akio raised an eyebrow but refrained from commenting on Eve's outburst.

They watched the information roll across the screen until the craft landed on the outskirts of Vladivostok, Russia. A large blond man climbed out.

Eve directed one of the drones to detach from the craft. She adjusted her controls, and a voice came through the

speakers that matched the movement of the blond man's
lips.

"Try not to antagonize Father while I am away," the
blond giant called into the craft's open door.

"Whatever," another male voice called from within.
"Don't get your fuzzy ass killed in Japan. You're a pain, but
you're still my brother."

The giant made an obscene gesture at the open door.
"You do the same. Seriously, quit pissing off Father."

The craft lifted a few meters into the air and started
back the way it had come. The drone hovering overhead
floated down at Eve's command and silently attached itself
to the pack on the man's back as he turned and walked in
the opposite direction.

"I will keep the carrier close. It will act as a relay so we
can keep an eye on this one." Eve pointed to the monitor
that showed a closeup of the material the man's pack was
made of. "I will track this one by satellite and get another
relay in place as soon as we see where he goes." She indicated the second monitor that showed a satellite map with
a flashing red marker instead of a live feed since the craft
had moved out of range of the relay.

Akio nodded. "Good work, Eve. I am going to prepare.
As soon as we know where the craft came from, the sooner
I can go there and see what they are doing."

Eve tracked the craft as it crossed Russia and continued
into China. It moved at a fast pace, but not as fast as it had
when she lost it before. She also noted that it was flying
close to the ground and avoiding populated areas, as
though the pilot was trying to keep a low profile. She
smiled as she watched the craft attempt to avoid detection,

its pilot never suspecting that he was already being tracked.

As the craft approached the area where one of her carriers was positioned, she put it on an intercept and soon had a live feed. The mystery craft flew over the unpopulated mountain terrain erratically—swooping low into the valleys and shooting up and over the peaks before diving again. She tracked it doing this with no seeming purpose or direction for almost an hour before it landed on a mountainside overlooking an isolated valley.

Eve directed the carrier to launch a swarm of drones into the area in hopes of finding the hidden base. As the drones spread out, one of them approached a drab gray two-story building hidden deep in the valley. She directed the drone through a door that was not properly secured, and her eyes opened wide when she saw many Nosferatu locked in cells on both levels. She sent in more drones to get a count of the feral beasts.

"Akio, you need to see this," she called tersely over her chip.

"I'll be right there, Eve."

When Akio entered, he saw what was on the monitors. His lips tightened in anger.

Eve directed a drone to show the positioning of the guards as she spoke. "This is a prison complex hidden in the mountains in northern China. I count one hundred and twelve Nosferatu locked in the cells. There are also three guards on each level."

Their pale skin and the way they stood, unmoving except for their eyes, told Akio that they were Forsaken. "Can you tell if this is their base?"

Eve shook her head. "I can't find anything but the prison here. There are bunk rooms and offices on one end, but nothing that indicates a research facility."

Akio frowned. "Where is the aircraft?"

"It's sitting on the side of a mountain overlooking the valley." Eve switched one of the monitors to a shot of a boxy black craft a little larger than their smallest Pod. A blond giant of a man identical to the one they had seen earlier leaned against the craft and stared at the prison with a disgusted look. His lips started to move on the monitor.

Eve touched her screen and his voice came clearly over the speakers.

"I can't believe Dieter doesn't see the wrong in this," the man intoned in a deep voice. "They are only humans, but no one should be turned into this type of unnatural beast. Vampires are bad enough, but to be turned into a mindless killing machine is nothing I would wish on any being. That bastard Heinz destroys everything he touches. First, my father, when he resisted his using the pack for experiments and soldiers for Anton. Then he killed my mother when he was so cocky that he traveled in the daylight. I wish those soldiers had blown his damned truck up and sent his leech ass into the sun. I can't believe my mother died protecting him."

Akio didn't need the speaker to transmit the man's frustration.

He snarled. "I hope the Dark One kills him slowly, and I am able to watch as he breathes his last polluted breath. He doesn't deserve a quick death after all of the suffering he has caused over the years." He looked at the prison for a few more minutes before he spat disgustedly and got back into the craft.

"Are you tracking the craft?" Akio asked Eve when the audio cut out.

Eve nodded as the craft lifted slowly and continued through the mountains until it had traveled a few hundred kilometers. There the craft slowed and descended into a dark valley. When it reached the bottom, a door opened in the side of the mountain and the craft slipped silently inside.

Eve's drones continued to show the location. She put another carrier on a vector for the area to act as a relay and send out more drones.

Akio silently watched until the live feed came up on a monitor. It showed the craft sitting in a manmade cavern carved into the stone, and a dark tunnel leading deeper into the mountain. He continued to watch as Eve maneuvered the drone down the shaft toward a light. The shaft opened into a brightly-lit room with multiple tables spaced evenly throughout. Several men dressed in black fatigues were scattered around the room.

"Welcome back, Horst. Did your mission go well?" one of them called.

The blond giant nodded. "*Ja*, there were no problems. Dieter is on his way and should be there in a few days."

"Good, I'm ready for some fun. I look forward to getting out of this place and somewhere that there are willing women."

Another of the men snorted loudly. "When has it ever mattered to you if they were willing or not, Gerhart?"

Gerhart sneered. "Huen, I find that they are all willing

—with the proper motivation."

Horst grunted as he moved through the room, his head down so Gerhart couldn't see his disgust. The group consisted of the remains of his true father's pack that Heinz had brought from Germany when Anton sent him to Japan near the close of the war, and some Asian Weres who had similar traits. They were the ones who served the vampire willingly; the cruel and twisted ones who did whatever Heinz asked because he regularly allowed them to play their sadistic games with humans. Gerhart was the worst of the bunch. He was a sadist and truly enjoyed terrorizing and killing humans. Horst had never been one for senseless killing or torture and was disgusted by them all.

When he entered the living quarters, Chang called to him, "Your father wants to see you."

Horst ground his teeth together in frustration as he turned toward the laboratory down the hall. "You wanted to see me, Father?"

"You were gone longer than expected. Did you get Dieter to the ship?"

"*Ja,* he should be on his way now."

"There were no problems, then?"

"No. I did as you said. Low and slow. There was no sign of any other craft, and yes, I steered away from populated areas."

"Very good, Horst. Dismissed." Heinz turned back to his work.

Horst stalked out of the lab and took the stairs up two levels to the surface facility.

When he stepped through a door into the afternoon

sun, the drone attached to his boot sent out a signal to the other drones in the area. Soon, multiple small drones entered the structure and silently worked down through the levels. They took video and mapped out most of the facility in no time. The carrier dutifully relayed the information back to Eve in the command center.

Akio's lips turned up in a half-smile when a face he knew appeared on the screen. "Well, hello, Heinz. It's been a long time. I will see you soon, and this time you have no one to stop me from killing you for the things you have done," he stated in an icy tone.

Eve looked up at him, startled by the coldness in his voice. Whatever history Akio had with this Forsaken, she had no doubt that it would end soon. Most probably with Akio's sword meeting his neck.

"Please let Yuko know when she returns that I am taking a Pod to recon the prison. Those Nosferatu need to be dealt with first. Keep monitoring the drone feeds and see if you can determine what they are planning. I want to be sure that all of them are removed this time. Whatever they have planned must be stopped. They will not be allowed to cause more destruction and death like was done to the people of Kume."

"Should I load out a Black Eagle with pucks?" Eve inquired.

"*Hai.* I believe you will get your chance to demonstrate your master puck-handling skills before this is done."

Eve grinned as he told her this. "Saint Payback is going to have her day after all," she mumbled.

Akio's smile didn't touch his eyes. "*Hai,* a day that should have happened to *some* long ago."

CHAPTER TWENTY-SEVEN

Tokyo, Riko's Noodle House

"Our gambling and protection numbers are up by twenty percent this month," Sero read from the screen on his pad.

Muto waved his hand impatiently. "What's the news from our men watching for the people our friends from China are interested in?"

"I was getting to that."

"Well, don't keep me waiting. I just received a communication from the captain of the *Guro*. He has one of their representatives on board. It took a few days for the message to get here, so he will be docking in Joetsu in about three days."

"Did he say who it was?" Sero asked. "I don't want to have to deal with Chang again. There's something off with him. He makes me uneasy."

"Yeah, it sounds like that German who was with him before. He's a big rude bastard, but still, nothing like

Chang," Muto mumbled around the cigar he had stuck in his mouth.

"Well, now we have something to report. Kosha was able to sign on as a worker with the construction crew at that building where the woman was seen. He reports that there are two different companies working there. He is with the one doing the first level, but the other is what really intrigues me." Sero paused long enough for Muto to roll his hand impatiently. "It seems that the other company is building living quarters on the second level."

Muto's eyes narrowed and his brow wrinkled as he took in this information. "Do we know if our targets are moving in?"

"Kosha doesn't know who they are for, but the woman and that strange child have been there daily, along with the two young women."

"Daily?" Muto confirmed.

"*Hai*," Sero confirmed. "The work is ending soon. They're putting on the finishing touches. He overheard the woman talking to the foreman for that job today and thinks that the apartments may be for the two girls. He said he only caught a few words, but he believes that is the case."

"I assume we are still no closer to locating where they come from?" Muto grumbled.

Sero shook his head as he spoke. "No, that is the most puzzling thing about this whole affair. We see them leave the building, and they manage to disappear shortly after."

"Keep working on it," Muto ordered. "I hope to have this nailed down by the time our guest from China arrives.

If nothing else, we have regular sightings at the construction site so we know where they will be."

Muto paused. His eyes closed, and he stroked his jaw with the fingers of one hand. His eyes opened as his hand came down with a loud *thunk* on the desk. "Sero, I want you to take one of the women."

Sero's eyes widened. He had been dreading this since Muto had first mentioned it. Chang had told them to watch and report, but he had insisted that he would deal with the people once they were located. "I thought Chang said to watch and gather information, not take direct action."

Muto grinned. "That's correct, but they did offer a significant amount for the location. I think that if we take one of the women, we can make her tell us where they come from."

Sero knew that Muto acted without thinking at times and when he got an idea in his head, he didn't always consider the possible ramifications. "Muto, that may not be the wisest action. There are rumors that the woman has some important connection with the government. We don't want to bring the authorities down on our organization over this. Your brothers, not to mention *Oyabun*, would look unkindly upon anything that did this."

Muto looked askance at Sero. He often had advice, but this sounded like open defiance. His lips tightened briefly, and when he spoke, his tone left no doubt that he was angry. "My brothers run their territories and I run mine. As for our leader, it is my place to worry about that, not yours, Sero. Do as I ordered and do not question me on this again."

Sero felt a sense of dread when he heard this. Once Muto took that stance, there was no option but to do as he said.

"I'll get a snatch team on it today," Sero assured him. "We should have some answers by the time the ship docks."

"See that it is done before the representative arrives. Now go, and send in that new girl on your way out. I need to have a meeting with her." Muto wagged his eyebrows at Sero as he said this.

Sero nodded as he stepped out of the room, amazed as always by Muto's mercurial mood swings. Menacing one minute and thinking of carnal delights the next. Sero hoped that his bad feeling about this latest decision was wrong, but he couldn't shake it as he issued the orders for the snatch.

CHAPTER TWENTY-EIGHT

Northern China, Prison Complex

The black Pod silently drifted down through the night sky into a valley with sparse trees and light underbrush. Akio stepped out as the ramp lowered and sent his senses out searching for danger.

Satisfied that he was alone, he sent the Pod up into the moonless sky to hold position above him until he called for it. He moved out of the valley in the direction of the hidden prison, his armor making him invisible in the darkness. He paused as he approached the top of a ridge overlooking the complex and crouched in the notch of a large boulder that had been split by some unknown force in the past.

The two-level prison was dark and appeared abandoned, but his keen hearing picked up the sounds of bodies shuffling about and the occasional snarl from a Nosferatu locked in the cells. Each time he heard a snarl, it was followed by a strong sense of a Forsaken as the guards exerted control over the beast. He sensed that the Forsaken controlling the Nosferatu were strong enough to keep them in check but had to constantly monitor them to keep them calm.

After ensuring that he wasn't visible, Akio surveyed the valley below for several minutes before he silently slipped behind one half of the boulder, out of sight of the building. He touched a slot on his armored right arm and a small screen slid out. It dimly lit up and showed him a live video from the second level of the prison cell block.

A Forsaken lounged against the wall two feet directly below the drone, leaning casually against the wall. As Akio watched, he heard a pair of snarls come from close by the drone. The Forsaken pushed off the wall and walked to one of the nearby cells. Seconds later, Akio's senses again detected the stronger sense of a Forsaken as the Nosferatu quieted their snarls and movement.

After cycling through several more feeds from the drones Eve had managed to scatter throughout the complex, he slid the screen back into his armor and slipped over the lip of the ridge. He carefully worked his way down, stopping often and casting his senses about for any other Forsaken that might be around. He slowly made his way into the shadows at the base of the wall without sensing any Forsaken outside of the complex. He made his way to a closed door that led into the prison and stopped.

As he crouched in the shadows, he heard voices from inside.

"How much longer are we going to be stuck out here watching these things?" one man complained.

"Until Miko tells us otherwise," another responded curtly.

"I wish he would hurry up, Miyabi. I'm tired of sitting on these things for who knows how long. Any idea when Miko will get back? He's been away for days now," the first complained.

The other voice came back. "Tanji, you need to understand something right now. We sit here until Miko says differently. If you don't like that, then take it up with him when he gets back from meeting with Heinz, but you don't want to piss him off. Remember what happened when you and those two idiots with you killed off that village instead of bringing them in as ordered?"

Akio heard a grunt, then the second speaker continued.

"That was Miko in a good mood. How many did you have to gather to make up for that? What was it, twelve for the four you killed?"

"Fifteen," the first speaker mumbled. "He sent me for more when one I brought back was too far gone to survive the change."

"Exactly. If that was Miko in a good mood, do you want to see what he does when he is unhappy? That is, if Chang or Heinz don't hear about it first. You *really* don't want either of them to notice you questioning orders."

"I...I'm not questioning orders. I j...just wondered how much longer until we can move these things to T-t-tokyo and turn them loose. I'm just bored," was the stammering reply.

"Be bored on your own time. For now, keep the damned things in your area quiet and don't ask so many questions. We will be told when it's time and not before."

Light footsteps moved away, and only the sounds of the caged Nosferatu could be heard.

Akio silently made his way back over the ridge to the next valley and called down the Pod. He directed it high into the sky and headed back to Tokyo at speed, then activated his chip. "Yuko?"

"Yes, Akio?"

"I'm done at the prison and have found what they plan for the Nosferatu being held there. They plan to bring them to Tokyo and let them loose on the populace."

Yuko's voice took on a harsh deeper tone. "They all need to die! I will not allow what happened on Kume to be repeated again if I can stop it."

"Agreed, but we will be...*smart* about this. Won't we?"

"*Hai.* I will be smarter this time," Yuko answered contritely.

"Good. I don't want Eve mad at *me,* again," he deadpanned.

"Message received, *Sensei.* I promise to control my emotions."

"We were fortunate that Eve was able to locate this place when she did," Akio assured her. "We will put an end to this before they can cause more pain."

"This would have been a disaster if we hadn't discovered them in time. Can you imagine the destruction that many Nosferatu could do in a crowded city?" A chill coursed through her as she spoke.

"*Hai*, it would be a massacre of innocents. Now it will be them who die. Is Eve back from her business with Koda and Asai, yet?"

"No. When I heard from her a little while ago, she said it would be roughly another hour."

Akio thought for a few seconds. "These Nosferatu aren't an immediate threat, but I'm not willing to wait long. Although they can't get to Tokyo anytime soon, if they get out in this area, there are many small farms and villages all through the region that they could destroy. We need to take them out sooner rather than later."

Tanaka Electronics Boutique, Tokyo, Japan

"This is awesome!" Koda exclaimed when they stepped inside the electronics store. There were multiple displays with bright screens showing all types of entertainment throughout the space.

Asai hesitated at the entrance, squinting against the glare of so many flashing screens. "It's so bright in here. How can anyone make heads or tails of all this?"

A young man wearing a green shirt with the name of the store sewn on the pocket approached them with a smile. "Welcome to Tanaka Electronics Boutique. My name is Seki. What can I help you find today?"

Koda smiled back as Eve stepped around Asai.

Seki's smile grew brighter at her approach. "Eve-*san*, it's good to see you today. Thank you again for allowing me to try those amazing simulations you developed. That was the most fun I have had in ages. What can I help you," he raised his eyes to Asai, "and these lovely ladies with?"

Eve chuckled at his thinly-veiled flirting with Asai. "Seki-*san*, your input was very helpful. When you run the

Demon sim again, you will see some changes that I believe you will like. These *lovely* ladies need some equipment for their new homes. What do you recommend?"

His eyes lit up and he raised his arms as he turned, taking in the whole store. "All of the products we carry here are top of the line. What type of things do you like? We have the latest in 3-D televisions in any size you could want, as well as the best-sounding music systems on the market."

Koda pointed to a large television hanging from the ceiling. It showed an underwater scene with coral reefs and a multitude of brightly-colored fish swimming around. The image was so clear that the fish appeared to be real enough to reach out and touch. "What is that one?"

"Ah, that is the Hui Theater model. It has a three-dimensional screen with an active voice interface. This particular model also has an integrated stereo with wireless surround sound. It's one of the most popular models we sell."

Koda continued to stare at the screen. With a push on the remote he pulled from his pocket, Seki changed the scene to an all-girl band singing and dancing on a lighted stage.

"It's voice-activated, but we have to use a remote in the store," he explained. "It automatically detects the type of show you're watching and adjusts the sound to give you the best experience possible." He pressed another button, and Koda was immediately surrounded by music on all sides.

"Oh, ancestors. That is... Unbelievable." She spun in place, spotting small speakers anchored above her.

Seki chuckled at her response. "A magnificent device, indeed."

"That sound is coming from those tiny boxes?" Wonder filled her voice.

"*Hai.* Those are part of the Hui theater-in-a-box system. They are optional but are made to pair to the unit with no wires. Each one has a wireless receiver, and can be placed anywhere since they have the ability to run on house current or built-in rechargeable batteries."

Koda's eyes were wide when she was inundated with sound that was so intense she felt it in her bones.

"I think you have a sale here, Seki," Eve informed him. "Go ahead and put in the request and let's move on. Asai needs to get some things, too."

Koda's shoulders slumped as she looked at the price tag on the bottom of the case. "Eve, this costs way too much. I can't afford…."

Eve raised her hand and cut off her protest. "Don't worry about the prices, either of you. These are your housewarming gifts from Yuko and me. Price is not an issue since I am certain that the Palace will make whatever we spend here in a short time on opening day. Now, let's get done so we can get you into your new homes."

Two hours later, both girls had made multiple selections. Koda went for the flashier items with lots of features while Asai continued to be more conservative, opting more for basic function instead of a plethora of extra features. Eve paid for the order and arranged to have it delivered later in the day.

Seki had continued to flirt with Asai at every opportu-

CHARLES TILLMAN & MICHAEL ANDERLE

nity. She had been hesitant at first, but seemed to warm to and enjoy the attention as time went on.

Once the sale was final, Seki hesitantly approached her. "Asai-*san,* my shift ends in ten minutes. If you would like, I would be happy to come by and show you how to get the most out of your new equipment."

Asai flushed bright red as she stammered. "Th-thank you, Seki-*san.* I, uh, I appreciate the offer, but all I have is a vacant room right now. My furniture is being delivered today as well, and I will be setting up my home and helping Koda with hers, too."

Seki's disappointment was evident on his face. "Ah, I see."

Koda stepped up and slipped her arm through Asai's. "Seki-*san,* you have been such a big help today. Would you do us the honor of being our guest at the Palace's grand opening?"

Seki's face lit up. "The grand opening? Of course, I would love to be there. I have been going by each day to check the building's progress since Eve-*san* told me where it was going to be."

"It's scheduled for two weeks from now," Eve told him. "I planned to send you and the others who helped test the games invitations next week. I guess you don't need one, now." Eve chuckled.

Seki laughed weakly as he continued to focus on Asai.

"We look forward to seeing you then," Koda told him with a smile.

"Um, ah, yeah, I will see you there, too," Asai finally managed, her blush getting deeper with each word.

Seki's face lit up with pleasure when Asai answered.

Eve smiled to herself as she realized that Yuko's fears that the young woman would be hesitant to engage with the opposite sex because of what Isamu had done to her seemed to be unfounded. She also knew that Seki was an honorable man and would treat her well.

CHAPTER TWENTY-NINE

Acheng, China, Research Laboratory

"You wanted to see me, Heinz?" Miko spoke respectfully from the doorway of the lab.

"Yes, Miko. Come in. I have something for you."

"You have information from Japan? The Nosferatu are ready. I would like to get a few more, but I have over one hundred and seventy ready to go now."

Heinz waved his hand while shaking his head. "No, we haven't got anything back on that yet. I sent Dieter to handle it. He should arrive there tomorrow, and I have decided we can't wait any longer. I'm going to send Gunter over in the craft the next day to get an update. Whether they have located the base or not, we're going forward with the operation."

Miko nodded, a satisfied look on his face.

"What I meant was that I have a new treatment for you. If my calculations are correct, it will give you several added benefits."

Satisfaction turned to concern as a troubled look crossed Miko's face. He remembered the first time Heinz had given him a *treatment* and what it had done to him. The increases in strength and speed were formidable, but the effects of the treatment were intense to put it mildly. "Benefits?"

"Several," Heinz informed him.

"What do I need to do?" Miko hesitantly asked.

Heinz held up a syringe that was filled with blood and motioned to a chair next to his workbench. "All you have to do is give me your arm. This will do the rest."

Miko hesitated. "Heinz, is...uh, is this going to be like the last time?"

"I don't think it will be as intense," Heinz assured him. "The negative effects didn't last as long nor were they as severe during the trials. I will keep you here for observation and testing for a few days, then we should have word from Dieter. You will get to try out your *benefits* in Tokyo soon after, I imagine."

Miko sat in the indicated chair and held out his arm. He knew from experience that Heinz would not allow him to stall for long.

Heinz wasted no time plunging the needle into the exposed flesh and pushing the plunger. Miko watched expectantly as the blood went into his arm. "How long before I feel the effects?"

Heinz removed the needle and placed the syringe into a rack that contained three more full ones. "It shouldn't take long. The test subjects all showed signs within a few minutes."

Miko sat patiently while Heinz looked on. That some of the test subjects had shown a less intense reaction to the mix was true. What Heinz didn't mention was that almost half of them had experienced a fatal response.

Warmth blossomed in Miko's arm and rapidly moved through his body from the injection site. The heat continued to move throughout him, and he started to tremble as his skin flushed red. The tremors quickly became a continuous shaking that gained strength until his whole body spasmed violently and uncontrollably.

His eyes were clenched shut as he fought to control his body until he let out a low moan and collapsed to the floor, his body still shaking but the tremors growing weaker with each passing moment.

Heinz watched dispassionately until Miko's body lay unmoving.

Heinz consulted his watch as he pulled a pad from his bench and made several notations while he continued to observe the inert form. After several more minutes elapsed, the body jerked once, twice, and on the third spasm, Miko's eyes flew wide open.

"How do you feel?" Heinz asked, his pen poised over the pad.

"Fuck me! What the hell was that?" Miko groaned as he slowly pushed himself off the floor and crawled back into the chair.

Heinz waited until he was settled before repeating, "How do you feel, Miko?"

He was silent as he sat for almost a minute before he looked up with wonder in his eyes. "I-I feel... I feel different."

"How so?"

"I'm, uh, I'm not sure," he finally managed.

Heinz tapped the pen against his chin, a pensive look on his face. In the blink of an eye, he hurled the pen through the air toward the befuddled man.

Faster than thought, Miko's hand blurred, and when it stopped, he was grasping the pen between his forefinger and thumb, the point only a fraction of an inch from his eye.

Miko pulled the pen away as his face flushed with anger. "What the hell?" He paused and looked at his hand, still holding the pen as he had caught it. The anger was replaced by a tight smile.

"I feel faster," was all he said as he realized the pen he held would have surely lodged in his brain if Heinz had done that earlier.

"That's one benefit." Heinz nodded.

"Are there more?"

"*Ja.* Listen."

Miko, can you hear me?

Miko stiffened as he looked incredulously at Heinz. "I heard you, but you did not speak."

Ja, *that is another of the benefits I hoped for.*

Again, the words came into his mind without being spoken.

"You now have some ability to pick up the thoughts of others. There is no way to tell how strong this will be until you use it. I have some tests set up for you in the next room." Heinz stood and walked through a door leading into a larger adjoining area.

Miko followed and saw that it was a training area with

weights and other equipment along one wall. The other wall contained several cages, one of which had three humans locked inside.

Heinz made his way to the weights and motioned him over. There was a bar sitting against the wall that held multiple metal plates on each end.

Heinz turned a few pages of the pad he held and briefly studied the information on it.

"According to your records, you were capable of lifting three hundred kilograms with minimal exertion after your last treatment. Pick this up." He motioned toward the bar.

Miko eyed it questioningly. This bar held considerably more than three hundred kilograms.

He positioned himself over the weights and slowly squatted, grasping the bar with each hand. He drew a deep breath and tensed as he prepared to lift the bar. With an explosion of motion, he stood, lifting the bar as he went. The bar stopped with a sudden jerk as his arms reached their limit and locked.

Miko's mouth hung open as he stared at the weights he held suspended almost effortlessly over his head. The bar started to bend, the weights pushing it down on each end.

"Put them down," Heinz ordered.

He complied and stepped back, his eyes going from the weights to Heinz and back before he stammered "That... that's three hundred kilos on each side. How? What?"

"Another benefit." Heinz smiled. "Now for the last test. I want you to focus on the meat in the cage. See what you can pick up from each of them."

Miko stepped in front of the three humans, two men

and a young woman. The woman pushed to the back of the cage as far from him as she could, trying to hide behind the men. One man stared defiantly at Heinz. The other watched Miko, curious but surprisingly showing no sign of fear. Miko silently studied each one in turn.

"This one," he indicated the defiant man of about fifty years, "wants to kill you. He blames you for the deaths of his wife and sons and wants to see you torn limb from limb. He has no fear because he has nothing left to live for."

Heinz nodded for him to continue.

"This one is confusing." He pointed to the young woman. "She is afraid, but it's like her thoughts are muted and I can only detect bits and pieces, more jumbled images than whole thoughts."

Heinz raised an eyebrow and motioned for him to continue after making more notations.

Miko's eyes narrowed. He turned to Heinz, confusion on his face. "The last one doesn't belong."

Heinz nodded and stepped across the space to the door of the cage. He took a key from his pocket and inserted it into the lock. The woman pushed hard against the bars at the rear of the cage while the first man glared defiantly at Heinz as he opened the gate.

He motioned to the third occupant, who stepped past the angry man and slammed his elbow into the side of his head as he came even with him, knocking him to the floor.

"No need to break him, Huen. He still has some limited use," Heinz told the Were as he went past.

"I only gave him a love tap. He needs to learn his place, even inside his own mind," the Were sneered.

"Go find Gerhart and prepare the pack to move out. You will go with Miko to assist him with moving the Nosferatu when he leaves in a few days. Tell Gerhart to take the pack hunting in the mountains and let them run off some steam for a day."

"We will be ready to go. I'm certain the men will enjoy the hunt. Do we need to bring any back for you?"

"No, just limit the hunting to one or two of the small settlements. I may need more human test subjects, and don't want the entire population in the area wiped out. I prefer to have some close when I need them."

"Yes, sir," Huen replied with an evil grin. "I'll make sure that they understand that they have to leave some for seed in each location."

Miko watched the exchange dispassionately. He had no feelings about the humans that Heinz had ordered slaughtered as entertainment for the Weres.

"Miko, you need to feed," Heinz ordered. "The serum will settle sooner if you do. Go ahead and take the girl, she is of no use to me. After you're done, see Chang about a room. You will remain here until there is news from Dieter. I plan to leave for Japan soon, so you will need to go back to the prison and get the Nosferatu ready to travel."

Miko stepped into the cage, grabbed the young woman, and dragged her out into the lab. She screamed as his eyes turned red and his fangs extended. Her cries were cut short as the vampire pulled her into a crushing embrace, then struck like a snake and latched onto her throat.

She struggled ineffectively as he drained her lifeblood. It was over in minutes, and the body fell lifeless to the floor. Miko wiped the blood from his face as her dull eyes seemed to stare at him accusingly.

Heinz went to the cage and pulled the unconscious man out, supporting him with one hand while he lightly slapped him to consciousness with the other. The man moaned and his head lolled from side to side. Heinz continued to slap him until his eyes opened and full consciousness returned. "So, you want me dead," he stated.

Pure hatred on his face, the man did not respond.

Heinz shook him violently. "Answer me."

The man stared defiantly and without warning, spat at his tormentor's face.

Heinz dodged back. The spittle missed his face but landed on his arm. He looked at the offending substance and then back to the man.

"That was unwise," Heinz growled.

The man smirked as Heinz looked at him. His smirk soon turned to a look of terror as Heinz allowed his eyes to turn red and slowly extended his fangs.

The screams of agony were heard throughout the complex as Heinz repeatedly plunged his fangs into the hapless victim. His intent was not to feed but to prolong the man's suffering for as long as possible.

Chang rushed through the door just as Heinz dropped the lifeless body next to the previous one. "What's going on, Heinz?"

"Have this mess cleaned up," Heinz ordered as he stalked out of the room without explanation.

Chang shook his head as he looked at the two bodies on the floor. One lay lifeless with little signs of injury. The other was torn and mangled, its eyes wide and mouth open in a silent scream.

"Gerhart," he called as he activated the intercom. "Have a disposal detail report to the laboratory for cleanup immediately."

"On the way," Gerhart replied.

CHAPTER THIRTY

TQB Base, Tokyo, Japan

"Eve, do you have any new information?" Akio inquired as he entered the operations center.

Eve had been monitoring the reports from her drones at both the prison and the lab for over a week. They now had a good idea of what they were facing, as well as what Heinz was planning.

"Nothing new. They still seem to be waiting for something," Eve replied. "I have managed to infiltrate all of the prison complex and have learned that there are thirteen guards and one hundred seventy-six Nosferatu."

"I believe it is time to deal with the Nosferatu," Akio advised. "The longer they have, the more villagers get taken. We have to be sure none of them get away. A Nosferatu running loose would mean death for any human who encountered it."

"What if we hit them during the day?" Eve suggested. "We could go in with the sun directly over the prison and drop pucks. The sun would destroy any Forsaken or Nosferatu who escaped the blast."

Akio chuckled. "I did promise that you could use the pucks if the situation warranted it."

Yuko entered the room as he said this. "Pucks? Don't we need to go in and see if there is any information on any others involved?"

"*Hai*. I don't plan to use the pucks until I know all of the Forsaken there are dead. Mindless Nosferatu should not be able to escape, but we don't know if any of the Forsaken there have resistance to the sun. Heinz has been experimenting with vampire blood for many years, and Isamu was much stronger than he had been before. Some of them have also been known to use heavy clothing and head covering to move about in the sun if necessary."

Eve grinned. "So, you two go in and take out the Forsaken. As soon as you're clear, I bring the pain down on the lackeys. Works for me."

Akio and Yuko looked at each other with raised eyebrows. Since she had ascended to AI status, Eve seemed to be more like Bethany Anne in her eagerness to unleash destruction. In this instance, they were all in complete agreement.

"What about the laboratory complex?" Yuko prompted.

"I haven't yet managed to get full drone coverage in the lab. Unlike the prison, it is built a lot better, and there always seems to be someone moving around. I had to be very careful about moving the drones. Not that I haven't managed to get into some key locations."

Eve called up a video feed that showed Heinz and Chang in an office. "I was monitoring this when you came in. I finally managed to slip one into that boot-sniffer Chang's office."

She pressed a button on her console and activated the overhead speakers.

"Are you sure we should go ahead and do this now?" Chang asked.

"I believe Dieter will soon have the information we need," Heinz answered. "If not, Tokyo will experience an abrupt decline in the number of Yakuza leaders."

Chang consulted a pad he pulled from a drawer in his desk. "Barring any unforeseen problems at sea, Dieter should be there sometime today."

"*Ja*," Heinz agreed. "I've already told Horst to take the craft and meet with Dieter tomorrow night."

"Do you think it's safe to go that close with the craft? I know I pushed you to use it, but I never intended that we go near the mainland of Japan."

"We have to move soon. The longer we wait, the more chance for that damned Dark One, as they have started calling Akio, to discover us. All it would take is for one of the Nosferatu to get loose and wipe out a village. That could get the attention of the Chinese government. I'm sure he has spies there who would get word to him somehow."

"Heinz, I know he's dangerous, but do you make him out to be more than he is? He is only one man. Granted, he has shown abilities that we can't duplicate, but surely you don't believe he is that dangerous?"

"Chang, you never met any of Kamiko's personal guard. They were all extremely dangerous before the bitch queen did whatever it was that upgraded Akio. From all reports, he is Walking Death now, so never take anything for granted when he is involved."

"If you say so. Did you send Miko back to the prison, yet?"

"Not yet. I've been monitoring him to see how the new serum performs. I plan to send him back tomorrow with Gerhart and the pack. I want the pack to go along and provide daytime security during the transit."

Chang nodded in agreement. "Did the serum work as well as you anticipated?"

Heinz raised his hand and waggled it back and forth. "His speed and strength increased to about twice what he could do before. He's also able to heal injuries much faster than before, so that alone was worth the risk. His ability to get into the minds of others is hit or miss. Some he can read as easily as a book, but others he only gets impressions and feelings. It isn't always reliable, but I hope it gets stronger as time passes. He did show some improvement during the week. Once that bastard Akio is dead, I hope to obtain a sample of his blood before it degrades to see what kind of benefits can be reaped from it."

Akio's lips curled up in a slight smile when he heard this. Heinz would have a hard time obtaining anything from him other than a quick death. Although not at Bethany Anne's level, he had trained with her and had no doubt that none of the people Heinz had, no matter how much he had tinkered with them, were anywhere near his or even Yuko's level.

"Can I just drop pucks on them and turn their base into a smoking crater in the ground?" Eve growled.

"Not until we have gone through and released any human prisoners he is holding," Yuko answered. "You have found some there, haven't you?"

Eve looked startled by this. "You're right. I got so angry when I heard him so casually discussing killing Akio that all I wanted to do was destroy him and everything he represents. That is highly illogical."

Yuko nodded slowly.

Akio spoke up. "Eve, I thank you for your concern, but don't worry about me. I am certain Heinz doesn't have a chance of reaching that dream. I have you and Yuko watching out for me, after all."

Yuko spoke up soon after. "Eve, it is understandable that you would feel anger when he threatened your friend. It's only human."

"I'm not human, though." Eve huffed. "I will need to examine my programming and see where this is coming from. I will not let...*emotions* make me do things that endanger others."

"Eve, I don't believe you would have done anything to risk humans. You would have seen the flaw in the plan to puck them first when you ran the risk assessments," Yuko assured her.

"Perhaps you're correct, but I am not willing to risk it," Eve mumbled.

"That's why you have us," Akio told her. "We're a team.

CHARLES TILLMAN & MICHAEL ANDERLE

We will always look out for each other and ensure that none of us goes off the rails, if you will."

Eve was lost in silent introspection for a moment and then nodded to herself as she responded. "I will upload the schematics I have mapped out with the drones for both of you. The area where they are holding humans at the lab will be prominently marked."

"See, that is what I meant. It's okay to feel angry, as long as you make the right decision before you act." Akio caught Yuko's eye. "Isn't that right, Yuko?"

Yuko blushed as she remembered her last experience with anger and how it had gone when she had reacted to Isamu's words without thinking. Akio had since made sure during her training sessions that she would not soon forget that lesson.

"*Hai,*" she softly answered.

Akio's lips curled in a slight smile. Satisfied that they had properly dealt with Eve's personal crisis, he brought the topic back to the mission. "Eve, what about the Were? Do you still have a tracker on him?"

"Yes. He is approaching the port at Joetsu and will be there in a few hours. Do you want to take care of him tonight?"

He was silent for a moment and then answered. "No, let him think he has made it undetected. I want to see who he meets with in case they pose a danger to us as well."

"I managed to work the drone into a pocket on his backpack. As soon as he gets into the city it will be able to access the local network. We will have real-time information wherever he goes, then."

Akio stood and started for the door. "We go in the

morning. I am going to prepare the Pods. Full armor for you, Yuko. I am not willing to run the risk of our puck-happy friend here blaming me if you get injured." He nodded at Eve and smiled.

"See that she isn't injured, and you won't have a problem." Eve chuckled over her shoulder as he left the room. She knew without a doubt that her friends would always have her back, just as she had theirs.

CHAPTER THIRTY-ONE

Cargo Vessel Guro, Joetsu Harbor, Japan

Dieter stood watching the crewmen rush to throw lines to the shore workers as the ship bumped gently against the dock. The voyage from Vladivostok had been uneventful, and the ship's captain had made full use of the cloudless skies and calm seas to get to Japan in four days instead of the five he had expected. That gave him an extra day to deal with the Yakuza and find where the Dark One hid before Horst arrived.

The captain interrupted Dieter's thoughts as he called to him. "Dieter-*san,* would you like me to send word to Muto that you are here? I know he would send someone to pick you up if you desired."

"No, I will make arrangements tomorrow. It was a long voyage, and tonight I think I wish to sample some of the local, ah, flavor. Could you recommend a good restaurant and perhaps an establishment that caters to the needs of a man who has been at sea?" Dieter leered.

"I know just the places you need." The captain grinned. "If you'd like, I can take you once the ship is secured."

Dieter cringed internally, not wanting to deal with the annoying man any longer than necessary. He could always kill him, but the man had proven to be a capable sailor, and it would be a waste. Dieter had plans for the shipping industry once Heinz had secured control of Japan. "That sounds good. How long will it take you?"

"No more than three to four hours."

Dieter shook his head. "I appreciate the offer, but I have a busy few days ahead and don't want to wait. If you point me in the right direction, I will be on my way."

"Okay, I understand." The captain sounded disappointed that he would probably not get his cut of the fee for bringing in customers to the eatery or the brothel. "Maybe next time."

As soon as the crew dropped the gangplank Dieter left the ship, armed with the location of the establishments he had asked about and the assurance that if he told both that Yamaguko from the *Guro* had sent him, he would be treated like a king.

Dieter waved his thanks as he strode down the dock, having no intention of doing either. It was only nine, and he figured that if he shifted, he could easily cover the three hundred kilometers to Tokyo by morning. Then he could explain to the Yakuza why it was a bad idea to upset his father.

Riko's Noodle House, Tokyo, Japan

"Muto, the representative from China is here," Sero

announced as he pushed through the door to Muto's private office.

Muto growled as he pushed the scantily-clad brunette who was sitting in his lap to the floor. "Dammit, Sero, how many times do I have to tell you to knock?"

"Ow! That hurt," she complained with a pout as she rubbed her backside where she had landed.

"There's no time for that, Muto," Sero continued, nonplussed by Muto's and the woman's protests. "The representative is here. As in, *he is less than a block away from here right now*. You need to get ready to deal with him."

Muto shot to his feet from the overstuffed couch he had been entertaining his guest on, he hastily worked to straighten his clothes to a presentable state. "I thought you sent someone to pick him up? How the hell did he get here unannounced?"

"I don't know. He just showed up. If Lai hadn't recognized him walking this way, we wouldn't have had any notice."

Muto pointed to the woman. "You. Out."

She started to protest, but one hard look from Muto made her pale, and she backed out through the open door.

"Fix yourself before you go out, idiot. Straighten your clothes before any of the customers see you. Jeez, Sero, what do you do? Search extra hard for the ones with good faces and no brains?"

"Focus, Muto. He is coming this way now." Sero pointed through the one-way window that showed a blond giant of a man pushing past the host and stalking through the dining area toward the office.

Muto finished straightening his clothes and pointed at

the office door again as he told the woman, "Don't go far. I'll probably need you after I finish dealing with this ass. Now, get out of here."

As the young woman stepped out, the man pushed into the office. Ka, the loudly protesting host, and several other of Muto's employees followed him.

Sero stepped in front of the host, blocking him and the others from entering. "It's okay. He's expected. Go back to your business and leave us. Oh, and close the restaurant. We don't need curious civilians around."

The host nodded to Sero and then quietly went to the few tables occupied by diners who were not Yakuza. He told them the restaurant was closed. They all left swiftly, not wanting to be caught up in whatever was going on.

Sero closed the door and turned to see the huge man staring at Muto, a look of disgust on his face.

Muto half-smiled. "Welcome…Horst, is it?"

"Dieter," the blond man growled.

"My apologies. You favor the man who was here last time with Chang," Muto explained.

"Enough small talk," Dieter snarled, cutting him off. "Do you have the information we paid you for, or have you spent all of your time and our money chasing tail?"

Muto bristled at the tone, unused to being talked to with such disrespect by anyone, especially in his seat of power.

"What I choose to do or not do is not your concern," Muto snapped as he pushed his coat back, revealing the pistol hidden underneath. "You're a guest in my house. I suggest that you remember that."

Dieter sneered at him, then turned to Sero. "You are his second in command?"

Sero looked between the enraged Muto and the too-calm man speaking to him. He nodded slightly, acknowledging the question.

"Good."

Dieter turned back to Muto and smiled, a smile that did not come close to reaching his eyes. "Maybe you will be more effective than this…ass."

Although Sero was watching, when it was over, he still didn't believe his eyes. Muto's face flushed with rage as he snatched the pistol from his belt. Before he could bring it to bear, Dieter's form blurred. Sero heard what sounded like a ripe melon bursting after being dropped on the ground and saw Muto slam back into the couch.

When the scene settled, Dieter was across the room from where he had been, standing in front of Muto's seated form.

Dieter turned, and Sero stared in horror at the sight before him. The wall behind the couch was spattered to the ceiling with blood and brain matter. Dieter's right hand was covered in the same, and Muto's head looked like it had been hit by a train.

Dieter dispassionately watched Sero over the top of his gore-covered hand for several seconds. "Do you believe you can be more effective than this piece of *scheisse?* Or should I send for your second and start over?"

"I-I'm… You…" Sero stammered as his mind struggled to grasp the scene. "You killed him," he finally croaked.

Dieter allowed his eyes to briefly flash yellow. *"Ja.* We

do not deal with feckless fools who can't provide the services we pay for. Are you a fool, Sero?"

Sero paled when he saw this, realizing the man in front of him was not entirely human. "N-n-no."

"Good. Now, tell me where you are with locating the people we *paid* you to find."

Sero swallowed hard, his eyes involuntarily focusing on Muto's broken body. "We have not located their base, but the woman has been seen multiple times around a site under construction in the city."

"So, you're telling me that the oh-so-powerful Yakuza can't follow a mere woman from a location she has been at frequently to their base?" Menace leaked from his tone.

Sero's heart rate increased and he started to breathe hard as the man's tone caused him to have to fight the urge to run. "We, uh, my men have tried to follow her several times. She disappears like a spirit each time."

"Bah. Spirits. Superstitious fools. I come here expecting news and get tales about spirits."

"Sir, uh, Dieter, I have men watching the site around the clock." He paused for a minute as a low rumbling growl came from the man. "Uh, I have a plan to locate them," he rushed on.

"I hope your plans are better than that fool's," Dieter snarled while pointing at Muto's slumped corpse. "If not, I hope your second has a better one."

Sero lifted his hands in a submissive gesture. "Just wait here a moment. Would you like something to eat? Drink? A girl, perhaps?"

Dieter shook his head. "What I would like is for you to do your fucking job and find that base."

Sero bowed as he backed out of the room, his bladder threatening to let go at any minute.

"Get someone in here to clean this mess up. He's starting to stink," Dieter yelled as Sero closed the door.

"Diago, Yasou, get down to the construction site and find one of those girls. Take her to the house that Madame Yono runs," Sero called to two hard-looking men sitting by the door.

"Madame Yono?" Diago questioned. "That's the freak house, isn't it?"

"Yes. We don't have time to waste. Show her what's in store for her if she doesn't tell us where the base is located. Send word as soon as you have one of them."

"What the hell is going on?" Yasou wanted to know.

Sero kept looking toward the office door, expecting Dieter to come out and start killing everyone. "The people from China want results now. Muto's dead, and we're all next if we don't give him what he wants."

He leaned over to Diago and whispered, "Take Hon out and tell him to load a silver magazine into his gun."

Diago's eyes rounded with surprise, and his head jerked as he looked toward the office. "Silver?" he whispered.

Sero nodded once as he stepped back and yelled. "I don't care that it's your mother's birthday. Follow your orders!"

Sero turned and rushed back to the office, stopping briefly to compose himself before he went through the door. As he started to enter, he remembered Dieter's shouted words as he left.

"Hino, Sogo, get a tarp and come to the office. Have one

of the girls bring cleaning supplies. Move!" he yelled as both men looked at him as though he'd gone crazy.

They looked at each other and jumped up to do as he had ordered, not wanting to deal with whatever had the usually calm and unflappable Sero in such an agitated state.

Sero went back to the door and drew several deep breaths before he entered. "I sent two of my best men to deal with this problem. I should hear back from them soon."

"Why are you just now putting your best on it? " Dieter snarled. "You should have done that from the start." His patience, already short, was wearing even thinner.

"I wasn't running this." Sero shrugged as he nodded at Muto. "He was."

"You'd better hope that you get results." Dieter glared at Muto's body. "I told you to clean this up. I am staying at the inn down the street. Contact me when you have some results. I suggest you do not fail."

Dieter stalked out, knocking Hino into the wall as he stood outside, poised to knock. "Get the hell out of my way," he snarled as he pushed past him and stormed out into the street.

These idiots can't do anything right, Dieter mused as he walked down the sidewalk toward the inn. He neither noticed nor cared how people shied away and gave him a wide berth as he passed. *I told Father to let me handle it, but he is so scared of this so-called Dark One that he can't think straight.*

CHAPTER THIRTY-TWO

TQB Base, Tokyo, Japan

"Yuko, Eve, are you ready to go?" Akio called over their chips.

"*Hai*," Yuko replied.

Eve responded seconds later. "On my way. I was putting the finishing touches on something in my workroom."

The elevator opened a short time later, and Eve emerged, carrying a short carbine. "Okay, I'm ready."

Akio tilted his head. "What do you have there, Eve?"

Eve held the weapon out to him as she explained, "It's from a schematic that Jean left for me. She was working on a shoulder-fired weapon that uses the same ammunition packs as your Jean Dukes Specials. This one is heavily modified for me. It can be turned up to eleven." She grinned. "Although I wouldn't recommend that someone without a reinforced titanium skeleton try to fire it on that setting. It packs quite a wallop."

"Hmmm. Eleven, huh?" Akio handed the weapon back to her. "If all goes as planned, you won't have the opportunity to use it this time. You will have to be satisfied with delivering the pucks."

Yuko arrived in time to hear this and laughed. "We're dealing with Forsaken, Weres, and Nosferatu—what could possibly go wrong?"

Eve nodded and smiled. "My thoughts, exactly."

Akio shook his head at the two and got into the elevator. When they arrived on the surface, he wasted no time exiting into the dark inner courtyard and boarding the waiting Pod. "Let's go before it gets light. We don't want to attract any more attention to this location than we have to."

Yuko joined him in the Pod as Eve climbed into the sleek and deadly Black Eagle beside it.

"I saw your message about a more secure location with a hangar. I have made some inquiries and hope to have an alternate location soon," Eve told Akio before the Pod closed.

"That is excellent, Eve. I hope you are successful. I like this place, but it is more exposed than I think is safe. Plus, if we were attacked here, there are too many innocents in the area for us to really cut loose with our defenses," Akio answered over the comm as both craft shot into the early morning sky.

Northern China, Prison Complex

Akio knelt beside a large boulder and looked down into the valley at the drab building. "Looks like they're all tucked in for the day."

Eve stood just below the top of the ridge, consulting a

tablet held in her hand. "There are two Forsaken on each level. The two on the lower level are each at the doors that lead outside. The two on the second level are together at the stairs closest to the living quarters. There is a door there that goes through the barracks, but it's barred from the other side. They appear to be playing cards instead of keeping a proper watch," she reported.

"What of the others?" Yuko inquired.

"I count ten lounging around in the rec room on the first floor of the offices and living quarters," she replied. "Number fifteen is not here. He is the one Heinz was talking about giving the serum to the other day. Miko was the name."

"At least the Weres haven't arrived yet," Akio commented as he slipped over the top of the ridge to join Yuko and Eve. "I was concerned that they would be here on guard duty by now and we would have to deal with them. This will make it easier to surprise the Forsaken inside."

Eve slid her tablet into a compartment that opened in her chest. "How do you want to do this, Akio?"

He thought for a moment. "Yuko and I will go in through the doors on the first floor and neutralize the guards there. You fly overwatch in the Black Eagle and take out any who try to escape, or watch them burn if they aren't daywalkers. Position yourself where you can see both sides of the living area. Anything that comes out of there is fair game."

He sketched a crude diagram of the complex in the dust. "Yuko, we will take the Pod down. I will drop you here." He indicated the door on the end farthest from the living quarters. "I will take the other door. When I give the signal, take out the guard by your door and meet me upstairs. We will silence those two and then move on to the ones in the other section."

They worked their way silently down the ridge to the waiting craft. Eve climbed into the Black Eagle and waited until the Pod lifted to deliver Akio and Yuko.

As the Pod dropped to the first door, Yuko stepped out, her red Jean Dukes armor standing out against the drab gray of the building. The Pod lifted again. As it passed over the other door, Akio stepped out and landed on bent knees in front of it.

"Go!" he called to Yuko as he slammed the heavy steel door with his armored boot. The guard was leaning against the door when Akio kicked it, and his body flew across the short hallway to slam face-first into the unyielding steel bars of the cell block with a loud crash. Before he had recovered, Akio's katana flashed down and severed his bloody head.

On Akio's signal, Yuko pushed open her door. The sunlight streaming in caught the Forsaken as he looked toward the disturbance at the other end of the cells. He hissed in pain and jumped forward away from the light. The last thing he saw was a blade that reflected the sunlight into his eyes, held by a woman with a face full of wrath like some kind of vengeful goddess. Before the pain of his burning eyes registered, his head was bouncing against the cells.

The hunger-crazed Nosferatu went wild as the combination of sunlight and the smell of blood broke the limited control being exerted by the two Forsaken upstairs. The shrieks of pain made by the ones caught in the sunlight almost drowned out the snarls and growls of the ones pressing against the bars to reach the bodies on the floor.

Akio darted up the stairs and smashed into one of the card players as he jumped to his feet. The other snatched a heavy machete from his belt and started toward him. Akio's lips turned up in a hint of a smile as Yuko's blade erupted through the front of the machete wielder's face. A quick downward slice of his blade stopped the other before he stood fully erect from where he had landed.

"That was uneventful," Yuko deadpanned.

"*Hai*, that's always the best kind of fight to have," Akio replied.

Angry shouts from the Forsaken in the barracks for the guards to quiet the Nosferatu came from below. Yuko stepped across to the steel door that led into the living area and cocked her head. "Do you want to do the honors, or should I?"

Akio's reply was to take three running steps and slam his armored shoulder into the door. The heavy door held, but the cinder block wall could not withstand the force of the blow. The door frame burst out of the wall in a shower of concrete and dust.

Akio bowed with a flourish toward the opening he had made. "After you."

Yuko nodded and pulled her Jean Dukes from the holsters on her side, glancing at the settings she paused for a beat and thumbed them both from five to six. Her face set with grim determination, she stalked through the swirling dust toward the startled yells of the Forsaken a level below.

CHAPTER THIRTY-THREE

The Palace, Tokyo, Japan

"Gah! I didn't know interviewing people could be so tiring," Koda lamented.

"We found some good people yesterday and more today, Koda. I believe the grand opening will be a success," Asai told her.

"I know, but the applicants all sounded alike by the end of the day. 'This one time at band camp, I...' how are you supposed to find the best people when your brain is numb? If I must listen to one more story about a school project, I think I will scream."

"What are you going on about? What's this 'band camp' you're talking about?" Asai looked confused.

Koda giggled. "Oh, it's something from an old movie I watched the other day. There was this character that started everything with that line. It was funny then, but after today I will never think of it the same way again."

"You know you're weird, right?" Asai chuckled.

Koda stuck her tongue out and crossed her eyes, causing Asai to burst out laughing.

Asai caught her breath and wiped her eyes. "We're done for the day. That was the last one. Now that we have them all picked, we need to meet with Yuko for the final interviews."

"Final interviews? What else is there to ask? That's just what I don't need, more interviews." Koda complained.

"That's right!" Asai exclaimed. "You were off with the guys who are putting on the laser show opening night when Yuko told me about that. Something about a last check that she has asked Akio to do before the final hiring decisions are made.

"We've both been so busy trying to get everything done that it slipped my mind. She said it has something to do with security and insisted that it be done."

"Security?" Koda furrowed her brow. "I thought we had Takumi to handle that."

Asai shrugged. "Takumi handles physical security and everything else related to running the facility. This is something Yuko called operational security. I asked her what that was, and she said it has to do with making sure everyone we hire is honest. She told me that there are some companies that send in spies to steal other companies' secrets. Akio has some means of finding these people."

Koda looked skeptical as she answered. "Uh, okay. I won't question Yuko's judgment, but I really don't want to do any more interviews."

"If I understood Yuko, all we have to do is ask them a few simple questions, and Akio will do the rest. It is her business, so if that's what she wants, then that's what we do. That's all I know about it." Asai's tone let Koda know that she was done with this conversation and the interviews were going to happen.

"Maybe I can be busy doing something, *anything* else that day?" Koda whined.

"We will have to see." Asai got a calculating look in her eyes. "What's it worth to you?"

"What do you want?" Koda asked. "I'll do almost anything to avoid having to do any more interviews."

Asai rubbed her hands together. "You go to the market for me for, let's say the next four weeks, and I will handle it."

"Go to the market? That's all?"

"Market, and any takeout we get," Asai added quickly.

"Two weeks," Koda countered.

Asai smirked. "Interviews start day after tomorrow at nine."

Koda gasped. "Wait a minute. I thought we were negotiating."

"Okay. Six weeks, then."

"You suck!"

"Four weeks, and be thankful I didn't add laundry to it," Asai finally relented.

"Deal, but you still suck." Koda shot back before Asai followed through with the laundry.

"Goody! You can start today. It's time for lunch, and I want a bacon and egg burger from Happiness."

"That's three kilometers away! Surely you don't want me to have to walk that far after working so hard today. Plus, it would be cold and yucky when I got back," Koda whined.

"You're such a drama queen, Koda. I should make you go to that one just for that. You're in luck, though. They just opened one on the next block this week. It's a few doors down from that sushi place you like."

Koda laughed. "Why didn't you say so in the first place? Even though I would walk three kilometers for one of those burgers."

"Then let's lock up and you can be on your way," Asai told her. "After we eat, we can do a final walk-through and be sure everything is ready for the workers to start. The foreman assured me that everything we had noted on his punch list was finished when he came by this morning. We can check this while we do the rest." She picked up a sheet of paper from the counter and held it for Koda to see.

"Works for me. Is there anything else on our schedule for today?"

Asai grinned. "I have a bath scheduled from two to four."

Koda smiled back. "You know, now that you mention it, I think I remember something like that on my calendar, too."

Asai laughed. "Well, the sooner you go, the sooner that scrumptious burger is in my hands and we can get on to the serious business of the day."

"Okay, okay. I'm going." Koda chuckled as she headed out the door.

"Takumi," Asai called after Koda had left.

"Yes, Asai?"

"Lock it down, please. We're done seeing people for today."

As Asai finished the command, most of the lights

throughout the building shut off and she heard the distinct sound of the lock sliding into place in the door.

"Level one lockdown initiated. May I be of further assistance?"

"Thank you, Takumi, that will be all for now."

"Acknowledged."

Koda squinted as she stepped out into the bright midday sun, her eyes dazzled and spots forming in her vision. She turned and crossed in front of the arcade, heading in the direction Asai had told her to go. Her thoughts focused on the additional ingredients she planned to have on her burger. In her partially blinded and distracted state, she didn't notice the two rough-looking men watching her intently from the corner across the street.

"Isn't that one of the girls Sero wanted us to grab, Yasuo?"

"She fits the description closer than any of the others I've seen come out of there today."

As Koda came abreast of them on the opposite side of the street, she stopped for traffic, turning to watch a sleek yellow sports car with two young women as it flashed past.

"Yeah, that's one of them," Diago confirmed as he motioned to the driver of a windowless van parked down the street.

Both men cut across the street. Yasou angled to get in front of Koda and Diago moved behind her. When the van screeched to a halt next to the oblivious young woman,

Yasou turned and faced her, blocking the sidewalk in front of her.

"Someone wants to talk to you," he growled when she stopped to avoid running into him.

Koda looked up and saw the scarred face and grim visage of the man blocking her path and some inner voice told her to run. She turned to flee and ran directly into Diago.

"No need to be that way." He grinned as he caught her by the shoulders. "Nobody's gonna hurt you, we just want to ask you some questions."

The side door on the van slid open, and Diago pushed her toward it.

Koda screamed when a dark bag was pulled roughly over her head. She felt herself being picked up and thrown into the open van, where rough hands grabbed her and held her in place.

"Go, go!" Yasou yelled to the driver.

He put the van in gear and cut into traffic. The whole thing took only seconds from the time he stopped until he was moving again. It happened so fast that none of the people in the area noticed anything.

CHAPTER THIRTY-FOUR

Northern China, Prison Complex

Yuko moved through the dust from the smashed wall with Akio on her heels. A figure appeared at the top of a stairwell and the Jean Dukes pistol in her right hand barked once. The projectile hit the Forsaken in the chest and hurled him back down the stairwell, a hole the size of a grapefruit through his chest.

"Mad, much?" Akio chided.

"These vile creatures need to be eradicated from the face of the earth," Yuko growled. "To take innocents and turn them into Nosferatu is an abomination."

"*Hai.* But remember, kill them calmly," he warned.

"I am calm," Yuko told him. "Now, can we finish this? The Forsaken stench is getting in my hair. It takes forever to get it out."

The yells of the Forsaken below increased when the body landed in their midst. The sound of feet pounding up the stairs heralded the arrival of two more. Yuko aimed her pistols and fired. The one on the right went down, his head a mangled wreck. The other managed to dodge at the last second and Yuko's round punched through the wall to the outside.

Akio stepped to the left behind Yuko. Before she could reacquire the fast-moving Forsaken in her sights, Akio lashed out with his katana and opened the Forsaken's throat in a spray of dark blood. Yuko fired again, and the round took him on the bridge of his nose. The body slammed against the wall with a wet *splat* as the top of his head disintegrated.

Yuko started down the stairs but was stopped short by Akio's hand on her arm.

"My turn." He disappeared in a blur down the now empty stairs.

"Eve."

"Yes, Takumi?"

"I have detected an anomaly outside of the security perimeter."

"What is it?"

"Video upload commencing."

Eve waited a few seconds until a video scrolled across the HUD of the Black Eagle. Her eyes widened as she saw the two men accost Koda and throw her into the van.

"Takumi, locate Koda Rii," Eve commanded.

"Koda Rii's location found. She is in the closet of her apartment," Takumi answered. "This is not logical. Locator beacon is active in Koda Rii's residence, but scans do not detect biomass inside."

Eve swore under her breath. "She left her communicator at home."

Akio stopped at the foot of the stairs, appearing in front of the remaining Forsaken as if by magic. They all stopped and stared at the armed stranger dressed in a dark tunic and pants holding a blood-covered sword as he stared at them with bright red eyes.

"Your lives are forfeit, by command of Queen Bethany Anne," he growled.

One of the Forsaken noticeably paled as he backed up until he hit a wall. "The Dark One," he whispered.

Akio nodded in acknowledgment. The others leapt into action as if it was a sign. Six Forsaken armed with swords and machetes rushed him, as did one giant of a man who was built like a sumo wrestler and armed with what looked like a medieval battleax.

As they converged on his location, Akio blurred. When they arrived, he was no longer there. The group milled about, searching for him. As they stared up the dark stairwell, a skinny Forsaken with his hair in a long braid down his back was knocked forcefully back into the giant with the battleax behind him by a round from Yuko's Jean Dukes Special. The headless body took him down in a tangle of limbs.

Akio moved in from where he had stopped behind the confused group and casually flicked his sword through the throat of one standing to the left of the stairs. Another Forsaken joined the two on the floor.

The remaining Forsaken scattered, seeking whatever shelter they could from the angel of death that was among them.

Yuko emerged from the dark stairwell. Her Jean Dukes barked again, and another Forsaken was thrown across the room. He hit the wall. When his body bounced off, Akio's sword met it. His head separated from his still-moving body and landed on a table against the wall.

"The head, Yuko. Always aim for the head," Akio admonished.

Yuko answered with a shot that hit one of the fleeing Forsaken in the back of the neck. The round severed his head from his body and dropped both amid the other dead and dying on the floor.

"Seems to me that the neck works fine, too," Yuko retorted.

Akio smiled, and then his eyes opened wide as he was pulled to the floor by the huge Forsaken from earlier, who had untangled himself from his dead compatriot and grabbed Akio's armored leg.

He twisted as he fell and landed hard on the arm that held his katana. The Forsaken rolled over on top of him and started to pummel him with his fists.

Akio snatched the tanto from his belt and plunged it repeatedly into the beast's torso. The Forsaken howled in pain and rage, his shirt turning black as his lifeblood leaked out of multiple wounds. He reared back, preparing to hammer both fists onto Akio's head. Akio was set to plunge his tanto into a pain-filled eye when the Forsaken's head exploded, showering him with gore.

He surged to his feet, disgust evident on his face as he wiped the remains from his eyes. "Was that necessary?"

"Oops," Yuko replied calmly as she sent another Forsaken to hell with a well-placed round to the face.

The last Forsaken, the one who had recognized Akio, was still frozen against the wall. His eyes were round with fear. When Yuko turned her attention on him, he ran toward the door that led to the cells.

"Yuko," Eve called over the comm.

"A little busy here at the moment, Eve."

"Koda's been kidnapped."

The sound of a rapidly firing Jean Dukes was heard. Dust and concrete flew out from the wall as Yuko shot at the fleeing form.

"Hold still so I can shoot you. *Gott verdammt* Forsaken," she grumped. "Ha! Got you!" she exclaimed as the fleeing Forsaken went down in a spray of blood and bone when a round took him in the back of the head.

"What was that again, Eve?"

"Takumi just sent me a video showing Koda being grabbed by two men and thrown into a van on the street in front of the Palace."

Yuko's face went pale. "Do you have a location on her?"

"Negative. Her communicator is in her residence."

"Akio!" Yuko called.

He paused and looked up from a wounded Forsaken, his sword poised to take his head.

"We need to get back to Japan," Yuko told him. "Koda has been kidnapped."

Akio's face flushed with rage as he severed the head from the Forsaken he held and wiped the blood-covered blade on his body. "Eve, bring the Pod to the door," he commanded.

Akio and Yuko rushed out of the rec room that now resembled a slaughterhouse and boarded the waiting Pod. Akio directed it to a position several hundred meters above and to the left of the complex.

"Level it," he ordered tersely.

Eve moved the Black Eagle into position away from the end that held the cells. She launched two one-kilogram pucks from the craft. Seconds later, they slammed into the prison complex like the hand of an angry god. A plume of dust and debris shooting five hundred meters into the air. When it settled, nothing remained except a deep rubble-strewn crater where the prison had stood.

Akio looked down from the open door of the Pod, his senses extended as he searched for signs of any Nosferatu or Forsaken still alive. Finding none, he closed the door.

As one, the Pod and Black Eagle shot higher into the sky and headed toward Japan.

CHAPTER THIRTY-FIVE

Pod, Between China and Japan

"Takumi," Eve called.

"Yes, Eve?"

"Where's Asai?"

"She is inside her residence," Takumi replied. "That has been confirmed by the presence of her communicator and a biomass that matches previous scans."

"Is anyone else at the Palace complex with her?" Eve asked.

"Negative. Asai Ono initiated level one lockdown when Koda Rii departed."

"Initiate level three lockdown protocols and contact the police," Eve commanded. "Send them the video so they can try to find that van."

"Acknowledged. Level three lockdown is in effect. Contacting Tokyo Police."

"Yuko, I have ordered Takumi to initiate a level-three lockdown at the Palace and to contact the police. I think you should go there to meet with them as the Vicereine," Eve advised.

"Where's Asai? Is she safe?" Yuko queried with worry in her voice.

"She's in her apartment. Takumi won't let anything happen to her."

"Has she been told about Koda, yet?"

"That was my next question," Eve admitted. "How do you want to handle it? She's going to panic and want to run out and save Koda, but Takumi won't allow that. She's going to be angry and upset when you arrive. She's calling me now."

Asai was hanging the brown skirt and white blouse she had worn for the interviews in her closet when Takumi's voice came over the intercom and her communicator simultaneously. "Attention, please. Level three lockdown protocols are in effect. All defensive measures are authorized and engaged. Please remain in place and await further instructions."

She looked up in surprise since she'd never heard that message before. "Takumi, what's the matter?"

"Eve has initiated a level three lockdown of the complex," Takumi informed her. "I have been authorized to repel any unauthorized personnel attempting to gain entry with extreme prejudice. That is all of the information I am permitted to divulge at this time."

Asai pulled the communicator Eve had given her from the pocket of the skirt and pressed the center. "Eve?"

"One moment, Asai," Eve answered.

Seconds later, Yuko responded instead. "Asai."

"Yuko, what's wrong? What is this level three lockdown Eve has ordered, and why is Takumi not permitted to tell me more?" The young woman's voice showed hints of strain.

Yuko drew a deep breath. "Eve ordered the level three lockdown because we believe that you and the complex may be under attack."

Asai panicked. "Attack! Who? What? Oh, my God. I sent Koda out for burgers. Is she okay?"

"I'm on my way there now," Yuko assured her. "Remain calm. I will explain everything when I arrive."

"Yuko, Koda's outside! I have to warn her!"

Yuko sighed, wishing the Pod would go faster as it streaked through the stratosphere toward Tokyo. "Asai, please remain calm. Akio and I will be landing in a few minutes."

"Yuko, you're scaring me. Is Koda okay?"

"One moment please, Asai."

Yuko switched her comm and called Eve. "Eve, can you get into the video feeds around the complex and try to see if you can find where they took Koda?"

"I've had access to them since before we bought the site," Eve informed her. "I need to get closer to do any real-time tracking, though. The signal is too slow for the number of feeds I need to review from this distance. I already sent a command to Abel. He is compiling and sorting the video as we speak. If they took her on a route with any public or private surveillance, traffic, or other security cameras in use, he should have an answer soon."

"Thank you," Yuko told her before switching channel again. "Asai, I'm sorry for the delay. I am handling multiple issues right now. To answer your question, we believe Koda was kidnapped by two men when she left the complex. Eve has Abel trying to track her location using the cameras in the area."

"Why the cameras?" Asai exclaimed. "Can't you track her communicator? Eve told us they were designed for that."

"Koda doesn't have it with her. Takumi located it inside her apartment after he witnessed the kidnapping on his external security system."

"NO!" Asai yelled. "She knows not to go out without it. I had to let her in yesterday—she promised me she wouldn't forget it again."

"We will find her, Asai. Akio and I will be landing in a few moments."

Takumi interrupted. "There is a Tokyo policeman approaching the front of the complex. Instructions?"

Akio had been sitting quietly, watching something on his pad while Yuko and Eve talked to Asai. "Takumi, advise the officer to contact his superiors and notify them that I am invoking the Bitch Protocol and will speak to him in a moment."

"Acknowledged, Bitch Protocol invoked on Akio's authority."

Yuko looked up, startled. "Do you think this is related to the UnknownWorld, and not simply a random thing?"

"*Hai.* The arrival of the Were from China and Koda's kidnapping are connected. I should have intercepted and dealt with him last night instead of continuing the surveillance," he spat. "I just reviewed audio data from the drone Eve tagged him with before he left China, and I have a location to start *asking* questions."

Yuko saw a faint flash of red in his eyes, but even without that small clue, she knew from his cold and deadly tone that Akio was willing to kill to get the answers he required.

The Pod touched down in front of the entrance, startling the policeman who was speaking into his radio. Akio stepped out of the open door. The officer's eyes widened in surprise as he took in the grim visage of the heavily-armed and blood-covered figure approaching him. He backed up in fear, drawing his sidearm and shakily pointing it at Akio. "*Stop!* Don't come any closer!" he ordered.

Akio stopped, his hands held out in a non-threatening manner. "I am Akio. Please contact your superiors. They will advise you further."

The officer keyed his radio and stammered, "Sir, ah, uh, sir, there is a man here who says his name is Akio. He just came down from the sky. He is heavily armed and covered in what looks like blood."

The reply came back instantly from a different voice that carried the force of a command. "This is Commissioner General Watabe. Assist him in any way he requests and advise him that I am on my way. Whatever you do, do not make him angry!"

The officer turned pale as the blood drained from his face. He lowered his weapon and managed to get it back into his holster after three attempts. "Understood, Inspector General, but I think it might already be too late for that."

CHAPTER THIRTY-SIX

Tokyo

Koda landed hard, the breath knocked out of her as she was thrown into the van. Rough hands grabbed her and shoved her against the floor before she could catch her breath.

"Hold still, sweet thing," a harsh voice said from above her. "We won't hurt you—*much*."

She tried to twist her head to see out of the heavy cloth bag which covered her head. It stank of fish and other unpleasant odors that made her gag. When she moved, a hard blow on her head left her seeing stars.

"Be still, bitch. I won't tell you again," the voice snarled.

The van made several hard turns and stops before it came to a halt and she heard a door open.

"Yasou, go tell Sero that we have the girl. We'll take her to the house. You can meet us there."

"Will do, Diago. Save some for me." He laughed cruelly.

The van pulled off with a screech of tires and continued for what seemed to Koda to be an hour, but in reality, was only twenty minutes. When it next stopped, the doors opened and she was pulled out by her arm.

"Don't try anything stupid," the same harsh voice from before warned.

Koda's arm was wrenched behind her back, and she was pushed up a flight of steps, stumbling and smashing her toes on each one. A door opened, and she heard several screams that sounded like people in agony coming from inside. She panicked and tried to twist away but could not break the crushing grip that held her.

"None of that, sweet cheeks," the voice chuckled as her arm was forced higher, making her go up on her toes in an attempt to relieve the pressure.

Koda was duck-walked down what seemed to be a short hallway. A door with loud squeaking hinges opened in front of her, and rough hands propelled her over the threshold. She tripped and staggered forward until she ran into a hard object and fell to the floor, bruising her hands and knees as she landed on the wooden surface.

The door slammed closed with a metallic *clang*, muffling the agonized screams that had followed her down the hall.

Koda's head snapped back as her abductor yanked her to her feet. She muffled her cry of pain when she accidentally bit her tongue. One large calloused hand painfully held her wrists together as he snatched the bag off her head. She blinked, her eyes watering in the sudden light. When the room came into focus, she blanched in fear.

She was in a chamber of horrors. There was a wooden rack with wheels wrapped in chains that had metal cuffs on the top. Multiple manacles were attached to individual lengths of chain that hung from the ceiling at various heights in front of the far wall. The wall itself was studded with hooks and brackets that held all manner of whips, implements obviously designed to inflict pain, and other objects whose uses she couldn't imagine. The closer wall held a small cage roughly one meter high and less than a meter square made of metal bars. It appeared to only be large enough for the occupant to squat or kneel uncomfortably in.

The man spoke close to her ear. "How do you like my playroom?" His breath reeked of garlic and made her stomach clench as she fought not to retch.

He shoved Koda across the room and forced her to kneel inside the cramped cage. He slammed the door closed, leering at Koda as he goaded her. "Look around, sweetcakes. Imagine the worst things that can be done with all this stuff. Then understand that your imagination can only scratch the surface of what it will really be like."

Koda's stomach was in her throat when she heard this. She had thought she knew fear when she was held captive by Isamu and his minions, but it was nothing like the mind-numbing terror she felt now. The only thing she had feared from Isamu was death. This was much worse.

"Think about what I said while you wait. Someone wants to ask you some questions when he gets here. Answer him, and you can go free. Don't, and I get to show you what all these things are for." He gestured dramatically. "Please be difficult. I can't wait to have a go at you." He laughed as he walked out of the room and shut the door. The hinges gave off an unnerving shriek as it closed.

Koda surveyed all the implements in the chamber of

horrors. She tried to control her reactions, but her imagination ran wild and panic overcame her as occasional screams filtered through the door. Her breath came in short, fast gasps as tears streamed down her face.

After a few minutes, her breathing calmed, and the panic receded to a manageable level. A sudden thought sent her hand darting into her pants pocket. Her fingers searched, fruitlessly, and panic overcame her once again.

She had forgotten to take her communicator out of the clothes she wore the day before. She was on her own.

TQB Base, Tokyo, Japan

Eve brought the Black Eagle down into the inner courtyard of the base at high speed. It came to a halt inches from the ground, stirring up a cloud of dust and small debris.

She bolted out of the craft and sent it to hover five kilometers above the base, where she could call it back in seconds when she had a target.

"Abel, what do you have for me?" she called as she rushed down the hall from the lift through the door of the command center.

"I was able to identify the two men who accosted Koda as members of the local Yakuza," the EI replied. "Each of them has been arrested multiple times, but they have never been convicted. The witnesses have either refused to testify or disappeared each time."

"Yakuza?" Eve questioned. "Why would they want Koda?"

"I believe it is because of the drone footage Akio accessed a short time ago," Abel told her. The monitor in front of her came to life with a black screen, and audio of the conversation between Dieter and Muto started to play.

"Where was this?" Eve inquired tersely when it finished. "Why is there no visual?"

"According to the tracking data, it was at a known Yakuza front, Riko's Noodle House," Abel replied. "It is located only a few kilometers from the Palace. This is the drone you managed to put in that Were's backpack when he boarded the ship in China. It's still in the bag."

"Akio," Eve called over her comm. "I have an address to go with the footage you reviewed earlier."

Yuko's voice answered. "Stand by one moment, Eve, he's speaking with the police now."

CHAPTER THIRTY-SEVEN

The Palace, Tokyo, Japan

"My apologies, Akio-*san*, I was unaware of who you were." The still visibly-shaken officer bowed and then continued. "The commissioner general has ordered that I give you whatever assistance you request, and also asked me to inform you that he is on his way."

Akio inclined his head. "Thank you, Officer…"

"Sato," he replied.

"Officer Sato, no apologies necessary. I apologize for startling you. I'm sure it isn't every day that you encounter someone looking like I do coming from the sky in a strange aircraft."

Sato laughed weakly. "Or get personally called by the commissioner general. This has turned into a strange day, indeed."

Akio gave him a half-smile and continued, "One of the people who works here was taken from the street by two men in a van earlier today. Getting her back before she comes to any harm is my primary focus."

Sato nodded. "I was sent to investigate the reported kidnapping. What can I do to assist you?"

The sound of rapidly-approaching sirens reached the two men, although Akio had heard them when he stepped out of the Pod.

Sato turned to look in the direction they came from. "I believe that is the commissioner general now, sir."

A patrol car with flashing lights on top followed by three black SUVs turned into the parking lot and came to a screeching halt in front of Akio and Sato. A distinguished-looking man in an ornate uniform exited the passenger door of the middle SUV and approached Akio. A group of harried-looking officers piled out of the other vehicles and rushed to catch up with him.

The man bowed. "Akio-*san*."

"Commissioner General Watabe," Akio acknowledged with a bow of his own.

"What is happening, and what assistance do you need from me?" the commissioner general asked.

"One of the people who works here was taken earlier," Akio informed him. "I believe you have received surveillance footage of the incident. I need to find where she was taken. I will handle it from there."

The commissioner general's expression was grave. "I was informed that you invoked the Bitch Protocol. This is related to, ah, your side of society?"

Akio nodded once. "*Hai.*"

Yuko had waited in the Pod until the situation with the frightened officer was settled. Now that the commissioner general had arrived, she stepped out and walked down the ramp.

Officer Sato stiffened and instinctively placed his hand on his weapon when he saw her blood-covered clothes and weapons.

The commissioner general saw his reaction and turned to see what had startled him. "Yuko-*san!*" he exclaimed as he rushed over to her. "Are you injured?"

"No, Watabe-*san*, none of this is mine," she assured him as she swept her hand down in front of her blood-splattered armor.

His eyes widened in shock, and he started to speak.

"Pardon me for a moment. I need to speak to Akio," she excused herself as she motioned Akio over.

"Certainly, Yuko-*san*," the commissioner general answered, shock still evident on his face.

When Akio approached she told him in a voice so low that only he could hear, "Eve has the location for the recording you reviewed. I will deal with the police while you speak with her."

"Thank you." Akio stepped into the Pod and immediately called, "Eve?"

"Abel has located the place where the Were from China was," Eve told him. "It is Riko's Noodle House, a known Yakuza operation. I am sending the coordinates to your Pod."

"Good work. Have you managed to track down that van, yet?"

"Not yet," she admitted. "But we are searching through the data now to find it. Abel was able to identify the kidnappers as Yakuza members. They have been charged with numerous offenses in the past but never convicted. Witness tampering is suspected due to the

CHARLES TILLMAN & MICHAEL ANDERLE

witnesses' reluctance to testify or disappearing before the trials."

"I don't think that will be an issue in this instance." His voice was ice-cold.

"Agreed. I will let you know when I find more. I have dispatched a drone carrier to the Yakuza site. You will have real-time information available in a short time."

"Send it to the Pod," Akio instructed. "I will be going there next."

"Do you want me to assist you?" Eve inquired.

"No, keep searching for the van. I will contact you when I am done...*talking to* the Yakuza scum."

"Abel is into the government traffic and surveillance network," Eve assured him. "I am pulling the footage from any private networks. We will find her!"

"*Hai,* and the people responsible for this will be held accountable." Akio stepped out of the Pod and heard Yuko speaking with the commissioner general.

"We located a complex in China where they were holding creatures like the ones on Kume. They intended to set them on the people here. We neutralized that threat but had to return for this before we dealt with the person responsible for all of it."

"You say this is part of the same group that you dealt with on Kume?" the commissioner general asked in shock.

"*Hai,*" Yuko confirmed. "We were able to find the location of the one behind all of this. Taking my employee is an unexpected escalation of the ongoing hostilities."

"Your employee? I was told she worked here." He indicated the building.

"She does," Yuko told him. "Eve and I started this business as a way to raise money to help the people on Kume. The girl who was taken is Koda Rii," she explained. "My other employee is Asai Ono. They are both from Kume."

"Ono?" The commissioner general tilted his head. "Any relation to Yagi the Mayor?"

"His daughter. Koda is his niece."

His face flushed with anger. "Yagi and I are old school chums. As I told Akio, whatever you need from me, just ask."

"Commissioner General, I have some new information. Are you familiar with a Yakuza operation in the area called Riko's Noodle House?" Akio inquired as he joined the two.

The commissioner general motioned for a tall, thin, dark-haired officer wearing plain black BDUs and a pair of pistols on his belt to approach. "Do you know of a Yakuza noodle house around here?"

"*Hai,* Riko's," he answered. "That's Muto's place."

"Akio, this is Inspector Yonai. He leads the Organized Crime Investigation Unit as well as an elite Special Investigations Unit."

"Yonai-*san.*" Akio offered a slight bow.

"Akio-*san,*" Yonai responded in kind.

"Yonai, please answer any questions he has. I am authorizing the use of your team to assist him in this," the commissioner general ordered.

Akio wasted no time. "What can you tell me about Riko's? Is there a risk of innocents being present?"

Yonai thought for a minute. "Riko's is where Muto Koto handles his day-to-day business. He is a lieutenant in the organization and this is his territory. He's a particularly nasty individual, too. Murder, drugs, prostitution, you

CHARLES TILLMAN & MICHAEL ANDERLE

name it, he's into it. He also has a reputation for violence whenever things don't go his way. My people have been after him for quite some time, but have never been able to pin him down for anything."

He paused and pulled an electronic tablet from his pocket.

After consulting it, he continued. "The restaurant is a public place. Muto has an office in the back that looks out into the dining area. I had an undercover officer attempt to get in there a few months ago, he was found dead in a dumpster on the other side of town. He had been beaten to death. We didn't have enough to charge him but rumor is that Muto did it himself. Needless to say, he is at the top of my persons of interest list."

"Muto is no longer of any consequence," Akio informed them. "He's dead. Sero is running the operation—for now."

Yonai's eyes widened and excitement filled his voice. "What happened? When did this happen? More importantly, who did it?"

Akio's lips turned up in a half-smile. "It happened earlier today. He failed to deliver as promised to some very dangerous...people. They took exception to his failure and sent someone to deal with him. He was disrespectful to their representative and died because of it."

"How do *you* know this?" Yonai asked. "None of my people have reported hearing anything like it."

"We were tracking the person who did it," Akio told him. "My associate was able to record audio of their meeting."

Yonai was obviously impressed by this information. "I would love to talk to your associate sometime. We have never been able to get surveillance equipment to work through all of the interference and jamming in that place."

He nodded at Yuko, who was talking quietly with the commissioner general. "You would need to speak with Yuko about that. Technology-sharing falls under her duties as the Queen's Vicereine."

Yonai nodded and continued looking at the information on his tablet. "There are normally ten to twenty heavily-armed Yakuza soldiers present at all times when Riko's is open. They hang out in the dining room for the most part, with one or two watching the back door in the alley. The place is small, it only has around fifteen tables, so if there are any innocents there, it won't be many. I can send an undercover in to check if you like."

"That won't be necessary," Akio told him. "The associate I spoke of earlier is working on establishing surveillance there now. Is there any way that you can help ensure that there are no innocents in the area? What type of area is it?"

"It's businesses, for the most part. There are some hotels and apartments, but none too close to Riko's. There is a lot of activity during the day, but most of the businesses close at five. After that, the area is deserted other than skeleton staff, security officers, and cleaners."

Akio thought for a moment. "I don't like waiting, but if the area is that crowded, we may have to unless my associate finds information that leads us to act sooner."

"I can have my Special Investigations Unit secure the area around it. We can also go into the surrounding buildings and get the people in them a safe distance away. Do you need my men to raid the place?"

Akio shook his head as he looked at the sky. It was a

few hours before five. He was concerned for Koda but didn't see how he could hit the Yakuza any earlier. "No, when it is time to hit them, I think it best that your men stay back. There may be some people there who Yuko and I are best equipped to deal with."

Yonai nodded knowingly. He was one of the few who had been fully briefed on Akio and Yuko's true purpose. He also had experience with UnknownWorld beings and would rather let them handle it as well. "What about the Yakuza soldiers?"

"If they don't attack us, they get to live," Akio softly replied. "Otherwise, they are all complicit in Koda's abduction and their lives are forfeit."

Chills ran down Yonai's back. He didn't doubt that many Yakuza would die tonight.

CHAPTER THIRTY-EIGHT

Riko's Noodle House, Tokyo, Japan

Yasou rushed through the door calling, "Sero, we have one of the girls!"

Sero's head snapped up from the whiskey he was nursing at the bar. "Sogo, go to the inn down the street and tell Dieter that we have results," he ordered. "Ask him if he would like to be present when we question the girl."

Sogo sipped from the glass he held and stood. He then casually sauntered toward the door.

"Sogo, if you don't move your fat ass any faster than that, I will shoot you myself!" Sero yelled. "Now, run!"

Sogo hit the door at a full run and turned toward the inn. He was out of sight of the men watching him through the windows in seconds.

Hino snickered. "Damn, Sero, I don't think I've ever seen Sogo move like that. He acted like he thinks that you really would shoot him."

Sero stared at Hino, his eyes tight with anger. "If you think I won't shoot any of you, do something to make me

267

look bad to that bastard Dieter. That's if he doesn't smash in your skull like he did to Muto. Now, make yourself useful and have Jeo bring the car. I don't want to have to wait for him when Sogo gets back."

Hino's face went pale at Sero's outburst. Everyone was used to Sero being the calming influence on Muto. With Muto dead, he was worried that Sero was going to be worse. "*Hai*, Sero. I didn't mean anything by it."

Sero turned to Yasou without answering. "Were you able to get the girl without issue?"

He nodded. "Yeah, we grabbed her off the sidewalk at the corner. We had her in the van so fast, no one saw a thing."

"Good. Maybe we can salvage this before it goes completely to shit. I warned Muto that these people were bad news, but he wouldn't hear it. Now I'm the one stuck cleaning up his mess, literally."

"It's gonna work out, Sero. Diago has the girl, and he is going to scare the hell out of her at Yono's place. He plans to put her in one of the dungeon rooms so she can think about what he's going to do to her until he hears from you. He laughed. "He also told Madame Yono to have some screamers in the house tonight, and to have them put on a show when he brought her in. She should be ready to answer anything we ask after a little bit of that."

"If she doesn't talk, Diago will be doing more than putting on a show for her," Sero growled as he went back to his whiskey.

Sogo ran back through the door about a half-hour later. He was panting and covered with sweat. "Sero," he gasped, his face flushed red from exertion. "I… I found that…that guy. He said to wait, he wants to question her himself. He said that he will be here in a while and not to fuck this up."

He collapsed into a chair as he finally got the message out, and reached for a glass in front of Hon. He slammed back the clear liquid and his eyes bugged out of his head as the straight gin burned down his throat. He forced it down and fought to catch his breath, tears running down his face.

"Serves you right, dumbass." Hon laughed. "Next time, get your own damn drink."

Sogo looked at him with hard eyes. He was about to reply when Hino set a glass filled with ice water in front of him with a smirk.

Sogo grabbed the glass and chugged it to the laughter of the men watching.

TQB Base, Tokyo, Japan

Eve and Abel had been going through countless video feeds for several hours when Abel announced, "Eve, I have detected an anomaly in the data I have determined that it is related to the vehicle used to kidnap Koda Rii."

"What have you found?" Eve asked.

"It is not a matter so much as what I have found, but more what I have not," Abel replied. "I was able to track the vehicle into a residential section about ten kilometers from the Yakuza restaurant. There seems to be a section of about four square blocks where I am unable to locate any working surveillance. The cameras are listed in the government database, but all of them are inactive."

"Show me," Eve instructed.

A map of the city came up on the monitor and zoomed in to cover the suspicious area.

"The vehicle was last spotted here," Abel told her as a red dot appeared on the edge of the highlighted section. "I have located working cameras at these coordinates." More dots appeared, lighting up in a box that surrounded the same section. "There is no footage showing that the vehicle exited the area."

"Good work, Abel. Let me know if it shows up," Eve called as she ran out of the room to the elevator.

When she arrived in the courtyard, the sun had set and the sky was dark. She called down the Black Eagle and in seconds was over the area Abel had shown her. She hovered a kilometer above the area and released the surveillance drones from the launcher on the Black Eagle. It wasn't near the number that a drone carrier held, but the drones were larger and had far more advanced built-in sensor suites. She had also upgraded the propulsion system and armor on these units. This was the first time she had used them other than during an operational test.

She activated the Black Eagle's HUD and it separated into six individual screens with a command from her. The screens showed each drone's individual video feed. "Okay, dead men walking, where have you hidden my friend?" she murmured.

CHAPTER THIRTY-NINE

Acheng, China, Research Laboratory

"Horst, come to my lab," Heinz called over the intercom.

What the hell does he want now? Horst wondered. *I'm sure whatever it is, he will tell me how to do it in nauseating detail.*

"You called for me?" he asked as he entered the lab.

"I want you to take the craft and meet Dieter," Heinz ordered. "He should have had time to find out what those Yakuza idiots have learned, or gotten them moving in the right direction if they haven't cracked the case yet."

"I thought you didn't want to take the craft near Japan?" Horst mused. "You said it was too dangerous."

Heinz pinned him with a sharp look. "That's why you're doing it. I don't trust any of the other crews to do it. I know that you *will* do exactly as I say."

Horst dropped his eyes. "*Ja*, Father."

"You are to take the craft and go no higher than five meters from the surface all the way. When you get to Japan, it will be dark, so use your best judgment on how

271

close you can get to the city. I suggest you find a remote place in the mountains and go in wolf form from there into the city."

Horst ducked his head to hide his grimace. "What do I do when I find Dieter?"

"If he has the location of the base, come back so we can get going. If not, assist him until you find it."

"*Ja.*"

Heinz wasn't done. "Send Miko to me on your way out. I want him to take the pack tonight and get the Nosferatu ready to go.

"*Ja.*"

"Horst," he scolded.

"*Ja*, Father. I will take my leave now if that is acceptable."

"Don't fail me in this," Heinz ordered as he turned back to the blood samples he had been analyzing when Horst entered.

Horst managed to keep his body language under control until he was back in his room, gathering the items he would need on the trip.

That arrogant leech. He always acts like he is so much better and smarter than everyone. Horst, keep it low. Horst, do not fail me. Horst, fetch Miko for me. Horst, help Dieter. He should have died years ago. I hope the Dark One finds him and tears his black heart from his body while he still lives.

When he was done, he drew a calming breath and headed for the common room where he had seen Miko. When he walked in, Miko was sitting with Gerhart and a couple of other Weres.

"Father wants to see you," Horst told Miko. "He says

you're to take the pack and get the beasts ready to go," he called as he strode through the room, not slowing as he made his way toward the hangar.

He prepped the craft and took off at a slow speed. It was still a few hours before dark, and he decided to wait until the sun had set before he crossed the open ocean. He took the craft deeper into the mountains and flew close to the ridges and down through the valleys as he killed time.

When he crossed the ridge and swooped into the valley where the prison was, he pulled up short. His eyes bulged as he saw the total devastation.

I need to get back to base and warn... His lips curled up in a slight smile. *I need to find my brother and get both of us away. I should be able to get us to Germany with no problem.*

He landed the craft next to the crater that was once a prison, then got out and surveyed the damage.

"Ha," he barked. "Looks like Heinz has been found out. I would like to see the Dark One kill him, but from what I hear, he will probably kill everyone. I will say a prayer to the Old Gods that when he catches that leech, he makes him suffer."

He didn't notice the small drone that had detached from his craft and zoomed in to hold station above him while he thought out loud.

Riko's Noodle House, Tokyo, Japan

"Where the hell is he?" Sero wondered for the tenth time since Sogo had returned. "The bastard acted like it was imperative to get this information, and now he keeps us waiting on him for hours."

"Sero, what's the deal?" Yasou wanted to know. "He's only a man, he bleeds like everyone else. I think we should kill him and forget about this."

Sero cut his eyes toward Yasou and grimaced. "I'm not so sure he is *only* a man, and I know that there is something off with Chang. You were out dealing with a problem when they came here and set this up with Muto. I don't think we need to get on these people's bad side. It could cause problems higher up in the organization."

Yasou paled. "You don't think this is like those cat men we've been hearing about out in the rural areas, do you?"

Sero nodded. "*Hai*, I think they may be, or worse. That guy moved faster than I could see, and Muto's head exploded when he hit him."

Yasou went back to staring at his glass for a moment before he quietly pulled a large black pistol from his belt and carefully reloaded it with a magazine of silver-infused bullets. Several of the soldiers saw this, and the sound of gun actions echoed throughout the room as they too loaded with the precious bullets.

Dieter waited until the sun was setting before he left the inn and started toward the Yakuza shop. He chuckled to himself as he thought about how unsettled Sero must be after waiting for so long.

I bet he is pissing himself about now. Father always told me it was best to set the stage for how things are to be when dealing with inferiors. I might be able to use these idiots in some way when we control Japan. Provided they understand their place.

Inspector Yonai had ordered his team to stay out of sight until it was time for them to block off the area around Riko's. As it approached closing time for the neighboring businesses, he sent trusted officers in plainclothes into the buildings. They were to get the few workers still in the ones directly adjoining Riko's to safer locations. He also had them keeping the people out of the possible line of fire in the other buildings on the block. Akio had joined him in his observation post on the tenth floor of a thirty-story office building across the street from Riko's to wait.

"Akio, I have received information from one of the drones I was able to get into the shop," Abel called. "Sero is waiting for the Were to come before they go where Koda is being held."

"Thank you, Abel." Akio approached the table that Yonai was using as his makeshift command center. "Inspector Yonai, we are expecting another guest for the party and do not want to alert him. Advise all your people in the buildings to keep quiet and move to a secure location away from the street.

"They were instructed to do that when they went in," Yonai informed him. "Everything in the area has been reported secure. Who else are you expecting?"

"The one who killed Muto," Akio replied. "It will be better to go ahead and deal with him now instead of having to hunt him down. He could injure a lot of people if he runs."

"Akio," Abel called again a few minutes later. "The Were is leaving the inn and heading toward you, now."

Akio turned to Yonai. "Inspector, I just received word that he is on the way. He is a big blond European. Tell your people not to approach him, he is extremely dangerous."

Yonai keyed his radio and relayed the instructions to the officers concealed around the area.

Akio called Yuko on her implant. "Yuko, Dieter is approaching Riko's. Once he is inside, pick me up in the Pod. I will head to the roof of the building across the street from Riko's as soon as it is certain that he is there."

"Akio, I have a plan for when we hit the place," she advised.

"What's that?"

"I propose that I go in the front door and pose as a customer while you come in from the rear. I have been looking at the footage from the drones. There are several young women in a back room across from the office. I believe they are prostitutes that the Yakuza keep around to entertain themselves."

"It would be too dangerous to go in without your armor with that Were at the site," he replied.

"I have borrowed some clothes from Asai that are loose enough to conceal the armor," Yuko assured him. "I won't be able to wear the helmet, but I do not think that will be too much of a risk. I only need to keep them off-guard long enough for you to clear the guard at the rear, then get between the main room and where the girls are," she explained.

"What about the Were?" Akio reiterated. "Can you hide a sword under the clothes?"

"No," Yuko admitted. "But I can hide both of my Jean

Dukes Specials under them. They should be sufficient for the task."

He thought for a moment. "*Hai,* they should be enough, and I will not be long in the back. Just do not let him get too close to you."

"Akio, he just went inside," Yonai called from the window where he was watching the street below.

"Yuko, it's time."

CHAPTER FORTY

Near Riko's Noodle House, Tokyo, Japan

"Eve," Akio called. "Can you bring the Black Eagle and fly overwatch while Yuko and I deal with the Yakuza and the Were?"

"I can if you really think it necessary," she advised. "But Abel discovered that the van entered a neighborhood where all of the cameras are offline. It was not detected leaving the area on the surrounding surveillance network. I am currently over the area with the drones from the Black Eagle searching for the van."

Akio jumped into the Pod hovering above the roof. "No, keep looking for Koda. I'm certain that someone at the restaurant knows her location, but if you find her before I can get it, notify me and see if you can get her out."

"That's the plan," Eve agreed. "But, I can't make any promises about how big of a mess Saint Payback is going to demand once I have her secure. We need to send a message to these scum that we are not people they want to piss off."

"Be certain that any damage you do is limited to the people actually responsible," he warned. "We do not want to have an incident where innocents are harmed."

"Understood," Eve confirmed. "Keep the damage restrained to the wastes of oxygen who deserve it. Got it."

Akio cut the connection and slowly shook his head.

"What is it?" Yuko asked.

"Eve has found an area where she suspects Koda is being held. I have advised her to initiate a rescue if it is feasible."

Yuko nodded and then noticed that Akio looked slightly uncomfortable. "What's wrong?"

He pursed his lips before the corners turned up in a slight smile. "She says Saint Payback requires payment for taking Koda. I wonder just how much of Bethany Anne's personality ADAM incorporated into her initial code."

"Does it really matter?" Yuko argued. "I happen to agree that this requires a lesson to the organization responsible. We do need to send them a message, after all."

Akio's eyes widened. Right before he stepped out of the Pod, now hovering above the back door of Riko's, he deadpanned, "Perhaps I am mistaken as to just where Eve got this from."

Yuko chuckled as the Pod moved to drop her off for her part of the operation. "You never know."

Dieter stalked into Riko's with an arrogant swagger. When he spotted Sero sitting at the bar, he pointed his index finger at him and then at the office without speaking as he continued through the room and disappeared through the office door.

Sero sighed as he unsteadily pushed himself to his feet. *Damn, how much did I drink while I was waiting for this ass?* he wondered, unconsciously using the same word to describe Dieter that Muto had before he died.

He slowly made his way to the door, placing each foot carefully as he tried not to appear as drunk as he was. When he entered the office, Dieter was sitting behind the desk, leaned back in the high-back chair with his boots propped on the desk.

"Is this how you handle your business, Sero?" Dieter growled when he took in the man's bleary eyes, unsteady stance, and the odor of whiskey coming from him. "You get drunk instead of performing the duties you are paid to do?"

"I sent word to you hours ago that we had the girl. What took you so long?" Sero answered defiantly.

Dieter's eyes flashed yellow briefly, and a small growl rumbled in his chest at Sero's outburst. "I told you once, Sero. *Do not question my actions.*"

Sero blanched as he realized how close he was to meeting the same fate as Muto. As he started to apologize, Dieter glanced out of the window, movement near the door catching his attention. His eyes went wide and he shot to his feet, slamming the chair into the wall as he stared through the glass into the dining room, fear evident on his face.

"In position," Yuko called over her chip as she approached the door to Riko's.

"Rear door is secure," Akio replied.

Yuko drew a deep breath and walked through the door. She was immediately met by a man wearing a white shirt with the name Kaito embroidered on the pocket.

"Sorry, we're closed." He stood there blocking her way.

There were fifteen men lounging around the dining area, all bearing the tattoos that identified them as Yakuza. Yuko heard the faint *click* of a door opening in the rear and brief sounds of the city outside.

"Oh, that's so disappointing," she lamented. "I was told that you had the best Udon beef dish in the neighborhood."

She sighed and looked up at the man with her best innocent look. "Is there no way I could get an order to go?"

"Ah, Kaito, let her in." One of the soldiers leered from a table. "She's a cute little thing, and I could use some entertainment."

The remaining Yakuza all laughed at this. As Kaito turned back to invite her in, a panicked voice shouted, "Vampire!" from the office.

Black Eagle, One Kilometer above Tokyo

"Where are you?" Eve wondered out loud as she watched the feeds from the drones. She had been holding her position in the Black Eagle for fifteen minutes and still had not located the van.

"Gotcha!" she exclaimed as one of the drones hovered over the vehicle she had been searching for. It was parked behind a large two-story house. The area was an older, wealthy residential neighborhood that had once been the location of several foreign countries' embassies and consulates. The house was surrounded by a high stone fence and had room for several vehicles to park in the rear.

Eve summoned the other five drones to the area and surrounded the house, scanning for any sign of her missing friend. She set one of the drones to hover near a window on the first floor and activated the audio. At first, she couldn't hear anything. An analysis of the window composition showed that it was exceptionally thick, a common practice used to dampen the noise of the busy city. She turned up the gain, and the first thing she heard was a woman screaming inside.

Her eyes shot wide open, and she took direct control of the drone as she rapidly brought the Black Eagle down into an open space next to the van. She moved the drone back from the window and accelerated it toward the thick glass as she jumped out of her craft, the modified Jean Dukes-designed carbine gripped tight in her hands. The drone punched through the window like it was paper as Eve watched the video feed, scared of what she would see.

To her relief and confusion, the video showed her a man and woman sitting in chairs just inside of the door leading out of the room into the house. The woman was in mid-scream when the drone smashed into the room, startling both.

Eve directed the drone to hover above the confused pair, who were staring at the broken window, and activated an electrical burst to stun them. "I'll sort that out later," she murmured.

She sent two of the remaining drones above her so she

could maintain surveillance on the exterior of the house, and directed the remainder to join the one already inside. The drones split up and moved down the hallway, stopping to scan each door. When one of the drones stopped in front of a closed metal door, the scan showed a small form huddled against the far wall. Without hesitating, she directed the drone to punch through that door. The door reverberated with a deep metallic *clang* as the armored drone blew through it, leaving a hole a little smaller than a golf ball in its wake.

Eve focused on the video feed as the drone zoomed to hover over the figure. "Found her!" she cried as she burst through the closed and locked back door, leaving an Eve-sized hole as she entered.

CHAPTER FORTY-ONE

Riko's Noodle House, Tokyo, Japan

Sero looked out the window into the dining room to see what had Dieter so shaken. All he saw was an attractive young woman talking to Kaito near the entrance. He turned back to question what was wrong, and his mouth opened in shock as he found a white wolf in Dieter's place. The beast was huge, almost two meters tall, and stood face-to-face with Sero.

The drunken Yakuza boss screamed as the beast leapt at him. His bladder betrayed him as he stood frozen in place.

The wolf hit Sero with a shoulder, knocking him onto the bloodstained couch in the same position as Muto had occupied earlier, then ran through the open office door with a vicious snarl.

Sero tried to stand, but the combination of alcohol and absolute terror was too much. He slumped on the couch as his vision faded to black and unconsciousness took him.

Akio stood in the open Pod door as it hovered above the rear of the shop. There was one person watching the rear, a man who was sitting with his back against the dirty brick wall on an overturned box. He held a small electronic pad with a video playing quietly. Akio stepped out of the Pod and dropped the short distance to land on slightly bent knees directly in front of his unwary target.

The mobster shot to his feet while reaching for a pistol tucked at his waist. His pad clattered to the ground. Akio caught him by the throat and pulled him close, staring into his startled face. The mobster's surprise quickly turned to terror as Akio's eyes turned red and fangs protruded from his mouth.

Akio plucked the pistol from his unresisting fingers as he compelled the terrified gangster to sleep. He propped the unconscious man against the wall and smirked as he retrieved the pad and placed it on his lap.

He turned the handle on the door but froze when the latch bolt made an unexpected *click* as it disengaged. He smiled when he heard Yuko's voice. She distracted the Yakuza soldiers and covered any noise he had made.

He slipped silently down the dim hallway, his senses on alert as he detected the Were and a human in the office to his left and three humans in a room across from the office. He was moving toward the open office door when he heard a voice yell, 'Vampire!' and a huge wolf came tearing out seconds later.

Akio rushed forward at preternatural speed when he saw the wolf leap across the dining room, bowling over several men as he rushed at Yuko.

Yuko reacted to the wolf flying toward her. She slipped

to the side, catching him by his scruff with both hands and using his momentum to spin and throw him back across the room.

The Yakuza soldiers were momentarily stunned by the sudden appearance of the snarling wolf in their midst. He landed on a table, crushing it beneath him and sending the two men sitting at it reeling. The crash seemed to snap the remaining mobsters out of their shock. The room erupted into bedlam as they turned over chairs and tables while grabbing their guns.

Yuko reached out and lightly tapped the man who had intercepted her on the temple as he stared open-mouthed at the wolf. His unconscious body fell bonelessly to the floor as she pulled one of her Jean Dukes and leveled it at the room.

"I suggest you drop your weapons," Yuko commanded. Her face transformed from that of an innocent young woman to one of a demon with glowing red eyes and fangs protruding from her mouth.

An older soldier with his arms completely covered in tattoos, screamed and turned to run, only to be brought up short as the snarling wolf surged to his feet between him and the safety he sought at the rear of the building.

Akio had been watching the scene, one lip curled up in a half-smile at how effortlessly Yuko took control of the situation. When the angry wolf gained his feet, Akio stepped in front of him and blocked his way. Katana held ready to strike in a two-handed grip, he commanded, "Shift or die."

Dieter saw the vampire in a dark military-type uniform with a patch on one shoulder of a skull with hair streaming behind it blocking his way. *The Dark One*, he thought as he saw the glowing red eyes and deadly sword. Heinz had shown him a picture from years ago of him once, and compared to the other men in the calendar, he didn't look very frightening.

The picture had lied.

He turned toward the front door and saw the woman who had so casually intercepted his attack blocking the exit, her eyes red as she held twin pistols in her hands.

Dieter looked from one to the other, frantically searching for a way to escape when a searing pain shot through his rear leg, followed by the sound of a gunshot. He spun to see a young Yakuza soldier holding a pistol pointed at him. The burning pain drove him into a rage. He felt a primal need to rend and shred this lowly human who dared to injure him. With a deep-throated snarl, he lunged at the hapless man, his strong jaws and ivory fangs tearing his throat out in the blink of an eye.

Gripped in bloodlust and pain-induced rage, Dieter spun on Akio and tensed his legs to spring.

Akio watched him through hooded eyes and set his stance, ready to bring his sword into position when the wolf struck.

Dieter surged forward, jaws open wide as he aimed for Akio. At the last instant, he darted left, attempting to go past Akio and flee out the rear.

Akio caught him as he ran past, slinging his body across the bar where it landed in an explosion of glass and liquor when he crashed into the shelves behind it.

Yasou aimed his pistol at Akio's back with a shaking hand. Before he could pull the trigger, his body was slammed halfway through the office window, his torso shredded by the hypervelocity round from Yuko's gun.

"I said, drop your *Gott verdammt* guns!" Yuko roared as she took aim at the only other Yakuza member who was actively pointing a gun.

He looked at Yuko and then at the gun in his hand. His face held a look of surprise at seeing the gun held there. His eyes went round with fear as he flung the gun across the room and quickly went to his knees, his hands clenched tightly on top of his head.

Dieter fought his way to his feet, shards of glass falling to the floor as he stood, and his vision went red as Akio again ordered him to shift back.

Dieter bared his fangs and leapt for his tormenter, his only thought to maim and destroy the being who had dared to interfere with his father's plans. He didn't feel Akio's blade as it powered through his neck. His body continued for three unsteady steps, then it joined his head on the floor.

Akio turned to the Yakuza mobsters staring in shock at the grim man with the sword who had so easily dispatched the monster wolf. "The lady told you to drop your weapons." He spoke softly, right before he projected the crippling sense of fear that was the trademark of a Queen's Bitch. The sound of guns falling to the floor from numb fingers was quickly followed by bodies thumping to the floor as screams of terror filled the room.

Akio raised his blade in salute to Yuko, then turned toward the office where he planned to ask Sero the question that was foremost in his mind.

Yuko nodded to Akio and moved around the room,

gathering weapons and shoving the dazed Yakuza into a group in the corner. She stood by the entrance, a pistol in one hand keeping the shell-shocked gangsters under control while Akio...*talked to* Sero.

Akio's face wrinkled in disgust as he stood in front of the unconscious man. The smell of whiskey, coupled with the acrid scent of urine, that came from him was so strong, it almost made his eyes water. He caught the mobster's collar and pulled him to his feet.

He held him there for a moment and then called, "Sero. Sero. Sero, wake up." As he lightly slapped his face, keeping his anger in check so as not to break the man's neck.

The gangster stirred and mumbled incoherently. Akio shook him gently and called his name again.

Sero slowly opened his eyes, shaking his head as he fought to regain consciousness. When his eyes focused, he tried to pull away from Akio in fear. "What? Why? Who? What are you doing?"

"You ordered someone taken, a young woman. I want her back. Now!" Akio demanded, his eyes flashing red.

Sero screamed in terror. His mind was close to the breaking point from all of the shocks he had received today. Muto's death, Dieter turning into a monster wolf, and now this man with glowing eyes had all overloaded his brain.

When Akio entered his mind, he discovered that his thoughts were incoherent and fractured. He pushed harder, pulling on memories of the past. A man begging for his life, a young woman in tears as she was forced into prostitution, an elderly shop owner on his knees with a look of devastation on his face as his store burned. There was no doubt that Sero was an evil man.

Akio had no qualms about pushing strong compulsion into his addled brain. "Where is Koda Rii?"

"I don't know who that is," Sero whimpered.

"The young woman you ordered kidnapped," Akio clarified. "Where is she?"

Sero's eyes rolled as his mind tried to fight the compulsion, certain that he would die if he told this creature what he wanted to know.

Akio looked at him in disgust as he pulled this thought from his mind. "I won't kill you," he told him in a low, steady tone. "I can do much worse."

Sero's eyes widened, showing white all around as Akio projected mind-numbing, gut-wrenching terror at him.

Akio watched dispassionately as Sero's body reacted to the sensation. His breath came in quick gasps, his face paled, and his body began to shake uncontrollably. He allowed the feeling to continue for a while, hearing the cries and moans of the mobsters outside the busted window grow louder as they too were subjected to the emotion.

He allowed the fear to slowly subside. While Sero's mind recovered, he was able to pull the information he wanted with no problem.

Akio held the trembling man, and after a moment's hesitation, he smiled. "You will turn yourself over to the police and confess all of the crimes you have committed. You will also give them any information you have about the crimes and illegal activities of others. You will not make any deals for leniency, and will gladly accept whatever punishment the courts deem appropriate."

Sero tried to resist, but the compulsion was too strong. His face went slack and his body went limp. "I understand."

Akio lowered him to his feet and pulled him out into the room where Yuko held the others. "I know where she is," he informed her as he shoved Sero into the midst of the others.

"Abel, please contact Inspector Yonai and advise him to send his people in to take custody of these men," Akio called.

Abel responded seconds later. "Message delivered."

CHAPTER FORTY-TWO

Yakuza Brothel, Tokyo, Japan

When Eve burst into the house, she saw a short man in an ill-fitting suit looking at the hole the drone had punched through the door into the house.

He spun and drew a pistol, snapping a quickly-aimed shot toward her. The bullet impacted the top of her head and ricocheted into the ceiling. Eve fired her carbine from the hip while running. The recoil forced her to stumble and take two steps back as the mobster's body exploded from the force of the impact when her round hit him in the chest.

Eve caught her balance and continued to the metal door at a run. She slowed only enough to make the turn, slamming into the door and leaving it hanging from one hinge as her body went through.

Koda jumped and hit her head on the bars of the cage. The movement sent pain radiating down her neck and back. Tears blurred her vision as she struggled to hold her body still to assuage the pain. She had been kneeling for hours, unable to move in the tight confines of the bars. Her body was wracked with pain from the cramps that had taken up residence in her back and both legs hours earlier. The slightest movement caused the stressed muscles to knot even more.

Eve stopped and surveyed the cage for a second, then reached out and grabbed the padlock securing her friend inside. She wrenched the lock free and threw it across the room in disgust.

"Koda, are you injured?" she called as she pulled open the door.

"Wha...who? *Eve!*" she cried as her vision cleared and she saw her friend.

Eve helped Koda out of the cage, speaking urgently as she summoned another drone to her location. "We need to get out of here. Can you walk?"

When the young woman tried to stand her legs cramped viciously, causing her to fall to the floor in agony.

With tear-filled eyes, she gasped, "My legs. Cramps. *Aieeeee.*"

Eve growled as she saw her friend in pain. "Someone is going to pay for this. Who put you in that cage? Do you have a name?"

"I... Oh, God, it hurts," Koda mumbled through the pain. "I think... *Aarrgggh*! I think he was called Diago."

"Diago! Abel found that name on the mugshot of one of the men who took you. He is a dead man," Eve stated in a voice that held an edge of pure menace.

"Just get me home, Eve. I can't stand another minute in this horrible place," Koda cried as she slowly convinced her tortured legs to cooperate.

CHARLES TILLMAN & MICHAEL ANDERLE

Eve leaned down and gently caught her arm. "Let me help you. Lean on me and I'll get you out of here."

"Eve," Akio called, "I have obtained the location where they took Koda."

"I got it," Eve told him. "I have her. Now we're working on getting out of here."

Akio was quiet a moment. "We will discuss your failure to properly communicate with your team later. Do you need assistance?"

"My apologies," Eve replied as Koda climbed to her feet shakily. "I'm in the Black Eagle, so if you can spare your Pod for a few minutes that would be helpful."

"Yuko and I will be dealing with the Yakuza and the police for a little longer. We will not need the Pod if that is all you require."

"I'll go get Koda," Yuko cut in. "You can handle this, Akio."

"Wait," Akio commanded. "This is a matter for the Vicereine. Since there are multiple criminals, plus the ones we were forced to kill, your presence is needed here."

Yuko dropped her head in shame, knowing Akio was right and that she had once again acted impulsively.

Akio continued, "Your concern for Koda is honorable, but Eve told us she doesn't need our assistance. We must honor her wishes on this, as she must honor ours when we do the same. That is what being part of a team means. You trust and support each other, even if you do not always agree on the course."

Abel cut into the conversation by activating all their chips at the same time. "The craft from China is on the move. I have been tracking it since shortly after you returned. It has departed the China coast and headed here. I am uploading an earlier surveillance recording to you now."

"Why are you only now giving us this data?" Eve demanded.

"It was not as relevant as locating Koda Rii at the time," Abel replied. "Now that you have located and secured her, the information is more relevant."

"Remind me to take a look at your risk assessment code," Eve huffed. "The parameters need to be adjusted."

"My risk assessment programming is working within acceptable parameters," Abel responded. "As long as the craft was in China, ensuring the safety of Koda Rii was the primary concern."

"Abel," Akio called, interrupting a potential argument. "What are the projected arrival point and ETA of the craft?"

"ETA based on current speed is thirty-four minutes. Location is somewhere near Tokyo, based on intelligence received and current trajectory. I will continue to track it and provide more information as it becomes available."

"Thank you, Abel," Akio told the EI.

Eve was focused on Koda and the information Abel had sent. She failed to notice Diago as he quietly made his way to the door.

"Stop there, or I will shoot the girl," Diago called as he pointed a pistol at Koda's head. Eve turned her head toward the sound and saw he was using the wall for cover with only his gun hand and a small part of his head exposed.

Koda froze, her eyes wide and her face turning pale. "Eve, don't let him hurt me," she whispered.

Eve's circuits lit up in rage when she heard the fear in Koda's voice. She took control of the remaining drone in the hall and watched its progress as it slowly and silently moved into position above Diago.

"You are one of the fecal stains who took my friend. I suggest that you drop the gun while you still can." Eve's voice was devoid of any feeling.

"Whatever you are, you are in no position to give orders. Now, you drop your weapon and move away from the girl," he snapped.

"Last chance," Eve warned.

His face flushed with rage, and he lowered his aim until the gun was pointing at Eve. She brought the hovering drone down at high velocity. It hit Diago's wrist and punched through it in a spray of blood and bone.

Diago screamed in pain as the gun fell from his unresponsive hand. He grabbed his shattered wrist with his other hand as his vision blurred with pain.

Eve calmly aimed her carbine at him and braced herself for the tremendous recoil to come. "Diago Shimizu, you have been a parasite on society for too long. That ends now."

Koda had watched the whole thing and realized what Eve was planning. She called out to her softly. "Eve, do not do this. He has committed a wrong against me, and I am sure many others, but this is not the way. Let the authorities deal with him. You're not a murderer. If you shoot him now, that is what it is."

Eve froze, her finger a split-second from triggering the

hypervelocity round into the helpless man. She carefully raised the muzzle of the gun and released the pressure on the trigger. "You're right, Koda. Thank you. Abel, notify the police to send officers and a medical team to my location."

Abel answered a short time later. "Police and medical units dispatched."

Eve silently watched Diago until the first officer arrived and took him into custody. She realized that she had almost allowed herself to become a monster like him.

CHAPTER FORTY-THREE

Tokyo, Shinjuku City Section

Horst brought the craft down in an overgrown park. It was adjacent to an abandoned university complex just north of the Shinjuku section of Tokyo. He had ignored Heinz's orders, deciding that he needed to get to Dieter sooner in hopes of convincing him to abandon Heinz and his plans of dominating Asia before the Dark One destroyed him.

He concealed the craft with debris from a collapsed building and started walking in the direction of the Yakuza shop where he would locate Dieter. He had walked roughly four kilometers when he felt a prickling down his back, he sensed he was being watched.

He heard a noise behind him and stiffened as a low voice told him, "I suggest that you do nothing stupid. I wish only to speak to you."

Horst spun and saw a man dressed in dark clothing holding a bare sword in his hand standing about ten meters behind him.

Another voice, this one female, spoke from a position to his left and rear. "Horst, we don't want to hurt you. We really wish to talk to you."

He backed up, putting his back to a boarded-up doorway where he could watch both. "What do you want?" He demanded, though he had already recognized both from photographs and had an idea they wanted him dead.

The woman spoke again. "We know that you do not agree with what Heinz is doing. We also know that you chose not to warn him when you discovered what we did to the Forsaken and Nosferatu at the prison."

He stiffened at this, wondering how these people had this information, and more importantly, how long they had been watching him. "What of it? I know who he is, and also that he murders all others from our world." He nodded at Akio.

"No, you're wrong," the woman told him. "We do not kill indiscriminately or *murder,* as you say. Those who follow the command of our Queen that the humans are not harmed have nothing to fear. Those who use their power to cause harm and prey on humankind are dealt with appropriately."

She moved closer to Horst and he saw that she was a young-looking woman with an open look on her face, but his experience with vampires had taught him that looks were deceiving. "All I want to do is take my brother and go. I assure you I have no intention of going back to Heinz or participating in his mad plans any longer. I never supported this madness to begin with."

"We are aware of your feelings about Heinz," she informed him. "Chang too, for that matter."

His eyes widened in shock. Surely these people did not have the ability to hear his most private thoughts or the infrequent conversations he only had with Dieter. "How can you know this?"

"We have been watching since the day you dropped your brother off in Vladivostok," Yuko stated calmly. "We were able to track him here as well as gather intelligence on the prison and lab complexes."

"Dieter, my brother. Where is he?"

Yuko shook her head. "He was with a group of criminals who had kidnapped a human member of our team. When given the chance to surrender, he attacked instead. I'm sorry, but he is dead."

Horst slumped against the door, feeling empty inside at the loss of his twin.

Yuko cautiously stepped up to him and gently placed her hand on his arm. He jerked and started to push her away until he saw the sorrow in her eyes.

She felt his body jerk but did not pull away from him. Instead, she projected a slight sense of calm and let him see that she was truly sorry for his grief.

"He, he was my brother. My last connection to my true family," Horst whispered, his voice laced with grief.

Akio had been inside his mind since Yuko had approached him, poised to cut him down if he showed any sign of trying to harm her. He sheathed his sword, knowing that the Were was not currently a threat.

"Horst," he called softly.

Horst looked up at him questioningly.

"I know you are not like Heinz," Akio told him. "That your plan was to take your brother and leave. If you want to leave, that can be arranged, but if you are willing to live in peace with humanity, there is a place for you here."

Horst frowned. "How would you ever trust me not to betray you? I have been with Heinz for many years. Not to mention, you killed Dieter."

"I know you hated Heinz and what he is doing," Akio told him. "I can also see that although you grieve, you knew Dieter was committed to Heinz. Again, if you would like to stay here, as long as you do no harm, you will be left in peace."

Yuko gently squeezed the arm she was holding. "We don't have any quarrel with you, Horst."

"What about Heinz?" Horst spat. "Destroying the Nosferatu will set him back, but he will not stop until he has found you. He is obsessed with ruling all of Asia and will not stop until he is successful or dead."

"Heinz will not see the next sunset," Akio stated in a low voice.

"I know that you are powerful, but Heinz is, too," Horst argued. "He has had many years to work on making himself and others stronger. He is a dangerous foe." His hands squeezed into fists, his mouth a tight line as he thought about Heinz. "Do you plan to bomb him with your super bombs? Anything else would be suicidal."

"No," Yuko replied. "We know he has some human captives in the lab. They are innocent and need to be freed."

"How do you plan to get in?" Horst asked. "He has automatic gun emplacements hidden around the exterior. If you are detected, you will not make it to the base."

Akio raised one eyebrow when he heard this. None of

their surveillance had detected any remote defenses. "We will do what we must. Heinz has to be stopped."

Horst nodded his head, a distant look in his eyes for a moment. He pushed himself off the door he had been slumped against once he had made up his mind. "I want him dead. He is responsible for the deaths of my parents, and he poisoned my brother's mind to the point that he too was killed. I can get you into the base unharmed if you are willing to trust me."

Yuko looked at Akio. A few seconds later, he nodded. "He is being truthful."

Research Laboratory, Acheng, China

The sun had just risen above the mountains when Horst brought the craft down into the valley where the hangar entrance was situated. Two human servants opened the doors to allow him to maneuver inside, closing them as soon as the craft was clear. He went through his normal routine of shutting down before opening the door. Both men were standing unconcerned when the craft opened.

They both lowered their eyes to the ground when he exited. Although they were willing servants, they knew their place and did not wish to risk the ire of their masters.

"I have some supplies inside. Unload them and take them to the kitchen," Horst ordered as he strode toward the entrance to the common area.

The men hurried to comply. When they stepped into the craft, Akio knocked them both unconscious. He was tying them up when Horst returned.

"The way is clear," Horst informed them. "These are the

only ones on duty. I have disabled the air defenses. The trucks are gone, too, so the pack and Miko have left to prepare the Nosferatu. They left sometime after I did yesterday, so we have at least one hour until the soonest they could return."

Yuko stepped out of the door, her Jean Dukes holstered on her hip and her katana fixed to the back of her armor.

Akio followed, dressed the same. "We weren't able to get the full layout of this place," he told Horst. "We know that the humans are being held one level down and there are labs below that, but we do not have the full picture of that level."

"Heinz has his lab there," Horst replied. "It's the room farthest from the stairs at the end of the hall on the left. That's where he spends most of his time. He doesn't interact with the others here unless it's absolutely necessary. There is another level below the lab where he keeps his private rooms. Its only entrance is a stairway that leads down from inside his lab. He also has a bolt hole in his rooms that leads into the caves beneath the mountains. Even I don't know where it comes out."

"That could pose a problem," Akio mused. "Where is he normally at this time of day?"

Horst thought for a moment. "It's hard to say. He normally keeps to his rooms during the day, but if he's working on something, he will stay at it until he's satisfied."

"What about Chang?" Yuko questioned. "He's not in his office or the common areas right now. Where will he be?"

"He has rooms on the same level as the lab," Horst replied. "His is the room closest to the stairs on the same side as the lab. Dieter and I have the rooms on the opposite side. He will be in his rooms until around four unless Heinz calls for him before then."

Eve was holding her position in a Black Eagle high above the base, monitoring her network of drones.

"Eve," Akio called over his chip. "Horst says that the air defenses are now disabled, but the people Heinz sent to the prison could be returning soon. Keep watch for them."

"I'm already tracking them. They are about two hours out at their present speed."

"That's good. We will be done well before they return. Horst also says that Heinz has an escape route out of his rooms. Have you located any areas during your exploring that could be a cave that exits the complex?"

"There are numerous areas that could be cave entrances. I haven't mapped but a few, and they all seem to be dead ends."

"Saturate the area with drones. If Heinz gets away, we want to catch him before he is able to leave the caves in the darkness."

"Already done." She sent a command out to the drones. "Abel, take control of the drones and monitor their progress. Let me know as soon as you find anything."

"Control established. Locating and mapping possible routes," Abel acknowledged.

"Time to go," Akio stated. "Horst, come with me to the labs. Heinz expects you to report as soon as you arrive, correct?"

"*Ja.* He is also expecting Dieter, but I should be able to locate and distract him long enough for you to prevent his escape."

CHAPTER FORTY-FOUR

Research Laboratory, Acheng, China

Horst led them out of the hangar and through the passage to the common room. "Wait here for a moment," he requested before they entered the room.

He crossed the common room and went through a swinging door that opened into a kitchen. Moments later, four young women came running out and headed up the stairs to the surface entrance.

Horst followed closely behind and motioned for Akio and Yuko to come. When they met, he told them, "The cook was loyal to Chang, but the women were taken from their villages and forced to serve. The cook will never be a vampire now."

"We need to hurry," Akio urged. "I want this finished before the others return."

They quietly made their way down to the lab level and stopped on the landing. Akio turned to Yuko. "Are you ready for this, Yuko? I can deal with Chang while you free the prisoners if you'd like."

"No. Go and handle Heinz. I will give you time to get there before I go after Chang. That way, Heinz will not have any warning."

Akio pursed his lips and nodded. "Very good. Fight smart, Yuko."

Yuko nodded. "*Hai.*"

Horst had silently watched the exchange. He opened the door and started down the hall to the labs when they were done. Akio followed him, a silent, deadly shadow.

Yuko slipped across the hall and stood beside the door to Chang's quarters. When Horst entered the door at the end of the hall, she heard a voice ask, "Where is Dieter?"

Yuko opened the door and stepped into the room, her sword leading the way. Chang was sitting in a chair with a ledger on his lap. He looked up, prepared to punish whoever entered his quarters unannounced. His mouth fell open in shock as he saw the young woman standing there with bare steel in her hand.

"What is the meaning of this?" Chang yelled as he stood, letting the ledger fall to the floor.

Yuko growled. "By order of Queen Bethany Anne, you are sentenced to die for your crimes against humanity."

Chang jumped and flipped over the chair, twisting as he did so to snatch a thick, short-bladed sword from where it rested on a table against the wall.

He turned to Yuko, holding the sword in a ready position. "Your Queen is gone. You have no power here."

Chang rushed Yuko almost faster than her eye could follow, the blade pointed at her throat. She slipped to the right and brought her katana down in a fast arc. Chang stumbled briefly as her razor-sharp blade slashed his left shoulder to the bone.

He caught his balance and changed direction, slicing at her as he moved across the floor. She grunted as the short, heavy blade hit her side. Her armor saved her skin, but the blow reverberated through her body.

Chang stopped against the far wall and turned to face her, his shoulder already healing. "You're fast, woman, but not fast enough." He launched another attack as he spoke.

Yuko parried his blade and sparks flew from it. They exchanged a series of fast slashes and thrusts, neither able to get through the other's guard. The sound of clashing steel filled the small space for several minutes.

Chang pressed her hard, the heavy blade sending shock after shock into her arms with each blow.

Yuko stepped back to avoid a thrust to her head and momentarily lost her footing on an ornate rug that slipped. Chang saw the opportunity and surged forward, intending to run the short sword through her chest while her guard was down.

She allowed herself to fall to the floor, the blade barely missing her as it went over her body. She lashed out with her armored boot and caught Chang's knee as he stumbled, off-balance after missing her. She was rewarded by his scream of pain as her boot hit his knee.

Yuko surged to her feet and slashed his uninjured leg behind the knee.

Chang spun and tried to bring his blade to bear on her head, but his damaged knee gave out, and he fell to the floor.

Yuko struck in an instant, taking advantage of his vulnerable position. She drove her blade deep into his chest, twisting it to cause maximum damage.

Chang's mouth opened in a silent scream as she wrenched her blade from his body and followed up with a downward strike that split his head from crown to chin. She pulled her blade free from his bloody remains and deftly removed the head, unwilling to take even a small chance that he could heal the massive damage already sustained.

She wiped the gore from her blade with a coat hanging from a hook by the door as she set out to free the captives being held on the level above.

***

Heinz had a syringe in one hand and a vial of blood in the other. He was carefully injecting a small amount of a milky substance into the vial of blood. He didn't acknowledge Horst until he had completed the task and placed the vial in a rack with several more on the desk.

"Where is Dieter?" Heinz demanded. "You were to bring him back with the information."

Horst's face flushed with anger and his eyes flashed yellow. "He's dead," he snarled. "Killed because he was enamored of your sick dream of ruling the humans. Dead because of you!" he yelled before his body transformed into a large snow-white wolf.

Heinz's body blurred as he pushed away from the desk and leapt out of the chair. He stopped against a counter to the side, his fangs bared and deadly claws sprouting from the tips of his fingers.

His eyes glowed red. "You dare threaten me? I raised you as my own, and this is the payment I get?"

Horst lowered his head, his hackles up as he stalked toward the enraged vampire. His muscles tensed and he launched at the scientist, his jaws wide and his intent clear.

Heinz smirked as he swung his hand and slapped the enraged wolf on the side of his shaggy head.

Horst spun in midair and crashed into a cart holding an array of medical implements. He lay unmoving amid the scattered items on top of the wrecked cart.

Heinz stalked toward the fallen Were, his fangs extended and his sharp claws flexing in anticipation. "Get up, damn you. You ungrateful mutt, I should have killed you the first time you defied me. I will not make that mistake this time."

He was so intent on exacting his vengeance that he failed to notice Akio enter the room until he was standing at the entrance to the stairs leading to Heinz's private quarters. He froze in mid-step when he saw the katana-wielding figure watching him through hooded eyes.

"You!" Heinz screamed. "You're a traitor to your kind, choosing humans over their rightful lords and masters."

Akio raised one eyebrow and continued to watch, sensing that Heinz was stronger than he remembered him from years earlier, the same as Isamu had been.

"Say something, *Akio*. Or should I call you 'Dark One?'" Contempt dripped from his tone.

Akio shrugged. "What is there to say? It doesn't matter

what I say or what you think. You won't be around long enough for it to be of importance."

Heinz smirked, his attention laser-focused on Akio. "I am not as easy to kill as you may think, traitor." As he spoke, he palmed a large knife from a workbench and threw it at Akio in a flash.

The blade flew true and impacted Akio's armored chest. The Jean Dukes armor bent but did not break as the tip of the knife struck, the force of the impact sent Akio staggering back a half step.

Heinz used that minor distraction to bolt through the door into the hall.

Akio regained his balance, but as he started to pursue the running vampire, Horst crossed in front of him, his claws tearing gouges into the tiled floor as he lunged out the door after Heinz.

When Akio entered the hallway, he saw Heinz rapidly approaching the stairs with the wolf close on his heels as Yuko, stepped into the hall from the door of Chang's room.

Heinz was shocked when Yuko stepped into his path with a bloody sword in her hand. His steps faltered for a second. That was all Horst needed. He pounced in an instant, his strong jaws locking around the back of the vampire's neck. Both went to the floor in a sliding tangle of limbs and snarls.

Yuko jumped to allow the struggling wolf and vampire to pass under her. She landed lightly on her feet as the two combatants crashed into the unyielding stone wall. The sound of bones breaking was followed by a muffled yelp of pain from the wolf, his jaws still firmly locked on the vampire and a pained grunt from the vampire under him.

Akio stepped up beside Yuko, and they watched as Horst struggled to his feet. One front leg was twisted at an odd angle, his stark white muzzle covered in blood so dark that it looked black. He stood painfully on three legs and forced the broken one out straight as his nanocytes blocked the pain and started to heal it.

Heinz pushed himself up with one arm. The other was shattered to the point it would take several minutes to heal. His tibia protruded from the middle of his lower leg, and dark blood bubbled out around his lips.

He forced himself into a sitting position, his eyes locked on the wolf. He opened his mouth to speak and Horst surged forward, clamping his jaws around Heinz's throat and savagely pulling back. Heinz's face paled as blood sprayed from his ruined throat when Horst opened his mouth to disgorge a chunk of bloody flesh.

The nanocytes in his blood started to close the wound. Heinz grimaced as his throat started to heal and tried to get to his feet. His shattered leg had also started to mend, and he managed to push himself halfway up on his uninjured one.

Horst's form morphed, and a naked man stood where the wolf had been, his features flushed with rage and his body shaking with barely contained rage as he stalked toward Heinz. He scowled at the battered and torn vampire, his eyes glowing bright yellow. "You murdered my father," he accused, his voice sounding more like a growl than speech.

Caught in the grip of uncontrollable rage, Horst felt a tingling in his limbs. He glanced down at his hand as it lengthened. Fur sprouted to cover it, and sharp claws extended from the tips of each finger. He lashed out with his claw-tipped hand, opening the partially healed wound on Heinz's throat. "You caused my mother's death with your arrogance."

He growled and lashed out with his foot, striking Heinz on the knee of his uninjured leg. The sound of bone breaking was followed by a scream of pain from the wounded vampire as he crumpled back to the floor. "You caused my brother's death with your insane plan."

Horst drew his foot back again and slammed it into the helpless vampire's side. He was rewarded with another scream of agony and the sound of snapping bones. "Now it is fitting that I, Horst, son of Klaus, Alpha of the Rohr Wechselbalg, end your miserable life."

He reached down and grasped Heinz by his head, then looked into his eyes and twisted. His arms corded with strain and a sickening *snap* came from the neck.

Horst placed one foot on Heinz's waist and pulled until the already-torn skin broke free and the head came off in his hands. He gazed at it for a moment, numerous feelings running through him: sadness for the loss of his brother, anger that Heinz was so cruel, and the uncertainty of not knowing where his path now lay.

As he stood cataloging this, a thought came to him. He was free to do whatever he pleased, no longer bound to the beast who had insisted that he call him father. Of all the feelings that had been coursing through him, contentment was the strongest. Whatever tomorrow had in store for him, he would face it as his own man.

With a final look, he dropped the head to the floor and

turned to Akio and Yuko. "Don't we have some people to free?" He started toward the stairs.

Akio nodded once and Yuko called to Horst, "Perhaps you should clean up and find some clothes first. I don't believe a naked, blood-covered man would be very reassuring to a group of captives."

Horst looked down at himself, seeing that Yuko was right as Heinz's blood covered almost all of his naked body. He grunted in reply and calmly walked past them to his room to do as she said.

"He partially changed." Yuko murmured as the Were closed the door to the room he had entered. "I did not expect he would have the ability to turn Pricolici."

Akio nodded, a thoughtful look on his face. "He is strong, and extreme emotions such as anger have been rumored to trigger the change into the Pricolici form in wolves. He just confronted his personal monster, one that has haunted him for most of his life. I believe it had a... therapeutic effect."

Yuko looked pensive, and her lips pursed as she considered that. "You might be correct but, we will need to watch him. Making Heinz pay for the deaths of his family has been his driving force for too long. I don't want to see him slip into despair now that he has lost everything that has defined him up to now. Plus, I remember how the Weres had trouble controlling themselves when they were in that form."

"*Hai,*" Akio agreed. "He should be watched, but I believe you will find that our wolf will adapt to his newfound life easier than you think. That level of vengeance does help to bring things into a new and better perspective, as I have recently discovered."

Yuko nodded. "I hope that is the case with Horst," she whispered to herself as she started toward the stairs to free the remaining prisoners.

CHAPTER FORTY-FIVE

Research Laboratory, Acheng, China

Eve brought the Black Eagle down when Akio called and told her they had finished in the base. She met him at the hangar doors when Horst opened them. "Where's Yuko? You didn't lose her *again*, did you?"

Akio looked behind himself, feigning surprise. Before Eve could respond, he chuckled. "She's freeing the people Heinz was holding for his experiments. She will be along soon."

"Not funny." Eve huffed, then allowed a small smile to play on her face. "I had a drone follow her into Chang's rooms. Want to see the recording?"

"*Hai.*" He smiled, looking back again before he added, "*After* we get back to base."

Eve nodded knowingly and focused on the back of the hangar as Yuko entered.

"Did you get them all out?" Eve asked.

"*Hai.*" Yuko's reply sounded off.

"What's wrong, Yuko?" Akio inquired.

"There were only three people left alive," Yuko lamented. "One of the prisoners told me that Heinz had come there earlier and injected four of them with some concoction. They tore each other apart in their cell shortly after. The bodies were still there. Had we gotten here sooner, we could have prevented it."

"Yuko," Akio responded softly as he placed his hand on her shoulder, "we can't save them all. We can only do what is within our power to ensure that any Forsaken and Weres we find preying on humanity are stopped."

Eve took her hand. "Yuko, we stopped Heinz, and he can never harm anyone again. I know it hurts you when people die needlessly, but you are not responsible for the acts committed by others. You are responsible to see that they are punished when they step over the line. That is all Bethany Anne wants and requires of you."

Yuko stood silently for a moment, comforted by her two closest friends left on Earth. "What about the Weres who went to the prison? Do we need to wait for them, or let them go now that Heinz is gone?"

Horst spoke up before anyone could respond. "They are all beasts. They served Heinz willingly, and he allowed them to play sick games with the humans. They don't deserve to live."

Yuko's gaze snapped to him. "Do you believe they will continue that with Heinz gone?"

"They will be worse," he spat. "Heinz wouldn't let them hunt as often as they would have liked since he needed humans for his experiments. Without him to restrain them, they will go through the villages and settlements like a plague."

Akio nodded his agreement when he saw the images in Horst's mind. "Yuko, I will stay and deal with them. I can return in the Black Eagle when I am done."

Yuko thought a moment before she answered. "No, I will see this to the end. Although I am tired of killing, I know it is necessary."

Eve spoke up. "I believe you should all go back to Japan, Yuko. Koda and Asai need you and Akio to screen the applicants so we can open on time next week. I will stay and handle the Weres when they return."

Akio looked at her. "What do you propose to do, Eve?"

A big smile crossed her face as she answered, "Puck 'em."

Akio rolled his eyes as Yuko looked at her and shook her head.

Eve followed up quickly, her face taking on a hardness not seen before. "I followed them with some drones when they were sent to hunt. What they did to those people no one should see, let alone endure. I plan to wait until they are all inside and drop the whole thing on top of them. I think that is a fitting end, to be buried underneath tons of rubble in the very place where they tormented and tortured so many others."

Horst let out a short laugh. "That would be justice. They have been untouchable here for many years. To die where they feel safest would be a fitting end for those bastards."

"Eve, are you sure?" Yuko pressed.

"I'm quite sure. Besides, we have everything planned for the Palace's grand opening and still don't have the staff ready." She trailed off as she communicated silently with the drones shadowing the trucks. "They are only an hour away, now. Go. I have this."

Yuko hesitated briefly, then nodded once and walked toward the waiting craft.

"Eve, leave some drones in the area after you're done," Akio directed. "If any others show up here, it would be good to know."

"If you kill them and Miko, there are no others," Horst stated.

"Just the same, Kamiko's network was extensive," Akio replied. "It would be imprudent to assume that there are no others who know of this place."

Horst shrugged and headed to the craft.

Eve looked at Akio. "Thank you."

"For what?" he asked.

"For treating me like a member of the team and trusting that I will succeed," she replied.

"Eve," he replied solemnly. "You have always been and always will be a trusted member of this team, as well as my friend. Now, get ready to show them what a master pucker can do." He grinned.

Eve nodded and grinned as she turned toward the Black Eagle. "They won't know what hit them."

He shook his head, fighting to control the laugh that threatened to burst out as he made his way to the craft for the ride home. *She really is acting like Bethany Anne's child now.*

Horst maneuvered the craft out of the hangar once they were all aboard and set the heading for Japan. Once he had the course set, he leaned back in the pilot's seat and closed his eyes, seeming to rest but with his mind running all over the place.

What will I do now? I have no family and don't know if any of the pack is still alive in Germany. It's been many years since there has been any contact. The last time we had contact with anyone in Germany was when Heinz went there with Dieter and secured this craft shortly before the world fell apart. Dieter didn't care enough to look for them even if Heinz would have allowed it.

He continued with this line of thought until he was interrupted by Yuko.

"Horst?"

Horst opened his eyes. *"Ja?* Um, I mean, yes?"

"Have you thought about what you want to do now that you're free of Heinz?" Yuko inquired.

"I intended to go to Germany," he replied. "But I don't know if there is anything there for me. It's been years since we have had any contact with anyone there, and longer still with any Wechselbalg."

"If you will give me a general area to look, I can ask Eve to see what she can find," Yuko offered. "As you have probably figured out, we have advanced methods of obtaining information."

"That would be good. I would hate to go there and find nothing."

"There is another alternative if you would like. We have homes scattered around Japan. If you wanted, we could set you up in one of them. You are welcome to remain there until we find out about your pack or longer."

"I don't know. How could you trust me? It's not as if you know anything about me other than that I hated Heinz."

Akio had been watching the exchange in silence. He leaned forward, looking into his eyes. "Horst, I know you are trustworthy. I know you didn't agree with the way Heinz or the Weres treated humans, and that you refused to take part in their depravities. If you would like to stay, you will have a place here."

Horst was overwhelmed by the sincerity he heard in his voice, but his eyes narrowed when he tried to remember telling Akio that he didn't participate in the hunts.

"How did you know that?" he demanded. "I never said anything about not taking part."

Akio raised one eyebrow but remained silent.

Horst's forehead wrinkled, then his eyes shot wide open. "You have Michael's powers. You can see into minds!"

"I am nowhere near that powerful, but do you deny that anything I've said is not true?"

"No, it's true. I just don't know where I will fit in. I have been living in that bunker for the last twenty-plus years. I don't know if I can function in this world." He sighed.

"Horst, you function like everyone else does," Yuko told him softly. "Day to day, week to week, year to year. As long as you continue to move forward, the rest will take care of itself."

None of them spoke again for the remainder of the trip until they drew close to the Japanese mainland.

"Horst, please take us down into the overgrown area south of the section of the city where Riko's is. You know it?"

"The site where the old temple complex is?"

"Yes."

"Will my craft be safe there?"

"It will. After dark, it will be moved to a secure area," he explained. "For now, it is close to where we need to be, and we also have a place for you to stay nearby."

Eve had been waiting ten kilometers above the lab complex, watching the four covered trucks slowly make their way down the rough mountain roads. She had sent numerous drones into the complex so she could be sure her quarry was inside the trap.

When the trucks arrived, one of the Weres jumped out of the cab of the first truck and opened the doors to a garage. As soon as the last one was inside, he closed and locked the doors.

She switched to a live feed from the area and turned up the volume as she watched on the Black Eagle's HUD.

"Gerhart, where the hell are those damn workers? I'm going to rip one of their heads off and beat the other to death with it," Kurtz growled.

"Silence," Miko commanded. "Something is off. I smell blood."

The Weres all stopped and sniffed the air around them. "Kurtz, Franz, shift and scout the area. I smell it, too," Gerhart ordered.

Both shifted to wolf form, leaving a pile of torn clothing behind as they jumped to obey.

"Gerhart, take the others and spread out. Alert me if you locate anything." Miko directed. "I'm going to check the kitchen area. I smell something burning."

Gerhart nodded and motioned for the remaining Weres to follow. He went to a concealed door at the back of the garage and tripped the latch holding it closed. A section of the wall swung out, revealing a narrow stairway leading down.

Miko went through the side of the garage into a passage that sloped down to the common room. The passage had several closed doors that led to storage areas where the food and other necessities were kept. He passed them by, homing in on the strong odor of something left to cook too long.

When he entered the kitchen, he saw an oven with smoke leaking out around the closed door. When he made his way around the counter in the center of the room, he stopped short, seeing the cook's obviously dead body on the floor.

He took off out of the kitchen at a run. He ran across the common room, and as he entered the hangar, his body was thrown into the air by a huge blast. He landed on his back and slid across the rough floor, and the last thing Miko saw before everything went black was debris and dirt crashing down on him.

Eve finished reviewing the feeds from the drones she had secreted throughout the lab with a feeling of satisfaction. Each one showed that it was buried. The pair of one-kilogram pucks she had launched had dropped the complex in on itself. There was nothing left standing once the dust outside cleared.

She recalled the carriers and most of the drones, leaving a few around the lab to maintain the surveillance Akio wanted, then took one last look at the damage she had wrought and grinned. Satisfied she had taken care of the threat, she accelerated the Black Eagle toward Japan at the best possible speed.

CHAPTER FORTY-SIX

Tokyo, the Palace (Three Days Later)

"Asai, can you believe it?" Koda gushed as she looked at the line of excited people that snaked from the door all the way around the corner of the building. "Look at all the people waiting to get in."

"I can," Asai answered. "Eve has had advertisements running across all forms of media for a solid week. There is no one in Japan who hasn't seen or heard an ad for 'the most realistic experience you can have without being there yourself.'" Asai chuckled as she made air quotes with her fingers.

"I know, but this is still unbelievable!" Koda exclaimed. "There have been people camping here for three days, wanting to be one of the first in, and the line has gotten longer each hour today."

"Eve said she didn't think this place was going to be big enough. I believe she was right."

Eve laughed as she approached the two women. "Did I hear someone say I was right?"

Koda chuckled. "As if you would ever be wrong."

"That would be highly illogical," Eve deadpanned as she raised one hand and spread her fingers into a distinct V configuration.

Both women burst into laughter at her response and action, having been recently introduced to the old science fiction television show by Eve.

"Have we had a good turnout of the special guests we invited?" Eve inquired, looking at the door that was designated for the government officials and other invited guests.

Asai's face flushed red and Koda chortled. "Well, one *special* guest was the first in line at daylight this morning. I'm not sure if it was the place or my co-manager that inspired him to arrive so early."

"Eve-*san!*" an excited voice called.

They all turned as a young man approached.

"Seki-*san*, how do you like it?" Eve inquired.

"It's amazing! I see you used my idea in the monster maze. When that fire-breathing *Akuma* dropped from the roof, I could feel the heat from his flames."

"I thought it was a good idea. Have you taken the dinosaur tour yet?" she inquired innocently.

He laughed. "Oh, that one was evil. When the T-Rex broke through the barrier, my friend Tomi screamed like a girl. I thought he was going to soil his pants."

"I'm glad you liked it. I can't take credit for that one, though. Akio said the first version was boring, and it would be more exciting if the people had to get away from the dinosaurs at the end." She chuckled.

"I knew something was up when I saw the sign warning pregnant mothers and people with heart problems not to try it," Seki enthused. "I remember the version I saw. It was like going to a zoo. This one is much better."

"Have you thought about the job offer?" Eve inquired.

"Yes. I thank you for asking, but I am happy where I am. I was offered a manager's job recently and feel it is best that I stay. Besides, it wouldn't be proper to ask my boss out on a date." He looked hopefully at Asai.

Asai smiled and ducked her head, too shy to respond.

Koda gave her a gentle push forward. "Seki, Asai would be honored to accompany you on a date. Why don't the two of you go to the refreshment stand and discuss it over a Coke? They are quite good."

Asai hesitated for a moment, and then tentatively reached out and caught Seki's hand and pulled him toward the stand. "That is a lovely idea."

Koda was watching her cousin and snickering when she felt someone approach her from behind. When she turned, she was looking at a dark t-shirt stretched over the muscular chest of a very large man. She slowly looked up and found herself staring into the deepest blue eyes she had ever seen. She continued to stare until Eve caught her by the arm.

"Koda, did you hear me?"

"Huh? Uh, I mean, did you say something, Eve?" she stuttered.

"I said, I would like you to meet Horst."

"Oh, yes, it's very nice to meet you." Koda blushed and her heart raced.

Horst smiled down at her. "It is very nice to meet you, too. Did I hear you say there is Coke? I would be honored if you would accompany me to get one."

"I, oh…" She looked around, searching for an answer, and saw Yuko beside him.

Yuko smiled. "Horst, Koda says she would love to."

Yuko watched the two as they nervously walked away. "Eve, I think Horst might have found a reason to stay here instead of going to Germany."

"I think you're right."

EPILOGUE

TQB Base, Tokyo, Japan

"Akio," Abel called, "I have received information from the drones Eve left at the lab in China that you need to see."

"I'm on my way back to base now. I'll come by as soon as I get cleaned up."

"I'll have it waiting for you when you arrive."

When Akio walked into the command center, Abel had a video feed paused on the main screen. It showed the valley where the hangar had been. When the video started, a lone figure was making its way up the side of the mountain. Akio watched as they took several steps and then slid back on the loose rock.

The figure struggled, apparently injured or ill, as it made its way slowly to the ridge above. When it reached the top, the figure collapsed in an exhausted heap.

"Abel, please zoom in."

The feed switched to another view, this one at the top of the ridge. The focus zoomed in until the screen showed the dirt and blood-covered face of a man. It was after

328

midnight in China on a moonless night, and too dark to make out any of the features.

"Enhance lighting," Akio instructed.

The picture slowly became lighter. The face was undeniably that of a man, but the angle showed only the blood-covered side. His head turned slightly, bringing the other side into view.

Akio's legs went weak and he slumped into a chair as he stared at the screen. He looked like he'd seen a ghost. His mouth worked, but no words came out. He finally croaked, "Kenjii?"

THE END

RETALIATION

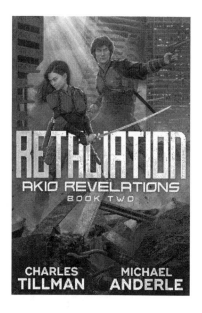

The story continues with book two, *Retaliation*, coming soon to Amazon and Kindle Unlimited.

AUTHOR NOTES CHARLES TILLMAN
JUNE 19, 2020

Hi, thanks for reading this book and reading these notes. This is the second time I have written author's notes for a published work. I'm still not comfortable talking about myself, but here goes.

First, I am so honored to write in The Kurtherian Gambit Universe. I found this series back in 2017 when some guy named Michael Anderle put an ad on Facebook that said, "Everything you knew about Vampires and Were-wolves was wrong, so very, very wrong."

I saw that ad several times over a few weeks and didn't click it. I mean who is this guy to tell me, a person who loves Dracula, Nicholas Knight, and the original Barnabas *Freakin* Collins, (Yeah, I'm that old) that I didn't know about vampires?

I'm an avid reader, one of those who before e-books were a thing, would have three or four books lying about the house all the time. I was looking for something to read and happened on that same ad again, challenge accepted. I got Death Becomes Her and was hooked halfway through.

The premise blew me away, and I couldn't get enough. Space aliens came here and screwed around with humans to make super soldiers. What a novel concept for, what I thought, at that time, was an urban fantasy.

One day after finishing one of the main series books, I liked it so well that I did something I had never dreamed of before. I reached out to Michael on Facebook and I sent him a quick message telling him how much I liked it. I figured he would never look at it but there was a *ding* from my computer almost immediately and when I looked he had responded.

OMG an Actual AUTHOR answered me!!!

We chatted briefly from time to time and I got to know him and found that he was really a super guy. I also found that he was a generous guy who helped other writers to learn and develop the skills needed to work in the indie market.

In 2018 I saw a post calling for short stories written by fans in another of Michael's Universes, Oriceran. I decided to give it a try and see what happened and wrote a story about a magic using bounty hunter from New Orleans.

I submitted the first story I had ever written in November 2018 and to my surprise they accepted it for publication. On top of that I had people messaging me wanting more.

November 2018 was a month of first for me. I submitted my first story and attended my first writers' conference. I finally got to meet Michael in person and talked to him a bit. No surprise what you see is what you get.

While I was there, I had the idea that I would like to do

a fans write short story based on one of his characters. The rules for fans write are that you can't use an existing major character in your story, so I searched Michael out to beg his permission.

Michael being Michael took my little idea up to eleven. I wanted to do a five to eight thousand word short story. He comes back with send me thirty thousand words and let's see what happens. I went into a panic and am not sure exactly what I said after that, but I exited stage right freakin now. (Michael says it didn't happen like this, but I have a witness who backs me up.)

I went back home and started working on a couple of projects, but this little voice kept nagging me in my head. As the months went by that voice started getting louder and louder, screaming that he had a story to tell. I gave in and contacted Michael again about writing Akio, only this time I was willing to take on a full-length novel.

That has since morphed into a three book series, the first of which you are holding in your hands. Please hold your sacrifices to the gods of rubber chickens and boiling Pepsi, the next one is written and will be released soon. All will be explained in due time.

I hope you enjoyed reading this as much as I enjoyed writing it for you.

If you want to reach me, you can find me on:

Facebook

Author Charles Tillman

https://www.facebook.com/CFTillman/

Or on my website

http://cftillman.com/

Join my mailing list if you would like to know what I'm working on and updates on future works.

Again, thank you so very much for reading this and hope to hear from you soon.

Charles
June 19, 2020

AUTHOR NOTES MICHAEL ANDERLE
JUNE 22, 2020

Have you ever had a situation where you built (or created) something, and yet you didn't feel that you were the right person to finish a part of it?

I have, and it's Akio.

When Charles approached me at 20Booksto50K® Vegas with the request to write Akio I didn't feel a sense of concern, but rather a sense of relief.

I knew that a lot of fans enjoyed the character I created, but I personally had NO WHERE I thought I could take his story. Not that I don't like Akio, I do. It's just that I believe to write the character correctly, you would need to do enough research to support who he was before Bethany Anne.

And Charles was willing to rise to the occasion, but not without a few checks and balances.

He is right that I'm not fond of authors taking control of major characters as they can accidentally get the character wrong. So, enter the Akio Beta Team (ABT). Charles' folks (he mentions in his author notes) helped steer him in the right direction, while allowing a bit of allowance for both who Akio was in the past, and who he is in the future having gone through the WWDE (World's Worst Day Ever.)

I'm happy to have Charles' work to bring Akio's story to life. I'm honored that he asked and honored that he 'put up' with all of the checks and balances (some self-imposed) to get the story down on the pages for the book(s). Not just one book, but three!

"If you're going to tell Akio's story, this won't be a small endeavor, you have to 'sign up' for the trilogy."

Damned if he didn't.

Thank you, Charles, for enjoying the Kurtherian Gambit, and Akio enough to see if you had a story, or three, inside you.

Thank you to everyone who stepped forward to help make this new series a success, to all of the teams that helped get it published, and (as always) to the fans!

Now, I hope you get fans asking YOU, "Hey Charles, where's the next book in the series?" That way, you get ALL of the experience.

Ad Aeternitatem,

Michael Anderle

BOOKS BY MICHAEL ANDERLE

For a complete list of books by Michael Anderle, please visit:

www.lmbpn.com/ma-books/

All LMBPN Audiobooks are Available at Audible.com and iTunes

To see all LMBPN audiobooks, including those written by
Michael Anderle please visit:

www.lmbpn.com/audible

Made in the USA
Las Vegas, NV
21 June 2024